Introduction

This book is a collection of writings by Writing at the Ledges, a group of poets, novelists and short story writers, who have been meeting in Grand Ledge, Michigan, since 2005. They come together to share their work, give and receive feedback, encourage each other and generally enjoy, over a cup of coffee, what they like to do best ... writing.

Small Towns: A Map in Words is an anthology of some of their favorite pieces, loosely designed to reflect life in one of the many small towns that make up the landscape of the United States.

For further information about our group, or to purchase a copy of this book, please visit our website at *http://writingattheledges.com*.

Small Towns:
A Map in Words

An Anthology by Writing at the Ledges
Grand Ledge, Michigan

Published by Riley Press, Eagle, Michigan

All rights reserved. Printed in the United States of America. No part of this publication may be reproduced, stored in a retrieval system or transmitted in any form or by any means, electronic, mechanical, photocopying, recording or otherwise, without the written permission of the author of the piece(s).

Book cover design by Colleen McCord,
Ionia, Michigan

Grand Ledge book cover images provided by the Grand Ledge Historical Society

Writing at the Ledges map graphic by C. J. Tody

Rileydog image by Tina Evans, Artist
Traverse City, Michigan

Book preparation, layout, and editing by Lori Hudson, Candy Little, Randy Pearson, and Rosalie Petrouske

Copyright 2008

ISBN 978-0-9728958-6-6

Published in the United States of America by
Riley Press, P.O. Box 202, Eagle, MI 48822
http://rileypress.hypermart.net

Thank you to the following Grand Ledge sponsors for their support of Writing at the Ledges

"Ledges" Sponsors

Miller's Pharmacy and Gift Shoppe
(517) 622-3392

All The Rage Hair Salon
(517) 627-1310

"Bridge Street" Sponsors

About the Home
(517) 622-8288

Four Seasons Gift Shop
(517) 627-7469

Grand Ledge Sunoco (Michael Smart, LLC)
(517) 627-7779

Lambs' Gate Antiques
(517) 627-6811

Ledge Craft Lane
(517) 627-9843

Piece of Mine Pottery Studio
(517) 622-0727

Sweet Linda's Café
(517) 622- 2050

In Loving Memory of Dr. Gertrude Z. Gass
by Donnalee Pontius

Contents

At the Water's Edge

Along the River Tonight	.....Rosalie Sanara Petrouske	14
Island Dreams	.....Jan McCaffrey	16
Duncan Bay	.....K. L. Marsh	17
The Ledges	.....Jan McCaffrey	18
Lasagna and Sex Therapy	.....Randy D. Pearson	19
The Covered Bridge	.....Jan McCaffrey	45
Simple Gifts in the Park	.....Wanda Davison	46
Treasures Beyond Measure	.....C. J. Tody	48
Muddle in a Puddle	.....Jan McCaffrey	69
When Autumn Comes	.....Rosalie Sanara Petrouske	70
Night Pond	.....Diane Bonofiglio	75

Corner Café

In a Café	.....Rosalie Sanara Petrouske	78
Phil Kline is Dead	.....Marion Phillip Kline	80
A Quiet Rainy Morning	.....Jan McCaffrey	82
Death By Broken Heart	.....Candy-Ann Little	83

Country Roads

Can I Go to the Woods?	.....Diane Bonofiglio	164
The Old Barn	.....Diane Bonofiglio	166
Ghost Shoes	.....Kerry Tietsort	167
Red Bird	.....Diane Bonofiglio	168
Thankful Hearts	.....Diane Bonofiglio	168
A Hay-Day	.....Jan Sykes	169
Winter Forest	.....Diane Bonofiglio	171

A Wondrous Winter Scene	.....Diane Bonofiglio	172
My Gravel Road	.....Alta C. Reed	173

Main Street

Childhood of Yesteryear	.....Alta C. Reed	176
Don't Mess With Tradition	.....Randy D. Pearson	178
Eye O' the Storm	.....C. J. Tody	191
Fairy Touch	.....Alta C. Reed	213
For Sale: Americana	.....Alta C. Reed	214
The Heart and Center	.....Kerry Tietsort	216
Message From Max	.....Donnalee Pontius	218
Letter from a Small Town	.....Rosalie Sanara Petrouske	224
Main Street	.....K. L. Marsh	227
The Perfect Ride	.....Rosalie Sanara Petrouske	232
Where Are You?	.....C. J. Tody	235

Over the Garden Gate

An Act of Kindness	.....Lori Hudson	238
Birds of a Feather	.....K. L. Marsh	244
My Mother's Garden	.....K. L. Marsh	245
Neighborhood Watch	.....Randy D. Pearson	246

Steeples

Call Waiting	.....Lori Hudson	254
French Sunday	.....K. L. Marsh	258
Snowflakes	.....Candy-Ann Little	260
Second Tuesday of Next Week		
	.....Donnalee Pontius	261
Sunshine Again	.....Candy-Ann Little	262

Town Hall Meeting

He Loved Me	.....Diane Bonofiglio	266
One Sided	.....K. L. Marsh	269
So Much Mess	.....Rosalie Sanara Petrouske	271
The Philadelphia Six	.....Diane Bonofiglio	273
Snowballs	.....Lori Hudson	276
Tired	.....K. L. Marsh	278
Somebody's Hero	.....Rosalie Sanara Petrouske	279
The Psychic Buddy	.....Randy D. Pearson	289
About the Authors	....	296
Index	....	301

At the Water's Edge

Every town from the beginning of time has been dependent on water. Not only is it essential for sustaining life, but it's great for recreation, too. What would summer be if kids weren't swimming in lakes, fishing in ponds, or catching frogs and turtles in creeks?

Think of all the benefits of a rainy day. As the water falls from the sky, saturating the dry earth and renewing life, it also makes us slow down. Our hectic schedule is put on hold and we can finally read that book we've put off, or play games with the kids, watch a movie, or perhaps we can just sit and ponder about nothing.

Whatever your favorite water-related activity, you're bound to find something to whet your appetite in this chapter.

Along the River Tonight

Rosalie Sanara Petrouske

Along the river tonight, darkness deepens—
Overhead, a not quite oval moon
reflects in water where geese rest,
wings folded as they float.

Couples walk paved paths touching hands.
Tree frogs throw out their throaty opera.
Here in midsummer, a first cricket begins its
song, rubbing legs frantically against each other.

Next to me, my daughter walks slowly,
head down, hands tucked in pockets,
thoughts far away, up north at the big lake
where soon she travels to her father's home.

I want her to love the Grand, to be familiar with this
water the same way she knows Superior, and
    recognizes
its cobalt blueness as it rises to meet the horizon.
I can tell her what I have learned about lakes.

I'm just learning the mysteries of rivers.
Lakes have no tides, yet rivers rush.
Toss a stone into a lake and it is lost:
Toss a stone into a river; it skips and awakens ripples.

In the upper reach amongst swift water
algae clings to rock, smooth—polished
almost black by rubbing of water and time.
Evergreen, moss, pine—this is the river's color.

Trout feed on larvae of stoneflies, wait
for anglers' hooks to find them. Dippers perch
on river stones, search for food to feed their young.
There is danger here as well as beauty.

In the middle reach, water moves slowly—
Notice how plants put down stocky roots, snails hide in
    weeds
and under stones. Large mouth bass propel to safety,
a fleeting flash of silver caught only by discerning
    eyes.

Now in the lower reach, we watch
dragonflies hover, glassy wings paper thin,
translucent enough to see through.
Each wing glistens bits of shattered light.

Some rivers are straight; others meander,
carving out land as they travel onwards.
I have lived my life by water: lakes and rivers,
waterfalls bursting with anticipation.

Some rivers are quiet, unpredictable,
others cold and turbulent,
except for mallards sheltering under bridges,
hid beneath willow fronds.

It is almost dark now as we walk along the Grand.
At thirteen, my daughter grows stalky and thin as
    cattails,
bending in the swampy areas beyond this path.

It is easy to love a daughter too much,
with a heart overflowing its banks
like the river after snow melts in March.

People say that love is great ambition;
it curls under skin like mud under fingernails,
eddies around you, grabs at wrists and ankles
like fast-flowing water, can pull you beneath the
    surface,

and all you can do is hold on....hold on.

Island Dreams

Jan McCaffrey

If you ever lived on an island
You will never be quite the same
You will dream of sandy beaches
That blue ocean waters claim

Sunrise, sunsets, long walks along the shore
Remembering the ancient steps
That have taken this path before

If ever you lived on an island
As carefree as the breeze
You *will* return forever
If only in your dreams.

Duncan Bay

K. L. Marsh

Walked through the rooms in my mind
Beaches where children screamed delighted
The bridge decorated like a bride
Islands folded over like money
Nothing changed.

A comforting embrace
Cool, steady breeze, waves lapping at the shore
Sunlight sprinkled over the waves
As a martini with a twist of lemon
Making me warm where I was cold.

Soothed and relaxed
Freighters weaved back and forth
North to Duluth, South to Chicago
Carrying iron ore and baby bottles
Blankets for the Indians.

Memories in an album
Ten and vulnerable
Adolescent and edgy
Thirty and broken
Visited over the years
Like an old teacher who has watched me grow.

The Ledges

Jan McCaffrey

An ageless landscape
Daring to be
In the midst of life
Untouched. Free.

Protective vines grasp
The rocky edge
Of a weather-worn path
Ascending the ledge.

Gnarled roots reaching
The river below,
Its waters silently
Continue to flow.

Past the splendor
Of deepening dusk,
The gaudy colors
Changing rocks to rust.

Evening shadows embracing
The timeless beauty here
Within the lemon-glow
Of city lights so near.

Lasagna and Sex Therapy

Randy D. Pearson

My dreams always attacked with a vengeance. The images in my head, while vague, always brought a strong sense of panic and urgency. I grew accustomed to the nondescript objects raining from above, crashing all around me, as well as the screams emanating from newly formed piles of debris. However, this dream felt different. I had a new series of images protruding into my mind. A thick, acrid smoke caused my lungs to clog while the heat grew unbearable.

I awoke with a series of barking coughs. Directly above me, inches from my head, flames crackled and danced. Fire engulfed my home.

While crawling out of my cardboard box, I saw my left arm ablaze. Fortunately, I couldn't feel the flames yet as they swirled along the sleeve of my thick overcoat.

Once I cleared the box, I ran toward the river as fast as my legs would allow, while smacking at the fire with my other hand.

Even though the river could only give me a few inches of depth here, it sufficed. Falling to my knees, I plunged my burning limb into the murky water. I submerged my arm up to the shoulder, welcoming the hiss as the fire graciously subsided.

By the time I refocused on the large appliance box I called home, little remained unburned. I yanked off my charred overcoat, using it to grab at a remaining edge of cardboard. First, I tipped it away from my body, hoping to save some of my meager possessions by forcing them out and onto the ground. Then, after tossing the burning cardboard into the river, I jumped up and down repeatedly on my stuff, desperately trying to douse the lingering flames.

Once I had the fire extinguished, my adrenaline began to ebb. I sat cross-legged on the banks of the Red Oak River and examined my arm. Fortunately, due to the chill in the air, I wore three layers last night. The fire tore through my overcoat and sweater, but the tightly fitting long-sleeved shirt still remained, though in patches. As I carefully peeled the sweater off my arm, I saw several red splotches on my skin. Before I could continue looking myself over, I heard harsh whispering behind me, alerting me to something I had hoped and strived to avoid. I turned to witness several of the locals who had congregated in the clearing, up the hill from me. Once they realized I had noticed them, the throng came bounding down as one.

I dealt with the choruses of, "Are you okay?" "What happened?" and the like. While I knew them as residents of this small community, I did not normally interact with them, so I answered concisely.

A woman pushed her way through the crowd and dashed up to me, gawking with wide eyes at my charred sleeve, worry splayed across her face. "Oh my! Are you hurt?" She wore a white lab coat with the name Irene stitched in cursive above the festive Redi-Medi Urgent Care Clinic logo.

Before I could formulate an answer, she placed her hands around my charred forearm, one on my wrist and the other just above the elbow. "It doesn't look too bad, thank goodness, but let's get you to the clinic." Barely awaiting a nod of my head, she began sprinting toward the clinic, and since she still had a solid grip on my arm, I had little choice but to tag along. Her brow deeply furrowed, she asked, "Does it hurt?"

Not until she mentioned it. "Maybe a little, yeah."

We entered the clinic, rushing past two other patients seated against the far wall. A heavy-set lady with her right leg in a cast seemed annoyed at my preferential treatment, but the short, elderly man with the angry red rash painted across his right cheek looked at me with sad, understanding eyes. I tossed the fat woman a shrug as Irene pulled me past.

As she carefully cut the remaining bit of sleeve off my ailing arm, I felt the need to say, "Um, you know I'm a bum, right? I have no way to pay for this."

She smiled sympathetically. "That's okay. It's on the house. We take care of our own here in Red Oak. Besides, it doesn't look bad at all. Only first degree burns in a few spots. They're all superficial and should heal quickly enough."

As she applied some white goop to my arm, I gave this lady a once-over. She wore her long, black hair up in a tightly spiraled bun, a long stick smoothly piercing it at a 45-degree angle. While pretty enough for a woman I assumed to be in her early 40s, I couldn't help but wonder what she looked like in her 20s. I'll bet she turned a lot of heads.

"Okay," she said with a broad smile, "you're all set. So, what are you going to do now?"

"I dunno. I'll have to see if anything survived, and go from there."

She had a strange look on her face, like she wanted to say something else, but instead, her body language softened and she simply said, "Okay, well, good luck. If it gets any worse, feel free to come back."

After thanking her for the assistance, I walked out of the clinic and into the harsh sunlight, squinting until my vision adjusted. Still feeling the eyes of the town upon me, I headed directly for the river's edge.

Sadly, very little survived the blaze. I now owned a shirt with a missing sleeve and torso, a half-charred pair of jeans, one sock and lots of ashes. The only other remaining item turned out to be the lower half of a paperback book I had recently found. "Man," I said aloud, "I was only halfway through. Now, I'll never know who done it."

How could this have happened? I don't smoke and we had no lightning last night. The only possible explanation? One of the neighborhood children must have lit my box on fire. But while I slept inside it? What kind of monster would do such a thing to another human being, especially one obviously down on his luck?

This line of thinking disturbed me too much, so I decided to concentrate on my next move. With a heavy sigh, I knew I needed to head back into town. I preferred staying away from the village until after nightfall, to limit my sightings. Sneaking into Red Oak under cover of darkness, I could root around the dumpster of the restaurant, the used clothing shop or the grocery store. Generally, I could scavenge a meal or some duds while avoiding unnecessary harassment.

Today, I did not have that luxury. With autumn fast approaching, the nights became chillier. The clothes on my back would not suffice. Besides, all this excitement burned a lot of calories. As if on cue, my stomach rumbled its demands.

After taking a few steps, my left foot landed on something. Assuming a rock, I lifted my foot and saw a colorful item partially buried among the weeds. Dropping on all fours, I discovered a psychedelically colored disposable Bic lighter. I had to wonder if I found the device used to torch my box. Holding it by the top, I dropped it into the pocket of my dirty sweat pants. I had no idea what I would do with it. Perhaps, I'd go to the police. Of course, there was no proof this lighter burned my stuff. Besides, why would they care about some bum like me?

Returning to my more immediate concern, I stepped into town and headed straight for my favorite dumpster, behind Paul's Diner. I thought of this one as my favorite because it always seemed to have something fairly fresh and tasty waiting for me. A couple days ago, I happened upon a pizza box with three whole slices. Before that, I found a Styrofoam container with quite a bit of salad and even a small dollop of ranch dressing still enclosed in a small, plastic cup. Why, on several occasions, I even lucked into a candy bar, still in the wrapper. The stuff these people throw away!

I turned the corner and had the dumpster in my sights when I froze. The restaurant's side door flew open and out walked a tall, heavy-set man. He had a brown garbage bag in one hand and a Styrofoam container in the other, heading straight for the trash. Even from a distance I could tell the man towered over me by at least a half foot and certainly appeared to eat much better than I did. His belly protruded past his belt in a graceful cascade. With the red and white striped shirt he wore, his gut reminded me of a giant beach ball. He flipped up the lid to the dumpster and heaved in the trash bag, but then he paused. After popping open the Styrofoam "to-go" box, he stared inside for a moment. He glanced around, so I ducked behind a large oak tree. Then, he reached in the container and pulled out what appeared to be a large sandwich. Opening his mouth, he took a large bite out of it before setting it back inside. As he chewed, a smile grew across his pudgy face. He closed the container and gently set it inside the dumpster. Still smiling, he turned and walked back inside the restaurant.

I stood there for a couple minutes before creeping over, feeling a bit like a stray cat. While lifting the lid to the trash, I reached in and procured the Styrofoam box. Inside, I found a whole sub sandwich, less the one bite, along with a pickle spear and a handful of plain potato chips. Although I thought the whole thing peculiar, my hunger had no problems with this. Tossing the box under my arm, I shot back to the safety of my charred piece of earth.

As I sat on the ground, chewing away at one fantastic sandwich, I kept noticing my grubby hands clutching the food I shoveled into my mouth. Wondering how many germs and how much filth I had ingested, I decided I wanted to clean myself up. So I set the remainder of the meal down, and sprang to my feet to begin the journey back to Paul's Diner. Though I really did not like doing it, I had found Paul's the easiest place to sneak into, since the restrooms were in a hallway directly to the right of the entrance. I popped my head in the front door and after making certain no one saw me, I made a beeline to the bathroom.

Once in the men's room, I dashed over to the sink. As I bent down and thrust my hands into the warm stream of water, I couldn't help but notice my reflection in the oval mirror. The man who returned my gaze startled me. In fact, it shook me to my core. How long had it been since I last saw myself? My mind's eye remembered a clean-cut, shiny-skinned man with bright, clear eyes. The straggly, shaggy mane I now wore had turned a greasy shade of brownish-black, reminiscent of used motor oil, but the large streaks of gray added a bit of contrast. My thick, unkempt beard had turned almost completely gray, except for blobs of what had to be ketchup from yesterday's meal, a partially eaten hamburger from the trash can near the fast food joint.

I began to chuckle softly at the food I wore on my face, until I locked eyes with those of the hairy, scary man in the mirror. More bloodshot than brown, they looked at me through droopy eyelids. Never before had I seen eyes so sad and lonely, and worse yet, they belonged to me. It disturbed me to the point of uncontrollable shivering, so I forced myself to concentrate on the running water, lathering up my hands several times until the water stopped running black with my filth.

Continuing with my plan, Operation Shiny Hobo, I squirted more soap into my cupped hands and lathered up my thick beard. The sweet caress of the warm water felt exceptional on my face. I began working on my hair next, continuing until no more soap sprayed from the dispenser.

The gooey, filthy mess plastered on the sink and surrounding walls embarrassed me, so I tried my best to wipe everything down, using up nearly an entire roll of toilet paper. Then, I stuck my face in front of the hand dryer, hitting the button several times until my hair felt dry enough.

At least now, I could almost stand being stared at by the unkempt man in the mirror. Still, I avoided his gaze like I owed him money.

After creeping out of the restaurant and back to my safe haven, I finished eating my sandwich with some peace of mind.

Once I had a full belly, I sat there staring at my charred pile of stuff. Losing all of it made me sad, of course, but I found myself especially disappointed by losing the book. I continued gazing at the remaining fragment lying there in the grass, reading the title over and over, *The Clock on the Floor*, by Phillip Brammen, or actually just *on the Floor*, since that was all that remained. This delightful mystery happened to be the first book that enthralled me, as far as I could remember. I found it at the edge of Jeffrey's Park, buried facedown in the tall weeds. It kept me from getting too bored these past few weeks. It helped that I read slowly, so I'd been able to savor the plotline. Now, of course, I wish I had read it quicker.

The more I looked at it, *on the Floor*, the sadder I got. Then, I remembered this town had a local public library. I figured they would have a copy.

I sprang to my feet and began the journey, but it didn't take long before my insecurities began their nagging. I wondered if they would even loan a book to a bum like me. That thought made me pause, but I really wanted to know who shot old man Filibuster.

Creeping up to the Red Oak Community Library, I peered in a side window. After spotting the elderly librarian on the other side of the building with his back facing the door, I had hope that maybe, just maybe, I could get in and borrow the book without being seen.

I had barely made it in the front door when the librarian turned sharply, quickly confronting me. He stood rigidly, his thin, bony arms crossed. His face thickly creviced with wrinkles, he scowled as he furrowed his brow, giving his forehead the appearance of a Shar Pei puppy. "Get out. We don't give handouts here," he snapped.

Doing my best to disarm, I smiled broadly. "Oh, no sir, I am looking for a book."

"You need ID and an address to check anything out of this library. Do you have either of these?"

My smile dissolved. "No, sir."

The cranky old man jabbed a long, skinny finger at the door. "That's what I thought. Now get out of here, you mangy vagrant!"

When several people in the library turned to look at me, I quickly dashed out the front door.

After sprinting for several blocks, I finally ran out of steam. Standing on the sidewalk with my back arched and hands resting just above my knees, I panted like a dog.

As my breathing returned to normal, I began to feel more at ease. Then, a couple of pre-teenage boys saw me and squealed, laughing as they ran away. Their chorus of, "Hobo, Hobo!" penetrated me. I tried to imagine one of them, a colorful lighter in hand, applying flame to my home as I slept. A shiver shot through me.

Once I regained my composure, I caught a glimpse of myself, full-length, in the front window of Gus's Barber Shop. My stained, charred shirt and faded, ripped sweat pants helped to strengthen my embarrassment. "Man, I look like crap," I muttered softly.

Through the barbershop's picture window, I saw a thin, nearly bald man gesturing my direction while talking to a couple other guys inside. I felt that uneasiness welling up again and I turned to walk away when the man flung the door open, waved at me and proclaimed, "Congratulations, you're my one thousandth customer! You win a free shave and a haircut!" Before I could protest, he draped his arm around me and ushered me inside the shop.

The two men in the small, rectangular building stared at me as I entered. A tall beanpole of a man seated in a row of chairs against the opposing wall crumpled his newspaper into his lap, while a fat, ugly guy stood next to him.

Then the thin, shiny-headed barber walked past me and scooped up his electric clippers, sporting a wide smile. He pounded his free hand against the barber's chair and said, "Have a seat right here and let ol' Gus take care of ya."

I smiled politely and replied, "Okay, thanks."

"So, ya feeling okay after the fire?"

Oh, of course these guys had heard all about it, too. I must've been the talk of the town. Certainly explained why everyone had been so kind to me. I answered, "Yeah, I guess. I'm alive, at least."

"Irene fixed you up at her clinic, did she? Good woman, that Irene." After a brief pause, he asked "So, any idea what happened today? How did your box catch fire? Were you smoking?"

"No, I don't smoke. I didn't do this to myself. I hate to say it, but I think it was one of the neighborhood kids."

"No, I can't believe that," said the tall guy, "The boys around here are decent people, with good, small town morals."

"They torment me, sometimes." My voice softened. "They throw rocks, call me names. Occasionally, I catch some of them rooting through my stuff. But I never imagined they could resort to this. I could've been killed."

Resting both arms on the table and cradling his wide chin in his hands, the fat guy sighed. "I'll talk to some of the parents. We'll figure this out."

Not that it mattered, really, but I thanked him for his concern. I inhaled deeply, pausing for a moment before pushing it out with an audible sigh.

As Gus finished whacking at my snarled mass of hair, I gave myself a quick once-over in the mirror. "Looks great. Hard to believe I actually had skin under all that hair. Um, you sure you don't need some money for this? I don't have anything now, but…"

"What? Oh no, no worries. It's on the house."

Offering a sincere smile, I gave Gus my thanks and walked outside. After all this excitement, I felt the urge to be alone, so I went back to my home, or what remained of it.

Lying there by the river's edge, I thoroughly enjoyed the feeling of the sun upon my freshly-shaven face. Amazing, the difference a bit of hair can make. If I still had my beard, I'd be miserable. The tickling of the sweat drops as they oozed through my facial hair would be making me itch, like insects crawling upon my flesh.

Instead, the sun gently warmed me, dancing across my cheeks like a graceful ballerina. I lay there, eyes closed, feeling quite at peace, until I drifted off.

The sky tumbled around me, pieces crashing into the ground with metallic thuds. A grinding screech echoed from above as clouds twisted from their moorings and plummeted. Screams shot out from every direction, yells for help from people I could not see in the ever-widening dust storm. Then, a face emerged from the thick fog. It was that lady from the clinic, Irene. Standing over me, she had an accusatory look plastered across her face. Grabbing me by the neck and pulling me up to her face, she screamed, "How could you?"

I looked up just as a tree-sized baseball bat fell from somewhere above me, striking me across the right temple. I jolted awake with a yelp.

Sitting up, I gripped my head with both hands, squeezing until the pain eased. The lingering effects of the phantom blow still reverberated in my skull.

It took me a moment to realize I had company. The sight of Irene standing a few feet away caused me quite a fright.

"Sorry," she squeaked, "I didn't mean to startle you. I just thought you might need that dressing changed." Holding her arms up, she showed me a roll of gauze in one hand and some ointment in the other. Her smile looked sincere.

Pulling myself to my feet, I nodded my head slowly.

"Please," she gestured toward the ground, "sit. It'll be easier. We don't need to go to the clinic."

"Isn't it a bit soon for a dressing change?"

"Who's the professional here?" she asked with a nervous chuckle. As she unwound my wrapping, she added, "That must've been quite a dream."

"Yeah. They always are. How long were you standing there?"

"Long enough. The pain on your face…" Her voice trailed off. "You must have a terrible burden to bear."

Deflecting her question, I asked, "So, how's my arm looking?"

"Oh, fine, it looks fine. You'll be healed in a few days." She stood up and took a step back. Smiling a thin-lipped smile, she said softly, "I was wondering… would you be interested in coming home with me? For dinner, I mean. I made lasagna last night and I have too much left over. I'll never eat it all."

As I sat there, I couldn't help feeling a bit sorry for her. This thin wisp of a woman couldn't camouflage her sadness or her frailty. It bled through her ill-fitting blouse as well as the oversized skirt that tickled the tops of her ankles. While certainly pretty enough, the worries of life had invaded her face, evident not only in the beginnings of wrinkles, but the overall sorrow that adhered to her skin like poorly applied makeup.

I almost said yes when something occurred to me, something I wish I'd remembered before this. "Well, I do appreciate that, really, but I'm rapidly losing daylight and I need to find a new box and some clothing. What I'm wearing is all I have left and I bet it'll get cold tonight."

"Oh! Wait a sec. I can help you with the clothing. I have a closet full of my husband's old things. You can have as many as you'd like."

"Your husband? Won't he mind?"

Her vision momentarily dropped to the ground. "No. He's not around these days." When her eyes locked on mine again, the sadness burned off like morning fog. "So, whatdya say, a free meal and all the clothes you can carry?"

I had mixed feelings about this lady. She seemed trustworthy enough and had been very kind to me, but she seemed a bit too needy. However, a phrase came to mind at that moment: Beggars can't be choosers. I was a beggar, after all. "Okay, sure, thank you very much. It's awfully kind of you."

She perked up considerably as she spun on her heels. "It's all just going to waste, otherwise. It's this way, on the other side of Main Street." She reached for my hand, to guide me, but thought better of it. "Come on," she said with a sweeping gesture. After a small pause, she added, "By the way, you sure look a lot better without all that hair."

"Thanks," I replied with a shake of my head, "I feel five pounds lighter."

As we walked, I engaged her in conversation. If I could find out some things about her before I entered her house, all the better. "So, Irene, how long have you lived in Red Oak?"

She stared at me for a moment before answering. "All my life, like most people here. The house has been in my family for generations. So, how long have you been living by the river's edge?"

"Don't know, really. All my life, I guess," I answered with a shrug.

"Are people treating you well?"

"For the most part, yes," I said with a cheeky grin. "This is such a quaint town. I mean, sure, there are a few people who yell and scream and the children can be awfully cruel, but I'm continually shocked. It's like this place has adopted me as the village hobo. I caught the fat guy from the restaurant putting food in the trash, presumably for me. And it's not just him. I've managed to find clothes in remarkably good shape behind the consignment store. It's like I'm their pet or something!"

"As long as they don't try to scratch behind your ear, huh?" Irene asked with a boisterous chuckle.

I joined in the laugh. "Even that wouldn't be *so* bad, y'know? Just no flea collars."

"Or a bell around your neck." She pointed toward a charming two-story green house with a beautiful widow's walk around the chimney. "Here we are!"

I followed her up the porch steps and waited while she opened the door. Her house was elegantly decorated, with lots of antique-looking furniture, flowery wallpaper and feminine knickknacks. "Beautiful place."

She spoke a simple, "Thanks" without turning to look at me. As she walked toward the kitchen, she shouted, "Why don't you go upstairs and see if there's any clothes you like. It's the last door on the left, the master bedroom. Oh, and if you want, you can use the shower in the adjoining bathroom to clean up."

From the edge of the stairs, I yelled back, "Thanks, I'll do that. I'm sure I'm far too gamy for indoor activities." I heard her giggle as I trudged up the plushly carpeted stairs.

I found the master bedroom easily enough. Even though closets flanked either side of the bed, I opened the doors on the right without hesitation.

This woman obviously assumed her hubby would be returning someday. Either that or she had serious pack-rat tendencies. I had never seen so many clothes in one place, so tightly packed I had to use both hands and a lot of wiggling to remove a pair of blue jeans and a white button-down shirt.

Holding the clothes up to my body at the full-length mirror, it appeared they would fit me well enough. I tossed them onto the bed and trudged into the bathroom.

The shower felt fantastic against my dirty, oily skin. Amazing, the difference between being caught, fully clothed, in a cold rain and standing naked in a hot shower. I could have spent all day lathering and smiling, but I knew a hot meal awaited, so I tried not to dawdle.

Once dressed, I lingered momentarily in front of the mirror. Examining myself in my new clothes, my fresh, collared shirt and nearly brand-new jeans, I couldn't believe how different from yesterday I looked. My hand caressed my clean-shaven cheeks and I smiled at myself. My eyes, in stark contrast from earlier, looked much brighter and livelier. These peepers didn't scare me.

Irene quietly pushed the door open and breathed, "Wow."

Her voice made me jump. "Huh? Oh, jeez, you're always startling me."

"Sorry. Dinner's ready when you are. You look good."

I grinned at her. "Yeah, I clean up well, apparently. Thanks again for these clothes."

As she handed me a plastic shopping bag, she replied, "You're welcome. Here, you can put your old clothes in this. I'll go set the table."

She pivoted and left the room while I scooped up my nasty old clothes. As I snatched the sweat pants by a leg, the lighter tumbled out, its tie-dye colors clashing with the brown carpet. Bending over, I picked it up and tossed it in my new jeans.

During the meal, we chatted about all sorts of topics. I found her to be an easy person to talk with. I hadn't realized how much I missed simple conversation with another human being.

"Well," I said as we walked toward the living room, "that sure was a fantastic meal! Thank you."

"You're welcome," she replied with a huge smile. "Say, have you seen the latest Bruce Willis movie? It's been on HBO the past few weeks."

"Um... No. I never got around to getting cable in my cardboard box."

She giggled like a little girl. "Too funny! Well, it's on tonight. I hear it's every man's favorite new movie. Ya wanna watch it?"

I shrugged as I plopped onto her sofa. "If I do, I won't have enough time to locate a new box to sleep in before nightfall. So, Irene, the answer is yes, as long as you don't mind me sleeping on this couch tonight."

As she took a seat next to me, she nodded while tossing me a sly smile. It didn't take long before I understood what that smile meant. Before the dust had settled on the first movie explosion, she leaned in and gave me a small, tender kiss. I guess the haircut and shower did more for my appearance than I thought. I returned the kiss with one of my own, long, lingering and passionate. We explored each other thoroughly. Being with Irene felt natural and comfortable. Before long, we found our way to the master bedroom.

When I awoke, for a fleeting moment I felt completely at ease, like I belonged right here. I rolled over and saw the back of Irene's head, disheveled black hair splayed against her white pillow, and I smiled. I also realized I had just slept a few hours without any horrible dreams, which hadn't happened in a long time.

Still, the moment passed and even though a light rain fell outside, I felt a strong urge to leave. Being careful not to disturb her, I eased myself onto the floor and scooped up my clothes. I carried them down into the living room, where the streetlights streaming in through the rain-soaked windows pierced the darkness. Using that light, I began yanking the jeans over my hips.

While buttoning up my new shirt, my gaze fell to a picture on the opposite wall. Framed perfectly inside a rectangle of light from the street, the photograph showed a man and a woman, smiling gleefully in front of a large oak tree. The woman I instantly recognized as Irene, taken many years ago. I smiled when I saw how young and giddy she looked in the photo. She really must've been in love with the man standing to her right.

"Do ya like the picture?" Irene stood at the entrance of the room, her pink robe tied loosely around her waist.

My breath caught in my throat. "Jeez, woman. Give me a heart attack, why don't ya?"

"Sorry. The picture. Take a good look at it." She turned and flipped a switch, illuminating the room with blinding light.

After my eyes adjusted, I did as she requested. "You look so beautiful here. How long ago was this?"

"Oh, a decade or so. Now, look at the man. Whatdya think of him?"

As I stared, I asked, "This your husband?"

"Yup. John Millicutty."

Grinning as widely as Irene, he seemed a happy fellow with his clean-shaven cheeks and short, brownish-black hair. I wondered if it ever bothered him, being a couple inches shorter than his woman. I hadn't noticed it before, but I also stood a couple inches shorter than Irene. Looking back at the man, I said, "I can't believe this guy was dumb enough to leave you."

"Extenuating circumstances." She sighed loudly before adding, "You still don't remember, do you? I really hoped the lasagna and sex therapy would help."

I spun to look into her eyes. "Lasagna and sex therapy?"

"Oh, where to start?" She asked as she picked up her purse and pulled out a pack of Kool cigarettes. Her hands shook slightly as she lit the cigarette with ... with a vibrantly colorful lighter! "You see..."

"Irene?" I produced my lighter and held it at eye level. "I found this near the fire."

Her eyes widened and her mouth parted slightly. "No, I... Oh... John, I'm so sorry. I didn't mean..." She approached me, her hands outstretched. "You weren't supposed to get hurt. You were in the center of the box, so I thought... I thought you'd wake up before then. You were always such a light sleeper. I didn't mean for you to get burned, John. Please believe me!"

Instinctively, as she moved closer to me, I inched toward the front door. "What the hell?! Why would you do this, you psycho? What've I ever done to you?"

"I just wanted to shock you into remembering. John, don't you get it?"

"Get what? And why do you keep calling me John?" I had to get away from this nut. I had backed almost to the door, so I spun and reached for the knob. "You're insane! You need help, lady."

"Why won't you remember? It's been over six months!"

As I yanked the door open and bolted down the steps into what had become a steady rain, she screamed, "Wait!"

Sprinting as fast as my body could stand, I ran down Main Street as the storm turned violent. "Crap!" I breathed as I suddenly realized I had nowhere to go. Before I realized it, I found myself on the steps of the library.

Swirling wind smacked my face with leaves and rain as I yanked on the library door. It didn't budge and I quickly realized they had closed for the night.

I plopped down onto the steps, panting heavily.

Sitting in the shadows of the Library's ornate overhang, I managed to find some shelter from the storm. I slumped down and fell into a restless sleep.

Gigantic metal trees loomed overhead, neatly in a row. Several people stood by my side, looking to me for guidance. Surrounded by large animals, the elephants and rhinos leapt and frolicked. Suddenly, a rhino staggered, slamming into one of the trees. It began to tip. Cracking and popping filled the air, quickly joined by screams of terror. The trees fell one into another like colossal dominoes, the metal forest becoming a torrent of artificial hail. Pieces crashed down around me as I pulled into a fetal position. A voice screamed out, "Help me John!" I looked around, but I couldn't see who called to me. The forest ...

I woke to someone repeatedly kicking the sole of my shoe. "You can't sleep here. Go away!"

"Wha? Oh, sorry." As I pulled myself to a seated position, I hugged myself tightly. Even though the morning sun poked through the scattering rain clouds, I couldn't stop shivering.

He stared at me for a moment before he spoke again, clearly not recognizing me right away after my transformation. "Oh, it's you again. All cleaned up, huh?" The man smoothed his thin, gray hair, wiping his hand on the front of his beige slacks. After scrutinizing me for a few more seconds, his taut features softened slightly. "You look miserable. I may not like you, but I can't let anyone suffer like this. Come on in," he said with a loud sigh. Pulling out a large set of keys attached to a metal hoop, he fumbled through several keys before finding the one that opened the front door of the library.

Though I appreciated his attempt at hospitality, his hostility made me nervous. As I walked into the dry, quiet building, I felt compelled to ask, "Did you say you don't like me? What've I ever done to you?"

His forehead crinkled up and he gave me a harsh, disbelieving glare. "Seriously? This whole thing isn't some deranged act, to get out of your responsibilities?"

"Deranged act? What are you going on about?"

The old man shook his head slowly and walked over to the computer against the wall. "Come over here," he said with a sweeping arm gesture. He powered it up and after accessing the newspaper archives, I found myself reading a very miserable tale from April First, 2005. The headline read, "April Fools Day Tragedy Claims Two."

Two men were killed and one seriously injured yesterday when a series of steel trusses collapsed at a local area construction site.

Workers from the Johnson Construction Company were erecting the main supports for a building at 1543 Farhat

Road when one of the trusses collapsed. This caused a chain reaction, which brought down all seven of the supports.

Abe Billman, 41 and Jesse Mason, 23, were killed after being buried under falling debris. Foreman John Millicutty, 39, is currently listed in critical condition. The other three members of the construction team escaped with minor injuries.

It took rescuers over 25 minutes to remove the heavy steel beams that trapped Billman and Mason. Billman was pronounced dead on arrival at Mercy Hospital in Menson, while Mason died on site.

"We believe a brace was improperly installed on the support truss," said Jason Johnson, owner of Johnson Construction, "and when that gave way, it caused a cascade failure. Everything came crashing down. I lost two good men today."

Millicutty was admitted to Mercy with severe head trauma. He has not regained consciousness.

I sat in the Library's hard, small-backed chair and stared at the article for a while. Underneath, the pictures told more of the story. A grainy, black-and-white photo of the accident scene showed a pile of debris, but the headshots of the victims mesmerized me the most. Abe Billman's picture showed me a man with a gap between his upper front teeth and a head with more bald spot than hair. I stared for several minutes at the shiny spot where the flash reflected off his head.

A young man in the prime of his life, Jesse Mason looked vibrant and rebellious, with wild hair and a cocky grin.

Then, I shifted over to John Millicutty. This guy kinda looked like the picture at Irene's, with a similar vibrancy to his eyes and the same chipper smile.

"Okay," I said to the librarian, "I don't get it. I see that something horrible happened to these men. But why show it to me?"

He looked at me like I sprouted a second nose. Again, he said, "Seriously? That's you, moron. You're John Millicutty."

"Excuse me? If that's true, then why, for God's sake, don't I remember any of it?"

"You need to keep reading." I accessed the next several days of newspaper archives.

It chronicled the coma that encompassed John Millicutty's brain for the next three days, as well as the amnesia he experienced upon awakening. One quote from the attending doctor said, "we expect his amnesia to be short term, but when coupled with the emotional loss he experienced, there's no telling how long it could last."

I looked over at the librarian. "Emotional loss?"

"The accident was your fault," he said matter-of-factly.

"What?"

"Or at least you blamed yourself. After all, you were the lead foreman. Of course, I blamed you, too."

"You... what?"

The old man shook his head slowly and scowled at me fiercely. "You don't even remember my name, do you? I'm Mac Mason. Jesse was my grandson. The authorities labeled it a freak accident, and I've come to

accept that. But it's been difficult to get over the fact that your negligence killed my grandson."
    I stared at the man blankly. "I... I don't..."
    "Yeah, yeah, you don't remember. I know. It's either extremely convenient or a sad, sad situation. From what I understand, you didn't know my Jesse very well. But Abe... oh, his death must've really got to you. You and he were best of friends, inseparable as teenagers and just as close as adults. I know you guys went fishing a lot..."
    "Okay," I cut him off, "So I spent a few days in a coma, woke up without memory of anything, and to this day, months later, I still have no memory of any of this? That makes no sense. What did the doctors do about it?"
    "You didn't give them much of a chance. Keep reading." A couple days later, this article appeared: *Amnesia Patient Escapes Hospital.*
    "Oh now, this is just stupid! It says here I simply walked out of the place in the middle of the night." After hearing a hush from someone on the other side of the library who I hadn't even noticed before this, I turned my rant into a whisper. "Seriously, this occurred days after the accident. Why don't I remember it, Mac?"
    "Hey, you're asking me? No one completely understands the intricacies of the human brain. I certainly don't know why you snuck out of the hospital under cover of darkness, or why you don't remember. But this, John, is a fact. That man right there," he tapped the photo of John Millicutty, "is you. Your wife Irene searched for you, as did the rest of the town, but you disappeared rather thoroughly. No one even knew you were still around until a couple months ago, when Milner spotted you rummaging through the trash behind his Quik Stop. You've been the talk of Red Oak."

Looking over at the scowling old coot, I shrugged as I asked, "All right, so what do we do now?"

Mac hopped to his feet. "Frankly, I don't care what you do. I've come to grips with Jesse's death. It was an accident. Whether or not you're to blame for that accident, that's immaterial. At this point, it's up to you. Either you go apologize to Irene for abandoning her, or you crawl back under that rock. Makes no difference to me."

"Apologize? That whack-job set me on fire!"

Mac actually chuckled at me. "Wait, you're saying Irene did that? Oh, that's rich!"

"Rich? She could've killed me!"

"Well, now, you need to look at it from her point of view. You're in this horrible accident, then you wake up from a coma not knowing her. Then, you run away. You might as well've been killed in the accident. At least she would've had some closure. But instead, you slinked away to live in the woods."

"But I don't remember any of this!"

"And that's the worst part. She can't even be mad at you for abandoning her when she needed you the most. Maybe that's why she did it. Maybe she thought the fire might jar something loose. Hell, at least it got you motivated. Now," he added as he turned his back on me, "I have a job to perform here. Don't stay too long."

As it turned out, I did stay too long. I sat in that uncomfortable chair for hours, reading every article over and over, staring at the pictures, trying to burn them into my memory. Or force their release from the vault in my brain.

The sun hung low in the evening sky, hurling vibrant reds and oranges across the deepening blue of the horizon. Standing on Irene's porch, I beat loudly upon her door until she answered. When she did, I exclaimed with a deep scowl. "I need to know why you tried to kill me."

She turned pale. "I wasn't trying to kill you, John. You gotta believe me. I... I was... Oh, I don't know, John. I guess I was trying to force you to come home. You live here. You're my husband."

"Yes, yes, I've been at the library, I read the articles. So how does flame-broiling me help?"

She walked past me and sat down on the porch swing. After burying her face in her hands for a moment, she looked up and with tears on her cheeks, she muttered, "I didn't plan to do it. I had heard rumors you were living down by the river, so I went to see for myself. I saw you sleeping there, and I guess I thought if I destroyed the box, you'd have to come home. I thought you'd wake up long before the flames got to you. I'm so sorry. It all happened so fast and I panicked."

I let her sit there for a while, sobbing into her hands. Eventually, I sat down next to her. "I doubt I can ever forgive you, y'know. But having read the articles about the accident, I sorta understand. I get your loneliness, your frustration."

She looked up at me with a face that looked like it had been caught in a rainstorm. "Did it help any? Do you remember who you are?"

I shook my head slowly. "But I wouldn't mind hearing about this man named John. Apparently, he's so great you'd fry a homeless man to get him back."

The two of us sat for hours in her living room, sipping lemonade and looking at pictures. "This one was taken a few years back, at Carlsbad. You were so handsome."

Looking at this photo, I fought to stifle a chuckle. The man, clad in beige Dockers and poop-brown loafers with a pink knit shirt nearly brought a tear to my eye. "Pink? Are you kidding? What, did you dress me?"

"I could lie and say you always loved pink, but no. You're right, you wore this outfit to please me."

"Wow. I must've really loved you."

The look she shot me caused instant regret of my wording. I looked into her teary blue eyes and asked, "So, how long after this did the accident happen?"

Blotting her eyes with a tissue, she replied, "Three, four years, maybe. There are a lot of memories in this book. Oh, here's my favorite wedding photo."

Irene sure looked radiant in that flowing white dress. Her smile lit up the whole picture, probably the whole room, and I told her so.

She smiled as a fresh tear tumbled down her cheek. "The reception was so much fun."

"Yeah it was! The look you gave me when I crammed that piece of wedding cake into your face. Priceless!"

It took a moment for the reality to set in. "John? You remembered that?"

"Oh my. I did, Irene. I did!"

We sat on that couch, in our tight embrace, for what felt like hours.

Frankly, I felt a bit guilty, pretending to remember like that. After all, didn't everyone smash cake at weddings? All I knew for sure was I did not want to be homeless through a cold, Michigan winter. I needed a roof over my head. Besides, I'd be a fool to pass up this sweet deal. I could certainly get used to Irene's lasagna and sex therapy.

The Covered Bridge

Jan McCaffrey

There is a winding unpaved road
    That leads into the past
Sheltered by ancient oaks,
    Their midday shadows cast
Ghostly shapes along the way,
    Once traveled by horse and sleigh.

And then a covered bridge appears
    Weather-beaten and time worn,
A tunnel to yesteryear.
    Spanning the restless river
Weathered wooden planks
    Stretch across the rapids,
Connecting the river's banks.

Within its walls distant echoes
    Of horses' hoofs
Fill the dusty air
    Where initials were carved
By long ago lovers
    Seeking shelter there.

Rippling waters from the past
    Seep between wood and ridge,
A tribute to a slower age.
    The timeless covered bridge.

Simple Gifts In The Park

Wanda Davison

A child's hand in mine.
The crunch of twigs
and stones underfoot.
Rusty bridge
and creaky boards,
a rush of excited calm.

Hearty conversations
of runners sprinting past.
Birds, ducks, chipmunks
offering their beauty
and humorous displays.

Two ducks fighting while
others simply part around them,
knowing this is not their battle
to stop or start.

A wise old woman sitting true
on the bench.
Thoughtful old men resting
beside her.
Their warm, silent "Hello"
as we pass by.

Yackity geese overhead,
whoosh-landing on the river.
Excited response from
little one's heart.

Wide eyes, questions, thrills,
jumping on the path.

Mother with children
playing on the swings.
Empty soccer field and
basketball court
ready to be filled.

Litter on the river bank
seeking community efforts.
Evergreens, grasses and bushes,
somewhat empty but strong as ever.

All seeking to bloom,
awaiting Spring.
At one in consciousness,
simply because all are there,
together at that one moment.

Treasures Beyond Measure

C. J. Tody

Kayle turned off the northbound interstate, smiling. *Just a few more miles!*
 Autumn color abounded around her. Happily driving toward the lakeside home where she'd attended kindergarten, she basked in the fragrance of a brilliant overgrown canopy framing the highway. Vivid memories flashed through her mind, ricocheted off unsatisfied longings from the intervening years, and accelerated the craving to recreate her childhood experience. She peered around, realizing that in a few more miles she'd see Shady Shores Park again.
 Her recent departure from a long, grueling career, accented by wrenching endings and the rigors of single parenthood, provided Kayle with newfound freedom. So she'd carved out a little time from her semi-retirement business for a trip to explore her roots and Michigan's natural peninsular beauty. She longed to travel around the islands and waterways, too. Her vigorous, healthy, youthful zest allowed her to sample natural abundance as freely as she chose, without some of the limitations placed on her by companions.
 She had dreams which she felt only she could understand, and began to translate some of them into a few private thoughts: *Once I arrive at the Park, I'll sit by the water's edge and spend some time writing about my experiences while living there. I'm bound to recapture some of the imagination I developed while playing there as a young child.*

Oh, she'd had many dreams as a child, but some were now forgotten. She'd quickly discovered the meaning of the old adage 'not all dreams are meant to be shared.' In all her innocence, she'd once thought that others would help her fulfill her wishes. Until, that is, she'd heard them scoff and ignore or defuse her efforts. There simply *had* to be a way to uncover those lost dreams again.

As a young child sitting in the fragrant security of grandma's lap, she'd heard her say, "You have to find your passion. There's no excuse not to dream." But when Kayle asked her how to do that, Grandma would only reply, "You have to listen to your heartbeat and dance." While that didn't make much more sense to her now than when she was four or five, she vowed to at least use some of her free time to search for innate passions that were set aside at times when she was too busy to pursue them.

Armed with a minivan she playfully referred to as 'Babe, the Blue Ox,' Kayle felt safe and secure. It allowed her to turn in small spaces, accelerate into quick getaways, and gain broad perspective on her surroundings. With the push of a button she could open, close, or lock all access areas. With Babe at her command, she felt she could safely visit isolated locations.

For the time being, she decided to curtail remote expeditions and island hopping in favor of exploring the lush inland wilderness areas of Michigan where she'd lived for five decades. During that time, her father developed an internationally acclaimed natural resource career and she, in turn, shaped her adult life.

She'd always lived in Michigan, but she'd moved from an urban setting to a remote log cabin outside Vanderbilt when she was four years old. Part of a larger federal research station complex on the Pigeon River, the wilderness cabin skirted a compound that housed her wild pet, a blind elk dubbed Nellie. At various other times while living there she helped her father skin rabbits, held the pliers while he pulled porcupine needles from his hunting dog, and studied folk arts with her mother. She slept in the attic bedroom with her baby sister, and acquired skills in tap dance and baton in the nearby town.

At five, she moved to Shady Shores and began school. For the next two years, her father led a river diversion project, creating a new watershed. Her family resided in a seemingly enchanted green cottage with a steeply A-shaped roof soaring two shingled stories from ground level into the sky. It sat near the water's edge, flanked by a residential park that was, in turn, sandwiched between two recreational lakes.

Memories of the cottage swept across her inner field of vision like a motion picture while she mused to herself, *once I'm back there, I can see the quaint rental we lived in.* She immersed herself in the bittersweet memory for a moment. *When we moved there, it was as if a storybook had come playfully to life and I lived the tale from the inside out, just as it was being written. Only I was too young to realize it at the time.* To a small child moving from place to place, family life can seem like a fairy tale when the right elements are present: preoccupied parents, playful stories, imaginative spaces, and long, lonely hours to fill. With more freedom now to pursue her own interests, Kayle sought renewal by finding linkages to her past. She intended to immerse herself in an epic of self-discovery by uncovering and reigniting former passions, thus sculpting a new sense of depth to her ultimate life purpose of realizing her dreams.

Albert Einstein once said that 'Imagination is more important than knowledge.' By extension, this hints that allowing the imaginative magic of childhood to flourish is essential to a child's well being; and, in turn, to the creativity of the adult the child later becomes. If the flow of imagination is snapped off too early and the 'magical child' goes into exile, creative health can run dry and require a great deal of priming to restore.

Ah, to be able to tap into the wonder, the incredible awe of childhood, the perception that still holds the privilege and power to ignite artistic pursuit in adulthood. Childhood is a magical time, a period when images haven't yet been tucked away in little boxes, allowing them to be imbued with an organic sense of flow. Kayle still remembered some of her early experiences. But many were still tucked away in the cobwebby corners of rustic cottages, lodges, and relatives' homes. These were the stages on which her favorite memories played to her as a delighted audience while her tears dried up in the presence of love and acceptance, laughter, and the scent of flowers. But what had she hidden away in those dusty corners?

She reminisced again. *While living by the lake, I sometimes played with cottagers' children beside 'fairy doors' we found in our backyards.* To reconnect to the playfulness of her younger self, she wanted to rediscover the small still voice of the girl who accelerated too quickly from childhood. Due to changes in her family, she became saddled with early responsibility too heavy for a child. Naturally, some memories are painful, and like others in the same position, she simply forgot them when no close friend surfaced to share her experiences. Strict reality was the only state of being allowable to the daughter of a scientist, regardless of how harshly that might materialize. Fantasy and role-playing were discouraged as foolish behavior at home. But other children and relatives had freely shared their imagination, which had encouraged her suppressed nature to surface.

Long lost recollections bubbled into her awareness like a fresh, cool spring on a hot summer day. *We lived next to a big hill, the "enchanted fairy raft," holding aloft a souvenir store where the children gathered.*

In order to fuel her new career as a multimedia artist, Kayle needed more material to fill her personal treasure chest with the essence of that imaginative child. Naturally, she planned and set goals, and expected to fulfill them. Considered by some to possess a "Renaissance Soul" with many assets and abilities, she had mastered amazing adult challenges and didn't expect to lose that ability. Rather, she sought to enrich her creative abilities by building more elastic connections between her own stages of development and with new people and ideas she had yet to encounter. She also knew that unpredictable opportunities often arose while journeying solo. Her hopes led her forward. She hoped to reconnect with something more ethereal, a dreamlike quality that would allow her to begin thinking more like she had as an inventive child. So, instead of rigidly holding to all of her plans, she decided to leave enough room for spontaneity to occur before her next adventure came flying around the bend.

That decision encouraged more youthful memories to emerge and she found herself thinking abstractly again. *Our cottage doors shone like emeralds behind me as I walked up the hill, underneath which dwelt the king of the northern fairies...*

Instinctively, Kayle hit the brake pedal and froze, her reverie shattered.

"Ooofff!!!" she yelped in surprise, as a deer crossed the highway in front of her. Her speedy reflexes proved legendary this time. "Missed that one," she affirmed to herself. Then a huge smile broke over her face.

She sometimes spoke when alone, but it surprised her.

"At such a high cost, though, Mr. Deer," she railed impulsively. "Just when I'd finally started to make contact with a younger part of myself, too. Thanks to you, she's gone again," she hissed aloud, too upset to be quiet even though no one was there to hear her. Now a safe distance away, the regal buck turned his antlered head to watch her pass his densely forested hill. She looked quickly from one side of the road to the other questioningly to check for other deer. Seeing none, she resumed speed. She returned to meditation, mulling over a hodgepodge of scattered thought, wondering why it was significant to her that he turned to look at her once safe.

Most deer simply run off and never look back. Should I know why he did that?

Pondering randomly wasn't very effective, so she concentrated on past encounters. She knew this wasn't the first time. Deer-like creatures were always doing odd things around her when she drove, but she didn't worry about it because they never collided. Sometimes they ran from the woods as if pursued by the devil's own dog. Other times they sauntered or floated across the road like a spirit in the wind, like the huge elk that crossed her moonlit path on California's Lost Coast.

Another deer left her gasping when it ran at full speed between her car and another going in opposite directions, their oncoming headlights just a couple of feet apart before they slid by each other. When that happened, signs beside the highway pointed north toward Mt. Rainier and south toward Mt. St. Helens, so she knew that as she headed east toward Yakima, Washington, she drove through a remote, spiritual sort of area between the two mountains. It shook her up so much that when she reached Yakima, she heard her engine subtly cough and sputter. An oil change failed to resolve the situation; a damaged oil gasket nearly caused the car to break down on the highway, leaving her stranded and alone. With the advanced warning, however, she was quickly able to find a dealership to repair her car.

Something swung freely on her windshield and she focused away from the scene on the road outside.

Earlier, she'd hung a Figment bobble on the window to remind herself to use some imagination instead of always taking things at face value. An idea entered her mind as she silently reproached herself and decided to ask some thought provoking questions. How do deer feel about this highway? Is it intrusive to them? How awesome would these wooded hills have appeared to a deer two hundred years ago when moccasin-clad Indians walked freely through the unbroken forest? *Wouldn't the unbroken wilderness make a great painting?*

Another idea occurred to her, thanks to an awakened imagination. Is the repeated exposure to fleet-footed wild animals like deer and elk merely a random coincidence?   Or is it more, perhaps even an awareness raising?   Generally, she focused rather narrowly on her goals instead of considering what she could not see with her own eyes; getting from here to there mattered in her busy life. She vowed to keep her eyes open in case an unusual problem or opportunity arose. Something extraordinary was about to happen, she was certain of it!

Slick wheels of foresight quietly turned to matters she considered practical. She wondered if she'd even recognize Shady Shores Park after so many years. Thoughts of painting the unbroken wild invited her to consider a visit to an area art supply store. *Hmmm...wonder what's in stock this time of year?*

Soon Kayle entered a small but growing community spread thinly along the southern shoreline of Houghton Lake. Abundant seasonal activity often resulted in frequent turnover among local businesses and scarce tourist activity on early autumn weekdays, such as this. Creative souls, though, regularly outfit their studios at Arnie's Arts and Crafts. The store was hard to avoid, since it was conveniently located on the most direct route to her destination, Shady Shores Park.

Fortunately, Kayle reached Arnie's shortly before closing. With a half an hour remaining, she sped through the store bypassing all she might otherwise have lingered over in the comfortably slow shopping mode that she fondly referred to as an artist's date. By the time the store closed at four that afternoon, two bags of treasure rested safely out of sight under a blanket in her car. Her wallet felt considerably lighter.

"OK, no more of that!" Kayle declared happily under her breath as she reclaimed the driver's seat. Veering into traffic, she drove toward West Branch, intending to continue the journey until she reached the road leading to Shady Shores. However, two blocks later she spied a prominent gift shop sign on the opposite side of the busy four-lane street. "Oh, nooooo you don't!" she cried aloud, resisting the almost palpable pull of the steering wheel.

Kayle had recognized what was previously invisible to her. Normally, she'd stay narrowly focused on her intended destination, especially so close to dusk when the dense deer population traveled the same country highway. But the earlier deer incident awakened her imagination and raised her awareness strongly enough for her to believe that she had found something she'd known in her childhood so valuable she wanted to take the time and effort to explore. Something much younger and stronger surfaced deep inside her, and an inner voice gained strength until it loudly exclaimed, "Oh, gotta go see it!" In fact, it screamed so loudly that she veered into the gravel lane beside the store to preserve her option.

Sitting in the van, Kayle needed to decide whether or not to follow her childish intuition. She knew she should move on, since stopping so late in the day could result in endangered driving later in darkness. On the other hand, she didn't tend to attract accidents, with or without deer crossing the road, and the Indian Store could close permanently one day. From her studies, she knew that unexpected callings are likely to issue from the soul, so unanswered calls can lead to frustration or disaster, and she decided not to take that chance. She answered the call to adventure and pulled into the parking lot beside the store.

A sign in the window pronounced "Open." Colorful windsocks danced and flashed in the sunny roadside breeze. A half-open screen door provided an inviting entrance. Defying the inner pull to go immediately inside, she took a calculated risk. Quickly she cruised back out of the lot, hoping it would stay open awhile longer, and drove to the lakeshore two blocks north along a dirt road. Searching the shoreline for answers to the relentless questions that drove her here, she quivered in anticipation. Where was that weekly rental cottage her family enjoyed so long ago? She'd relived the experience for years, but only just now realized that it was probably on the beach behind the Indian Shoppe.

Kayle accessed a rich memory repository to give her thoughts free reign. She flashed back to envision

"Kay," her younger self as a child of ten, playing in the lake outside a pristine white cottage one sunny afternoon. Kay submerged and rose with a leap, splashing a giggly playmate. Another youngster surfaced nearby and the three laughed as they chased each other in the surf. Then they tagged each other in an underwater game of hide and seek.

Refueled by the pleasant recollection, Kayle reviewed the vivid week by the lake. Mom dealt with the four children all week so she helped watch her younger brother and sisters, who ranged in age from one to six. Dad left them there to enjoy the lake, but he hoped to join them later on when he returned from one of his frequent business trips into Michigan's outback. Summer homework kept Kay partially occupied, with freedom to play in the fresh air. *It was a great summer vacation!*

Kayle looked pensively out the van window, indulging herself in a flowing train of memories. Like most kids, Kay loved water. One day, though, she'd disobeyed her mother and kept swimming. Without sunscreen to protect tender shoulders from the harmful rays reflected by the shallow lake, the time was long past to don a shirt. She'd had to pay the consequences from exposure to radiation that fricasseed her back. Once the sunburn fully developed, she resembled a lobster with blisters, but the sunburn hadn't fully matured and she enjoyed a period of blissful ignorance. With dinner at least an hour away, she sought a few minutes to follow her heart's desire.

While riding to the lake, she'd sparked an interest in something she saw beside the road. A sign outside a Main Street shop glowed colorfully, sporting a painted, feathered Indian riding a horse into the setting sun. Desperate to explore the store's contents, she requested permission to walk there alone.

Indian lore fascinated her. Kay wore rawhide and feathers like an Indian maiden for costume events and small town parades. Colorful totem poles and cushy moccasins piqued her imagination, teasing her to enter. Besides, she wanted to see if she could buy an Eskimo Indian doll with a fur hooded white leather coat. "I know it's gonna cost more money than I have, Mom," she'd pleaded, "but I really only want a little lookabout, Mom, that's all. Please, please Mommy! Please let me go?" She cajoled and wangled.

Finally, Mom agreed to let her walk to the store, but only if she promised to return quickly. "OK, but you have to be back in time for dinner," warned Mom, who didn't yet know about Kay's sunburn. Her t-shirt covered the characteristic deep purplish-red hue and her cheek color revealed nothing remarkable.

With permission to visit the souvenir store, Kay sprinted off before Mom could change her mind. Soon she arrived at the shop. She entered and quickly located the Indian doll she wanted. As she had anticipated, it cost more than the money she'd brought to spend. Disappointed, she hunted for a toy with a friendlier price tag. On a nearby shelf sat a small, inexpensive Indian beading loom. Kay liked to make beautiful things, and the loom awakened in her an ancient longing for hands-on artwork. Besides, she had enough money for this purchase. She tucked the flat box under her arm and carried it, while she looked around to make certain this choice was what she really wanted.

The hunt for treasure engrossed her compellingly. She pawed through Indian-themed merchandise, so preoccupied that she didn't notice anyone else enter the room.

When someone tapped her back unexpectedly, Kay jumped several inches. "Yoweee!" she screamed. Distress rippled over her burnt hide. She hadn't seen anyone! The shock startled her into a painful awareness of the throbbing sunburn whiplashing her shoulders.

"Hi!" The friendly store clerk was a volcano of enthusiasm. She smiled and gestured toward the beading looms. "Like some help?" she bubbled over the brim of her horn rims. "It's great stuff, isn't it?"

"'Eeeyow-w-w-w!" Kay couldn't stop yelping. "It's my back," she sobbed between gasps.

The clerk tensed, involuntarily pulling her taut mouth into a grimace. Her eyebrows shot up as her eyes widened, though she didn't say a word.

Noting the salesperson's horrified expression, Kay stammered, "S-sun-b-b-burn."

After Kay explained the situation to her, the store clerk retreated almost as quickly as she'd appeared.

Kay expected that when she left, she'd soon return with some sort of special sunburn treatment for her, perhaps an Indian remedy. But when she failed to return, Kay decided that sunburn was such a common summer ailment by the lake that it was unremarkable. She moved on, stiffening when her frayed nerve endings rubbed against her woven shirt. Portions of it stuck to her blistered shoulders. She felt nearly paralyzed after the painful incident and further shopping became impossible. She shuffled cautiously toward the cashier and paid for the reasonably priced loom with her back sizzling and her stomach clenching into knots. Then she hurried quickly down the cool lane cradling her prize gingerly, afraid her legs might strand her at the side of the road before she reached her waiting dinner.

Later that night she made a frightening new discovery. She couldn't remove her clothes or put on pajamas. She could not get into bed either; every stiff movement she made led to painful stress on the burn. Finally she took a gentle, cool shower. Keeping her skin hydrated, she pulled together two stuffed chairs and sat in one. Slowly she pulled one leg after the other into the second chair, and spent the entire night restlessly napping upright under a damp towel.

That is how Mother found her the next morning, too burnt to sleep and too proud to ask for help. *Be stalwart like the Indians at Zeke's Old Indian Gift Shoppe*, Kay thought as she buffaloed her way through the blisters and peeling that followed. After all, she'd defied her mother when told to leave the water. Of course, Mom would have helped her anyway, and eventually soothed Kay's pain with ointment. But Mom also cared for younger children and Kay knew treatment at the lake could be hard to find without a vehicle. Despite being a recalcitrant, obstinate child who defied her mother and stayed out too long, Kay really loved Mama. She didn't want to cause Mom any more work, so she accepted responsibility for herself without complaint.

Despite that horrible incident, the summer vacation was a glorious, memorable time of family togetherness and endless play by the edge of sunlit water so shallow they needed no watchful lifeguard. But for her the Indian shop highlighted the entire experience.

Now standing at the water's edge, Kayle remembered that she wanted to revisit the shop. *Uh oh, must go!* She thought, bolting toward the van. *Oh, no...what if it closes?* Agonizing, she drove on.

As the Blue Ox turned toward Main Street, Kayle resumed her reflection, realizing fond memories of her lakeside vacation still persisted; in fact, it was one of the most memorable events of her childhood.

During the short drive, she puzzled over the old Indian shop. It did look familiar. She wasn't positive it was the same shop, though, and couldn't understand why she'd missed it on other visits to the lake. Had she been too busy, too preoccupied, or just narrowly focused on other purposes? Nothing had ever taken her on a journey into the past before her nest emptied of children, love, and career. Now she drove down the dirt street realizing that the present moment held a unique significance for her.

Moments later, she parked her car and looked at the half-open door. Every open door, she knew, held a question. In this case she knew just what to do. She strode confidently toward the gaping door, and stepped unabashedly back in time.

Anticipation stirred in her, found long-buried embers of childish excitement, and fanned them into furious flames of curiosity as she pushed forward in slow motion. Standing forty years later at the threshold of what must surely be the same Indian gift shop, she trembled. Exulted, the memory of her terrible sunburn overshadowed and forgotten by her fresh discovery, she shook with excitement and trepidation. Her dream of reconnecting to the past could burst if she were mistaken about the shop.

Feeling like a small child, she reached forward to touch the screen door handle. Focused like a powerful young woman, she turned the knob and pushed open the inner door.

Split, while temporarily existing in a startling paradigm in which both her childish attitudes and womanly perspectives paralleled and complemented each other, she observed neat rows of colorful souvenirs. Walking into them was like stepping into a motion picture setting re-created to honor her past and center her in the present. In fact, it was almost too much to believe.

Immediately she recognized the telltale sign of long-term residence, as a faint musty odor engulfed her sinuses. *Omigosh,* she acknowledged to herself, *this is the store!* Even the aisle layout was the same.

Glancing around, Kayle had to stop her hand midair from reaching for a lollypop. Strips of penny candy hung from a nearby rack. A Tootsie Roll sign stimulated her sense of taste, until she heard the deep, silent cry: *I want some of that!* Her hand reached out more as a reflex action than as a conscious move. As it froze in empty space, she reacted by wondering where that particular cry originated.

She needed to regain a sense of control, so she refocused onto practical matters. The cost of the candy sent her reeling. Vast price differences existed. But, despite her efforts to recognize that penny candy now cost a quarter, Kayle discovered that she truly felt as if she'd stepped into her own past.

Eventually she calmed down as she stood there quietly, not wishing to break the spell cast over her when she entered. She answered the question posed by the half-open door and a sense of relaxed indulgence began to resurface, along with the return of the presence of mind she needed to fully absorb her retrospective surroundings.

Yes, over there on the right side, bright turquoise Southwest Indian jewelry still glittered in the long glass case, only now it carried the name "Native American Jewelry." An open, revolving rack at the far end offered her the exact earrings she sought.

A sense of paradox between old and new arose when she noticed that the old moccasin shop still sat tucked away at the rear of the store, but with a modern twist: a computer monitor now rested among the leather goods.

Desiring uninterrupted time to absorb her surroundings, Kayle wandered around the store in silence. Indian dolls coveted so long ago by ten-year-old Kay still sat on their original shelf. But now they presented a more modern plethora of sizes and wore an even wider variety of leather garments. Kayle tempted herself, and then decided there was simply no display space at home. Still drawn to the dolls, she considered buying for her young granddaughters. Then she remembered seeing other leather clad Indian dolls packed into their crowded curio cabinets. She realized then that the Eskimo Indian doll she'd once wanted would not now be quite as special to children of abundance as it was to her when she was a child. So she tried on a few moccasins, poked at furry miniature stuffed animals, and looked around for an Indian beading loom without finding one.

She had a sudden realization. *Things are different now. I like the life I've built, and don't need an Indian doll or beading loom to be happy anymore.* She felt a sense of completion as she carried the cherished earrings to the cashier along with some stone arrowheads and sandbox toys for grandchildren that she found so irresistible they somehow seemed to have leapt into her hands.

Kayle possessed such an exhilarating sense of wonder and awe that she felt inspired to tell her story to the cashier. She shared how she'd come in so long ago with a sunburn while vacationing in a nearby lake cottage, how her memory of the old Indian gift shop was still indelible forty years later, and how she'd sensed the store's antiquity even before she entered.

The aging clerk brightened. "Yes, I remember you!" She exclaimed in recognition, her entire face at once glowing with both an inner light and as if backlit by an angel lamp. "You were just a little thing, floundering about in the shop looking for something special. I wanted to help you. But when I discovered how much I hurt you with my friendly pat, well, I just had to have a good cry and beg some sort of forgiveness from myself. It was obvious you were unaware that your sunburn had blistered. I heard the phone ring, and went to answer it with tears flowing down my cheeks. It was impossible for me to return to the floor in that condition to apologize. Thank goodness I had a young lady to run the cash register. I'm so sorry. Since then I've been haunted by the memory every so often. Can you forgive me?" she implored. "Please?" She paused, and then added, "Oh, where are my manners? I'm Faith, and I'm mighty glad to finally meet you again!"

"Of course I forgive you," soothed Kayle, taking the woman's aging hands in her own warm grasp.

Kayle decided not to dwell on the past, but to diverge into a little fun now that she'd solved the puzzle. "Would you tell me a little about the store?" She queried the shopkeeper. "How did it originate? Why is it still here, looking just the same as when I was a child?"

The elderly proprietor brightened even further as she talked with Kayle. "It's been in the hands of the same family for the entire operation."

"Why then," Kayle asked, "does it bear this name?"

"Oh," she remembered, "Zeke's Old Indian Shoppe... Oh, yes, Fred Zeke started the store back around 1952 and he only held it for a year or two. By the way, do you know that in all these years, this will be the first time we will be closing for the winter in November?

"That's only a few weeks away!" Kayle marveled

at that piece of information. "How amazing that I was able to visit you today," she said. "In fact, I think some sort of miracle has occurred. I could so easily have missed seeing you. I went over to Arnie's and the lakeshore first, and didn't get back here until after 4:30. I'm so glad you decided to close two hours later tonight. As a result, I was able to visit and spend a little time here. This is certainly a coincidence, wouldn't you say?"

Faith nodded her agreement. They both laughed and took a few minutes to sit and share a cup of coffee on a friendly basis before parting to pursue their separate lives.

Something very strange had indeed occurred. Forty years after her cottage stay, Kayle revisited the store and it remained open plenty long enough for her late arrival. There was sufficient time even though she'd come there rather indirectly, after allowing memories to resurface by the water's edge. Moreover, she was there in time to hear the announcement about the first winter closing and talk in depth with the same owner she'd met when she was only ten years old. The event seemed altogether extraordinary, even phenomenal. Later on, it would prove to be even more miraculous than it seemed at the time.

"Farewell," crooned Kayle. "It was wonderful to see you again, and thank you for an amazing childhood encounter!"

Kayle waved as she walked outside to the Blue Ox, put away her new treasures, and headed further down the road.

Sunset approached with stealth. With it arrived a time of dangerous darkness in the land of a million deer. Kayle decided that her dream of seeing Shady Shores would wait another day, as she'd already accumulated treasures beyond measure for her childhood treasure chest. Tonight she slept soundly at the water's edge. While she slept, she dreamed of the deer she'd encountered earlier that day. Again it turned back to look her in the eye. A rosy red bow wrapped around its neck and a caution sign flashed gently behind its antlers, steadily dissolving into the mist rising from the road ahead.

    Waking at midnight, Kayle realized that the deer was a sort of gift. It was an omen or warning sign sent to encourage her to slow down, be aware, and recognize those amazing circumstances lying in wait. It was also a reminder to exercise precautionary driving in an abundant land of wandering wildlife and she vowed to return to sleep so tomorrow could introduce its own new adventures at Shady Shores.

    One year later, Kayle returned to Zeke's Old Indian Gift Shoppe. A considerably younger shopkeeper helped her find jewelry this time. Otherwise, the store remained much the same as before.

    "You're the new owner?" Kayle gestured toward the young cashier.

    "Yes. I inherited the shop this winter when the former owner passed on," shared Jessica as she processed the jewelry sale. "Due to my long years of service, I was the closest thing to family she'd ever had."

    "Do you know that I saw her just before she died?" Kayle marveled. "I also visited the shop as a child. But I'd never had time to revisit until that day."

    As fate would dictate, when Kayle visited the shop on her way to Shady Shores the previous year, she'd shown up just in time to say good-bye to Faith, the store's proprietor for over half a century.

    "She told me about you," continued Jessica, "and what happened one day forty years ago when, in a mood of good humor, she clapped you on your back without realizing you were sunburned. When Faith suddenly retreated, it was because she was shocked to discover your pain. Just before she died, she told me: 'Thank goodness I kept the shop going for years until the day Kayle remembered us, found the shop again, and interrupted her travel plans to stop in.' By doing so, I think she found a sense of forgiveness she'd sought for years. Within weeks of your encounter, she departed this life, leaving me in charge of the only career I have ever wanted...this shop," Jessica concluded, almost tearfully.

Kayle stared blankly at the jewelry sack in her hand while the clerk told her about Faith's passing.

"Apparently, Kayle," continued Jessica, "even though it'd been a long time before you stepped back into the shop, it was still pretty much as when you were a child. Am I right? Must have been an incredible experience. What was it like?"

"Well," stunned, Kayle finally grasped the new topic thread and picked it up, "...well, it was like crossing a threshold into the past. An unexpected piece of my younger self lingered there and I connected strongly with it. This led me to feel vulnerable, flooded with the same feelings that I must have felt when I was ten years old, looking for a doll."

Kayle's face clouded. A tear snaked down her trembling cheek, leaving a faint trace of navy mascara along its trail. "I relayed the story about my long ago sunburn to the shopkeeper while I paid for the earrings last year, not realizing that she was the same person who shared my childhood experience. So many years had passed. Faith introduced herself excitedly and told me stories about the shop. After a while she warned me that the shop would close for the first time over the winter

...apparently that was only a few weeks before she died. Then we said our good-byes."

Kayle regained her composure as she spoke. She shook Jessica's hand as they bade each other farewell.

At long last, the Blue Ox moved on down the highway toward the shady little cottage that had lured Kayle to travel north. During the drive to Shady Shores, amazing childhood memories surfaced for her, primed by her visit to Zeke's. Silver skates flashed once more on the frozen lake in front of the cottage. Playmates climbed stony fences and skipped stones at the water's edge as their bare toes sunk into the soft, mossy bank beside the water lily cove. Youngsters bought gum at the village store near the entrance to the school and blew great pink bubbles at each other. Five-year-olds hunted for fairy doors and found them at the base of hollow trees. Kindergartners rushed by, dragging unhappily caged froghoppers trying frantically to escape.

Kayle knew that her long ago playmates were grown now. However, by the time she arrived lakeside she could almost see them again as children, skipping along gravel driveways between cottages, calling each other out to play.

Then she returned home to look for other half open doorways to her imagination. She wrote her stories, and successfully sculpted a series of clay creatures that reflected the spirit of playfulness she'd united with on such an amazing level. Her reconnection seemed to be just an everyday miracle, yet it was an extraordinary gift that contributed to Kayle's childhood treasure chest.

Muddle in a Puddle

Jan McCaffrey

What is it about a puddle
No matter what its size
That brings fascination
To a youngster's eyes?

What magnetic forces
Draws him ever near
As cautiously he pokes a toe
And watches rings appear?

One foot and then the other
Before we can object
Plunk! He's in the water
Nearly to his neck!

Mud is so inviting
Such fun for making pies
A curious tot can't fight the urge
Of trying it on for size.

When Autumn Comes

Rosalie Sanara Petrouske

On Lake Odessa, I watch the mallards swim up and bob for food, their small heads under water, tail feathers standing upright. It is late September, and I am here with a group of women friends for a writing retreat. We are sharing stories about our lives. As I sit by the window with an open journal in my lap, the antics of the mallards take me back to when my daughter was still a little girl. We lived in the Upper Peninsula of Michigan in Marquette, and often I took Senara on long walks. Down at Lower Harbor, we dropped bits of bread or corn kernels into the water and laughed as the ducks scrambled to gather the pieces into their bills. On other days, we drove to Presque Isle, past tall Lombardy poplar trees lining Lakeshore Boulevard, and walked into the island woods, Senara holding my hand. We gathered leaves from sugar maples, red oaks and white birches, tucking them into our pockets along with acorns and pinecones. We named each leaf a different color: kettle bottom bronze, bread crust brown, candy corn orange, until we ran out of metaphors. By the end of September in Northern Michigan, the air was already turning crisp with the coming winter's first chill. Life was simple then. I was learning to be a single mother and contrary to the traditional wisdom, finding it surprisingly easy. Senara at four and then five bounded through life full of energy, long light curls flying, dark eyes so much like my own.

In the woods, breathing in that loamy smell of damp earth, Senara listened for the ovenbird's call, *teacher-teacher-teacher*, or the red-eyed vireo chirping *look-up, up here*, and sometimes I told her "be quiet, very quiet" and we waited for the white-throated sparrow.

"Listen," I told her, and we heard its plaintive whistle for *old Sam Peabody, Peabody, Peabody*. I taught her to move softly on the pine needle carpet, her small feet pressing moss and dried leaves gently—the way Native Americans stepped in their moccasins long ago. If we were lucky, over the next steep bank, we'd find a white-tailed doe and her spring-born young foraging for food. The deer were so tame we could almost put out our hands to touch their warm, sleek coats. I showed her a striped maple, pointed out its greenish bark, and large three-lobed leaves. "My dad called this snakewood," I told her. Even as a little girl, she used to say, "I wish I knew your dad." My parents died long before her birth; my father when I was only sixteen. "What were your parents like?" she often asked. Sometimes my mother was sad, I wanted to tell her, but when she was happy our house smelled like vanilla and lilacs. Instead, I said, "she sang songs with me. She made up silly words. Sometimes we harmonized and laughed when we came down off high notes. I loved to sing with my mother."

"My dad loved nature," I told her. "He took me for walks in the woods and we'd pick thimbleberries for jam. Once, he put my hand over the black bark of the hemlock so I could feel the soft green lichen growing over it. We stood like that for a long time. In the spring, we looked for the first white trillium and pink lady-slipper," I said. "He told me about floating down the Mississippi River, working on an iron ore boat sailing across Lake Huron. He lived in Louisiana for awhile, ran a restaurant there. He always talked about the jazz bands of New Orleans, the taste of hot gumbo and smell of magnolia blossoms. 'Nothing in the world smells sweeter than the magnolia blooms,' he said."

"I think I'd like your dad," Senara said.

"Yes, and he'd have loved you so much," I said. "He always wanted to be a grandfather."

This seems far in the past now, our simple walks, her growing up. Now, she is thirteen. This summer we took out the old photos, looked through them and there she was, only two, tucked in the Lands End backpack. In the photo, I am bending over so Senara can offer a young deer some corn kernels. She is laughing as the deer licks her tiny fingers before she lets go of the corn. "I think I remember this," she said. I wonder, though, how much a young child truly recalls. Was it her real memory, or the memory of the stories we have repeated? Sometimes, I fear that she remembers her dad and me fighting, the raised voices, slammed doors, the time I chased his truck down the driveway when he strapped her in her car seat, threatened to take her away from me. I hope she has forgotten this.

The early teen years were hard for us. We argued often, not the usual arguments about clothes or friends, because I trusted her judgment and I have taught her to be careful and open-minded, but we argued about her going to live with her dad. "You've had me for years," she said, "Now, it's his turn."

In the summer, she goes camping with her dad, floats down the Escanaba River in a canoe, hikes to Trapper's Falls in the Porcupine Mountains. This is what I did with my dad, hiking, fishing, hunting for rocks. My dad taught me to drive our old Chevy Biscayne on country roads when I was fourteen. He was my partner in crime. Once, we put on snowshoes, plowed through the woods looking for wolves, following tracks of an ephemeral animal we never found. We kept many of these exploits a secret from my mother. Senara's dad loves her. The first and only time I ever saw him cry was when we left for Kansas. Senara, at only five, played her Walkman all though Michigan, Illinois, Missouri, and listened to the love song from the movie "Titanic" over and over. This summer after many disagreements, I decided to let Senara live the school year with her father and her stepmother up North. As I sit and watch the ducks swim across Lake Odessa, I realize this will be the first autumn we won't go to the Country Mill to drink apple cider, hunt for the plumpest pumpkin or eat sugary cinnamon covered donuts in the tourist packed picnic area. We won't decorate our front porch with the ghost we made when she was seven, the gangly skeleton we bought at Wal-Mart, or hang out the blinking pumpkin lights.

Last year, Senara banned me from Trick or Treating for the first time. Dressed as a rap singer, she roamed the neighborhood and gathered treats in a pillowcase with her friends. I knew then she was growing up. I took our dog Spencer for a walk, feeling lonely amongst all the parents still holding their youngster's hands as they coaxed them to approach a house and ring the doorbell. *Trick or treat, Trick or treat*, called in a cacophony of childish voices. I passed all our favorite homes decorated for the season, even the dog seemed sad to lose his little companion. I stopped at the display off Scott Street, the house with its whole backyard turned into a cemetery with a motorized spider and talking zombie. The crowd of parents and screaming children jostled me, and Spencer tugged at his leash wanting to move on.

I knew this day was coming, when I would have to let go, realize it was time to allow her to make more of her own decisions, and trust that I have taught her many values that are good; ones that will help her as she travels on without me. The poet, Kahlil Gibran, once wrote something about your children never truly belonging to you, about having them for a little while before they leave home to find their own way. I just never thought it would happen so soon. She still has four years of high school and numerous occasions I will miss, such as teasing her while she gets ready for her first official date, cheering for her to run faster at a track meet, or snapping pictures as she poses in her senior prom dress. I may be able to be there for some of these big events, but mostly time, miles and work commitments will interfere.

I don't want to make her feel guilty for leaving because I know that will make her push me away. I used to hate it when my mother made me feel guilty about something I said or did. Every night Senara calls me to tell me about her day, about the new friends she is making, her French and Drama classes. She misses her friends back home, and I know she misses me. Occasionally, she fights with her stepmother. She is learning life is not always so easy. She has to work harder; take on more responsibility. Sometimes, I know I was too easy on her. I didn't always set limits for her, or at least not always the right ones.

She bought a circle journal and last week she sent me her first entry with pictures of her school, her friends, and the horse on which she is taking riding lessons. She wrote, "Mom, I forgot it gets so cold up north, even in September. I forgot how the early morning frost turns your breath into white smoke, and rushes into your lungs until it hurts to breathe." I believe she has inherited my poetic talent. I will write back, tell her about this weekend at the lake, my students at the community college, how difficult it is to teach argumentative writing. I don't think I will mention the cider mill because I probably won't drive out there this year. The front porch of our house may end up less a jack o' lantern. Senara always helped me carve it; only she can carve the scariest faces. She's been scooping out the seeds since she was seven. Then again, maybe I will find a jack o' lantern to illuminate the porch on Halloween Eve.

Out on Lake Odessa, the mallards rise and fly away. Overhead, a V-formation of honking geese begins their journey to a warmer season. I pick up my pen and write to Senara, "Today is the first day of autumn...."

Night Pond

Diane Bonofiglio

The sounds from the little pond told of frogs leaping,
of air pursing through their throats in deep, loud croaks.

Ducks called to one another in special night songs,
telling the day's adventures.

Bass jumped, splashing as they fell back into
secret hiding places, happy to leap another day.

Golden light that sparkled on the water, faded with the
sun's goodnight and silence covered the night pond.

Corner Cafe

Although these days, our towns seem to be dominated by the big coffeehouses, it's the small, family owned ones that make us feel at home. The place where the proprietor knows your name and your favorite drink or sandwich.

Within the warmth and comfort of these cafés, we learn about life and the people living in our community. Over the steaming cups of coffee and creamy cappuccinos, we meet with friends and family, catching up on our daily lives.

It is this intimate relationship that is captured in the pages of this chapter. So, pour a good cup of Joe, put your feet up and enjoy the stories and poems.

In a Café

Rosalie Sanara Petrouske

I sit in a café looking out the window.
People stroll by, their mouths move
silently, while others step quickly, gripping packages,
or clutching tightly to handbags or children's hands.
It is late November, the afternoon ensconced in
    sunlight.

No longer a deep October glow, but not yet stark
illumination of winter. Most leaves have fallen,
tumbled in piles at curbs. Some branches still
hold a few maples or pale yellow aspens.
A handful of dried red berries hang limply
on a bush across the street, and in the opera house
garden, mums collapse under weight of matted blooms.

There is something peaceful here as day deepens.
My hands curve around the oval of my coffee cup.
In the background, voices mingle and become
    unintelligible.
There is a beauty to so many words spoken at once;
the different tones, high or low, create rippling
    patterns in my ear.

It is cozy inside the café, but outside I know
    the temperature is dropping.
Customers come in, blow on hands for warmth.
Some bend their heads over books, or write on
    lap top computers;
occasional poets scribble furiously in notebooks,
but most share amiable conversation,
enjoy buttery scones and cappuccino.

How simple this life is: quiet clatter of dishes,
smell of toasted bread, cinnamon sprinkled on top
and French roast brewing in the coffee maker.
Someone I know walks past, says hello. I nod,
my throat clotted with silence; I cannot utter a sound.
I feel I have not spoken for hours.

Soon I will pull on gloves, scarf, coat, step out
into the cold, begin moving toward evening.
I open the door to our house and my daughter runs
forward chattering, a school paper in her hand,
my husband calls from the kitchen where
he is roasting a chicken; the dog barks and jumps up
to lick my face as I bend down to remove my shoes.

Phil Kline is Dead

Marion Phillip Kline

If you had been at Mike's Village Restaurant between eight and ten on Saturday morning, you would know why I didn't write anything this week. A friend of mine walked in and announced to the crowd that Phil Kline had been killed in an automobile accident. The noisy conversation stopped, replaced by subdued talk. The place was filled with many of the locals, as village restaurants often do on a Saturday morning, and most of them were either friends or acquaintances. Mike asked my friend, who had made the announcement, how he knew, and he said, "I heard it from his ex-wife."

Art St. Clair, the township supervisor, heard the news and called my house to verify the information. Nobody answered, so he called my next-door neighbor, John. John said he had taken me to the hospital on Friday but hadn't heard anything since. He said he'd check it out. He called Art back ten minutes later with the news that there was nobody in the hospital by the name of Phil Kline.

Mike decided to verify what he'd heard, so he called my ex-wife. She told him she didn't say I'd died, just that she had visited me while I was on a heart monitor at Ingham Medical the night after my accident, but that I appeared to be okay. She called the hospital and located me because she knew I was not registered under Phil Kline, but under my real first name. She called my room, and I told her I was alive.

By the time this information got back to the restaurant, most of the people had already left and didn't hear the good news. I was released from the hospital

Saturday afternoon and given a ride home by John, who in the meantime, had called my ex-wife and discovered I was still alive. I stayed in bed for most of the next two days. On Tuesday night at the township board meeting, I was welcomed back from the dead by a couple of people who were surprised to see me still walking around.

The next morning, I went to Mike's Restaurant and one of the cooks, Judy, came out of the kitchen and hugged me. "I'm glad you're okay," she said. "I cried when I heard you were dead."

Cathy, the server, said, "I see we still have to put up with you."

Over the next week, I encountered many surprised people, who in a variety of ways, gave me something to write about.

A Quiet Rainy Morning

Jan McCaffrey

On a quiet rainy morning
    I sit alone in my kitchen,
Coffee steaming in its
    Brown ceramic mug.

I watch, mesmerized,
    In the grey humid dawn
As rain slithers across the darkness
    Of my window.

Softly, like a strand of
    Broken beads in slow motion,
It forms damp, shadowy shapes
    Frozen for an instant,

Then aimlessly exiting
    Out of sight.
My thoughts flow effortlessly
    With the rhythm.

As my finger slowly traces
    The lines of dampness
Across the steamy film of glass
    I am cleansed.

On a quiet rainy morning.

Death by Broken Heart

A Novella by Candy-Ann Little

Chapter 1

"Stupid exit," Bailey grumbled, and jerked the steering wheel, cutting off the car behind her. The blue van honked as it roared past her. "It's as bad as New York." Of course, the fact that she'd been fiddling with the radio and not paying attention had nothing to do with her almost missing the exit.

Irritation as thick as her grandmother's old quilt wrapped around her chest, its smothering hold more blistering than the summer heat. Ten years ago, Bailey packed her suitcases, along with a broken heart and a trunk full of dreams. Leaving this sleepy little town, she headed for the excitement of the big city. Now, she found herself coming back like a beaten dog with its tail between its legs.

The happy cadence of her heart felt like a betrayal. No wonder her life revolved around such chaos. She couldn't even control one organ! Grand Ledge, Michigan was the last place she wanted to be, so why did she feel glad to be home?

As she drove along Saginaw Highway, the hustle, flurry and commotion of stores and businesses gave way to the slower pace of small town life. Large, Victorian houses sprawled out with their lush green lawns accentuated by a variety of colors. Climbing roses and ivy clung to trellises and the sides of houses. Flower beds of begonias, snapdragons, pansies, and lilies dotted lawns, while white picket fences, evergreen and hydrangea bushes separated the lots. Children rode their bikes, and teenagers jumped and flipped their skateboards on the sidewalk. Couples held hands as they strolled under the large oak, maple and pine trees that lined the walkways.

Bailey smiled at the memory of playing hopscotch on that very sidewalk with her best friend. Although she hated to admit it, she missed the peaceful security of small town life.

She drove along Bridge Street, watching the old brick buildings slide by. Although new businesses dotted the landscape, some still remained from her youth. She parallel parked in front of the row of stores and went into Sweet Linda's Café. The soothing colors of pale yellow and rust brown greeted her, along with a beautifully decorated mantle over the friendly fireplace. The warm, welcoming atmosphere, however, was interrupted by raised voices.

"I'm telling you, Ralph, my parents already paid the rent."

"They didn't pay all of it, and they're late. I'll be posting an eviction notice if it isn't paid by tomorrow." Dark, round eyes narrowed under pointed, gray brows.

"You post what you want. We'll see you in court." The aggressive tone of the redheaded young man flustered the old man.

"I will not have any back talk from the sorry likes of you." His wrinkled face turned redder than a Traverse City cherry. "You will be out of here. I'm calling the police." A fine mist of saliva flew into the air while a line of spittle ran down his chin, disappearing into his gray goatee.

"You'll look like a fool, as usual. You know as well as I do that you have no legal grounds for an eviction." The young man folded his arms. His unruffled disposition making the old man even more furious. "The police actually suggested that we sue you for harassment."

"Bull!" Blue veins popped out of Ralph's thin, long neck, looking like a road map. "You're a liar. So are those sorry, lazy parents of yours."

The young man leaned closer. "Ralph, I will give you ten seconds to leave." The low growl bounced off the mirrored wall in the back of the shop.

"I own this place. You can't order me around."

"You own the building. We pay the rent. As long as we are tenants, you can't step foot in here unless we give you permission. Go check with your lawyer."

"You smug little ... we'll see." Ralph stormed out the back door.

A few customers tried to pretend they weren't eavesdropping. Bailey filled her Styrofoam cup with coffee, put the dome lid on top and walked to the counter.

"I'm sorry about that," he apologized. "I wish he'd stop coming in here when there are customers."

"It's okay. I'm used to hostility. It's all over New York."

"Bailey?" He looked dazed. "Is that you?"

Recognition dawned. "Randy?"

"Yes." His voice had grown deeper since their teenage years.

"I didn't recognize you without your nose ring," she laughed while handing him two dollars.

"I gave that up a long time ago." He shrugged. "There comes a time when you outgrow things like that." He rang up the order, giving back the change. "Do you still have your tattoo?"

"Unfortunately. It's a little harder to get rid of."

"I take it that you don't think it's so cool now?" Randy winked. He'd tried talking her out of it when they were seventeen.

"It's still cooler than that stupid nose ring." She snapped her wallet shut with a sharp click.

"We do lots of stupid things as kids." His tone turned serious. "Hopefully, we learn from them."

"Hopefully." She swallowed the lump forming in her throat. "I'll bet your wife didn't like the nose ring."

"Not married. I'm sure Martha has filled you in."

"Actually, Mom has never mentioned you, except when your grandmother died last year." She saw him flinch. "I was sorry to hear that."

"She lived a good life."

After a pause, Bailey said, "So, you work here?"

"My parents started this business a few years ago. I help out when needed." He locked eyes with her. "I hear you're a big shot private investigator now."

"Well, not that big."

"Just like all those shows and reruns you used to watch on TV. Magnum P.I., Simon and Simon, and, um, what was that other show you liked?"

"Murder She Wrote."

"No. She wasn't a P.I."

"But she solved crimes. How about Matlock?"

"He was a lawyer." Randy shook his head.

"Conrad was a P.I." Bailey insisted.

"True. You loved anything that involved solving crimes." His eyes crinkled in thought. "I'm thinking of the show about police."

"Miami Vice," she suggested.

"That's it." He snapped his fingers. "Although I still think you watched that show because you thought Don Johnson was cute."

"Are you still jealous?" She laughed.

"No."

"So, what's your real job?" She couldn't believe he'd wound up working in a café. He was too smart for this.

"I'm a teacher."

"Get out of here." They both laughed.

"No. It's true. I teach history at Grand Ledge High."

"Well. Wonders never cease." She shook her head. "After all the classes you skipped, you wind up working there."

"Yeah, well, someone has to keep these young kids in line." His brown eyes danced, reminding her of the teenager he used to be. "I love my job. What about you?"

"What can I say about the P.I. business?" She sipped her coffee. "Never a dull minute."

Randy crossed his arms and leaned a blue-jean clad hip against the counter. "Are you in town for the reunion?"

"Sort of. Mom basically browbeat me back."

"I can believe that." He paused for a moment before adding, "You look great, by the way."

"You're such a liar." She unconsciously smoothed back some loose strands of brown hair. "I've been sweating like Niagara Falls for the last twelve hours. The air conditioning in my car stopped working."

"Stop in and see Joe. He'll fix it for cheap."

"Nah, it's a rental."

"New York is a long drive. Why not fly?"

"I had some things I needed to think through. The drive helped." She smiled awkwardly. "Well, I better get going. Mom is waiting."

"It's good to see you again." He paused. "Maybe we can get together some time and talk over old times." It was a weak line, but it always worked in the movies.

"Maybe."

Childhood memories danced inside her head as she drove out of the business district and entered the farming community. The houses were separated by fields of corn, wheat and soybeans, while large barns sheltered cows, horses and pigs. Funny how she never took the time to recall her childhood. New York and work kept her so busy she hardly had time to think about much of anything.

Turning onto the lonely road at the edge of town made her heart beat even faster. *I'm home, I'm home*, it seemed to pound out. She couldn't deny the joy, no matter how hard she tried.

She watched as her mom ran out the back door and down the steps of the porch. "Bailey, you're home. You're home." Her mother's embrace was strong enough to take down a bull.

"I made it." She clung tightly to her mom. It had been nearly five years since they'd seen one another.

"Come sit down on the porch. I have fresh brewed iced tea and chocolate chip cookies."

That alone was worth the drive. "Leave it to you to bake cookies in July."

"You're looking way too thin. I'm going to have to fatten you up while you're here." Martha patted her arm. "Too bad I only have a few weeks to do it in."

"Let's not even go there." Bailey didn't want to hear her mother's lecture. "My life is in New York, and I will be returning."

"We'll see." Martha ignored the determination in her daughter's voice. The battle lines had been drawn years ago. Neither one had dared to cross over. But now her daughter was home. That had to be a positive sign.

The shrill ring of the phone etched its way into the peacefulness of the country.

"Bailey, it's for you." Martha handed her the phone.

"What." Her abrupt greeting earned a disapproving look from her mother.

"Randy, here," he sighed. "You don't have to bite my head off, just wanted to see about getting together?"

"Sorry. I thought you were someone from work. I've only been home a few hours."

"Plenty of time to unpack and catch up with your mom. Thought you might need a break by now."

"That offer sounds tempting." She shot her mom a glance. "Okay. Where and when do you want to meet?" Mom had rattled off the entire life stories of every person in town and Bailey couldn't take any more.

"I close the café at seven. How about I pick you up around seven-thirty?"

"I'd rather meet you." She hated relying on anyone, even for a ride.

"Meet me at the ledges. Do you remember where they are?"

"You don't have to be so condescending just because I want to drive."

"I'm not. I didn't know if you remembered. It's been a long time since you were back."

"So everyone keeps reminding me."

She turned onto Jefferson Street and headed north until she came to Fitzgerald Park, driving slowly down the lane as dust billowed out from her tires. Randy stood waiting by a blue pickup truck. He waved.

Bailey felt a warm sensation spread over her, something strange and familiar at the same time. It had been a long time since she'd felt anything. She liked it that way. *I'll have to guard my heart closely with him,* she thought.

He came over and opened the car door. "I wasn't sure you'd come."

"I said I'd be here." She got out and closed the door herself. "I keep my promises."

"Ouch." Randy physically recoiled. "Another jab like that and I'll need a doctor."

She shot him a sharp look and pulled her long, brown hair into a ponytail. "I'll call 9-1-1. They do have service out here, don't they?"

"New York has changed you." He shook his head.

"Life has changed me. You said yourself that people learn from their past."

"I said they learn from their mistakes."

"Have you learned from yours?" Her eyes narrowed into blue slits. Without waiting for a response, she stomped away.

"What is that supposed to mean?" Randy hastened to catch up. "Hey, don't you think I should lead?"

"Because you're a man?"

"No. Because it's been ten years since you've been on this trail."

"I can't believe anything has changed."

True to small town form, the trails were exactly as she remembered. The Grand River lazily wound its way along the bottom of the trail, while steep rocky formations stretched up the side of the hill. The two of them walked along the path, quietly enjoying the view.

"It's amazing how these trees survive." Bailey finally broke the silence. "I mean, look at them growing in the rocks. There's barely enough dirt to grow a flower, and yet these thick roots have grown down the side of these stones and survived all these years."

"Life can be hard, but things always find a way to adapt." Randy stopped.

"Sometimes transplanting is the best thing."

"You're harder than these rocks." Randy leaned against a large boulder. "Is there a heart somewhere in that chest?"

"What do you know about hard?" She crossed her arms. "You took the easy road your parents carved out for you. I made it on my own. Waiting tables at night while going to NYU during the day, and I graduated with honors in criminal law."

"I graduated, too. Just because I went to Michigan State doesn't mean I didn't work hard."

"And now you sit behind a cushy desk in the high school."

"You think being a teacher is easy?"

"It's easier than my job. I constantly have to prove myself. Just because I'm a woman people automatically think I'm an airhead and can't do the job. The P.I. business is tough, but it's twice as hard for a woman." She fidgeted from foot to foot.

"You chose your profession."

"It wasn't all my choice where I wound up."

"No?" Randy was stumped. Why did she seem so angry with him? "You ran away. Just like you always do."

"How dare you." Pulling the scrunchy from her hair, she raked her fingers through the long tendrils, gathering the loose strands and pulling the scrunchy tight again. "You're jealous because I got out and you stayed stuck in this 'little prairie' of a town."

"I'm not stuck. I want to be here. Unlike you, I love this place. I like the history. I care about the future, and the kids. I am a success in this town." He felt his face getting hot. He didn't know if it was from temper or lack of oxygen.

"You're a coward!" She pointed to her chest. "I accomplished my goals."

"Not without losing a piece of yourself." Randy crossed his arms, pressing his lips into a thin, hard line. "I remember a girl who wanted to gain knowledge and see the world." His brown eyes bore into her soul. "You may have gotten the education, but what about the other things in life?"

"Work is all I need. I get enough of real life there." *Probably too much at times*, she thought. The Big Apple had a way of eating at you from the inside out.

"Only problem is you're still searching for something." He leaned closer, barely whispering, "Or someone."

"I need to run." Moving always helped clear her head and regain her focus.

"Bailey, wait." Randy ran after her. "We should turn back."

"Why? Because you say so?" She sprinted down the path.

He tried to catch up but her lean body was merely a silhouette as the sun sank behind the treetops. She suddenly stopped.

Wheezing and gasping, he made it to her side. "Guess I'm a little out of shape."

"Not as out of shape as he is." She pointed.

Chapter 2

He followed her finger, carefully edging closer to the overlook. He leaned forward and almost gagged. The outline of a body lay below. A pool of red blood slowly crept out from the man's head, covering the grayish-white concrete.

Randy grabbed Bailey's head, burying her face into his shoulder. His first impulse was to protect her from the violence.

"What are you doing?" She pulled away. "We need to call the police." Digging the cell phone out of her pocket, she dialed for help.

"Amazing, you do have 9-1-1." She flipped the phone shut.

"Is this a big joke to you?" Randy shook his head. *How could she be so trivial about death?*

"Sorry." She forgot he wasn't used to crime scenes.

"What are you doing?"

"I'm going to look around." She started climbing down the side of the ledges.

"You can't do that. You'll contaminate the evidence."

"Now look who's been watching too much TV." She continued her descent. "I know how to look around without destroying anything."

When the police arrived ten minutes later, they also admonished her.

"Little lady, you can't go climbing around a crime scene." The officer scratched the back of his head with his ballpoint pen.

"I haven't touched anything. I'm a private investigator." She handed him her I.D.

"I see." He scratched his balding head again. "That makes all the difference." He checked the body. "Besides, you shouldn't be looking at something as crude as this."

"Mister." Bailey stood up to her full height of five-seven. "I have seen bodies split open from groin to neck. I've dug bullets out of hearts and helped the medical examiner decipher the remains of stomach contents. A few pieces of cement embedded in his head are nothing." She crossed her arms.

"The victim is Ralph Borlen." A young blond-headed officer approached.

At the mention of the name, Randy's head swiveled to look closer at the body. Up until now, he had not felt up to looking directly at the dead man, but hearing the name of his parents' landlord made him want confirmation.

"Are you sure it's Ralph?" Randy felt sick.

"Yes. It appears to be a suicide." The younger officer pointed to the ledge. "No sign of a struggle."

"It's mostly rock," Bailey commented. "How could you tell if there was a struggle?"

He looked from his partner to Bailey. "And who are you?"

"Bailey Rhodes. I found the body."

"This here is a big shot from New York." The older deputy gave back her license and I.D. card.

"And this may not be a suicide." She stuffed the I.D. in her pocket.

"Is that so?" The blond asked.

She hated the patronizing tone. "It's a known fact that jumpers take off their glasses. He's still wearing his." She pointed to the broken spectacles.

"Maybe so, but this here is our investigation." The blond made a notation, then flipped his notebook closed. "Guess old Ralph won't be bugging us anymore."

"Will you be quiet?" The older, balding officer admonished. "You can't keep spouting off information."

"You knew him?" Bailey's head snapped up.

"Ma'am, we have your statement. If we need anything else, we'll contact you." Both men walked away.

"Pompous, arrogant ... jerks." She looked at Randy, noticing his color was tinged green. "Let's go."

They climbed up the ledge, walking back up the path as the last of the sunset turned from pink to dark blue, finally fading into black. Fortunately, the half moon shined bright enough to aid their walk. A few stars dotted the sky. The cool, night breeze dried the light sweat from their bodies. Darkness wrapped around them like a shroud, concealing their thoughts and emotions. Neither wanted to talk. When they reached their vehicles, Bailey offered to drive him home.

"I'm fine. Be careful." Randy closed her door and walked slowly toward his own vehicle.

After a fitful night's sleep, Bailey needed some coffee. She headed to town, wanting a caramel latte, not just the plain ordinary coffee her mother had. Of course, a part of her wanted to see Randy, just to check up on him.

The aroma of fresh baked goods and coffee greeted her as she entered the cafe. She inhaled deeply, feeling a warm sensation spread throughout her body. Randy's mom waited on customers behind the counter. She hadn't changed a bit. Her dark hair was still pulled into its usual French twist. A red apron hung from her tall, willowy frame, covering her blue jeans and white cotton shirt.

A few customers dotted the black, marble tables, but most were grabbing their coffee to go. Bailey placed her order, then asked about Randy's whereabouts. Linda gave a quizzical look before smiling. "Bailey Rhodes, is that you?"

"It is." Bailey felt warmed by her smile.

As if on cue, Randy came out of the back room carrying a big box. He looked tired and his unruly red hair stood up on end, making him look like he'd just rolled out of bed. He set the box down and went to talk to three older men sitting at a table in the corner. He noticed Bailey standing by the counter and walked over to join her.

"Good morning." His smile seemed a little strained. "How are you?"

"Didn't sleep well." He cocked his head. "You don't seem disturbed at all."

"I've seen a lot of crime scenes." She shrugged. "You get used to it."

"There isn't much crime around here." Randy felt ashamed for being so squeamish.

"I know." She paused before asking. "Randy, how bad were things between Ralph and your parents?"

"He's always been a jerk, but things had gotten really ugly the last few months. He kept trying to kick my parents out so he could rent the building for a higher price to someone else."

"Do you know who?"

"No. Why?"

"I don't believe he jumped."

"You think it's murder?" His brown eyes clouded.

"It's possible. I don't understand why the police are just writing it off and not launching a full investigation."

"They're probably glad to be rid of him," came a voice from behind them. Bailey turned to see an older man with a green Spartan ball cap.

"How did you hear about Ralph so soon?" Randy asked.

"Are you kidding? This is the biggest commotion this town has had in years. Everyone knows."

"Dan is one of our regulars. He owns Lambs' Gate next door." Randy introduced them. "Dan, this is Bailey."

"Was Ralph your landlord, too?" Bailey asked.

"No, but that didn't stop him from trying." Dan paid for his coffee. "Nice to meet you." He headed back to the table where three men sat.

"That group comes in every morning." Randy smiled. He pointed to the tall, thin one with salt and pepper hair and round glasses. "Do you remember him?"

"I haven't finished my latte yet. I'm not awake."

"That's Burt Wilson."

"Mr. Wilson?" Bailey looked harder. "Our English teacher?"

"One and the same." Next, he pointed to the only man who still had a head full of black hair. His thick mustache moved as he talked. "Jerry Douglas is the football coach."

The man reading the newspaper noticed the two of them talking and pointing. "Hey, Randy. Quit being rude and introduce us all to the pretty lady." His gruff voice came out from under a short, gray mustache, which matched his hair. His glasses were square and his belly round.

"Bailey, this is Arthur Mackenzie, editor of the Grand Ledge paper."

"Call me Art." He glared at Randy. "I hate being called Arthur."

Randy laughed.

"He hates being called lots of things," Burt added. "But we call him names anyway."

"Well, I try to watch my step. He gives me bad reviews in the paper if I harass him too much." Jerry extended his hand. "It's nice to meet you."

"That's nonsense and you know it," Art defended. "If I give you a bad review it's because you called stupid plays."

"All right boys, settle down." Linda placed a steaming plate of breakfast casserole in front of Art and a scone by Dan.

"Have you had a scone?" Dan asked. "Linda makes the best scones and muffins around."

"No, I haven't tried one yet." Bailey winked at Linda. "However, I recall how good her muffins were as an after school snack."

"You've known Randy for a long time, huh?" Art arched a bushy brow.

"Since we were in kindergarten."

"I hear you're a P.I. in New York." Art's penetrating stare unsettled her.

"How do you know that?"

"It's my job. I'm a reporter."

"Then you would already know how long I've known Randy."

"Yep. I also know that you two dated all through high school and most folks thought you'd get married." He paused as he finished chewing his food and swallowed. "Surprised everyone when you packed up and left without warning." He wiped his mouth. "I also know that your nickname in high school was 'knockers.'"

That drew chuckles from everyone.

She glowered at Randy.

"I didn't say anything, honest." He held his palms up.

Her brows creased together. "Why do you have so much information on me?" She'd forgotten how small towns could be. In New York, nobody cared. Here, your life was open to the entire community.

"I also know that you and Randy found old Ralph last night. I hear you were giving the police some trouble."

"I didn't give anybody trouble." She pointed to her chest. "They gave me the hard time." She glared at Art. "Better get your facts straight before shooting your mouth off."

"Well, then, why don't you swing by my office and we can have ourselves a little chat that I can put in the paper."

"If you wanted an interview, why not just ask?"

"That's not as much fun." Art winked. "Knockers."

"Uncle Arty, are you being bad again?" A blond with long curly hair and a body as sleek as a panther approached. "I hope you didn't forget about our shopping trip."

Art groaned out loud.

"Uncle Arty just hates to shop," she informed no one in particular, "but Momma's birthday is tomorrow."

"I hate to break up this little love-fest but I have a store to open." Dan stood.

Bailey needed an excuse to get out of there, too. The foxy blond made her feel inadequate, something she hadn't felt since high school.

"My uncle has no manners at all." The blond held out a finely manicured hand. "I'm Kelly Peterson."

The name immediately registered, making Bailey want to disappear.

"Kelly, this is Bailey." Randy intervened.

"Bailey Rhodes?" She almost dropped her hand, but pasted a phony smile on her face instead. "I didn't even recognize you. What ever happened to you?" She didn't bother hiding her disdain.

"I live in New York now."

"Ohh." The fake smile showed her perfectly straight and unnaturally white teeth. "I'm a very important sales representative for a lucrative cosmetics company."

"Yeah, she sells the most Mary Kay of anyone in town." Burt laughed.

"Probably because she buys it all herself," Jerry added.

Randy laughed and Bailey hid her smile.

"I made nine hundred dollars last month." She snubbed her nose at Burt. "Randy, be a dear and get my usual."

Bailey's smile instantly soured. "Why, Kelly dear, is that shine I see on your forehead? Your products must not be doing their job properly, or you have very oily skin."

"Nonsense." Her hand instinctively went to her forehead. "I just lost my compact and haven't gotten a new one." She looked at Art. "I'll be right back. I just need to run to the powder room. Ohh ... I mean the restroom."

Randy winked at Bailey.

"I should get going." Bailey checked her watch.

Randy walked her to the door. "Don't let Kelly get to you."

"She hasn't changed at all. She still thinks she's the hottest thing under the sun. Does she realize that we are adults now and everyone is on equal footing? She isn't any better than the rest of us."

"You won that round. She's in there powdering her forehead as we speak."

"Do you remember how she was always powdering her face? I thought she would turn into one big powder puff before graduation." Bailey laughed.

"That's better." Randy touched her cheek. "Let me get her drink. Then we can go do something fun."

"Like what?"

"I don't know. Anything."

"No. I have something to do." She pushed open the door.

"Anything I can help with?"

She stopped. "Nothing you would be interested in."

"Try me." He'd do anything to spend more time with her.

"Breaking the law isn't what I had in mind." Randy grumbled as they traveled down the dirt path.

"We aren't breaking any laws. We're just investigating."

"Maybe P.I.s investigate, but I'm a teacher and crossing the line of a crime scene sounds like breaking the law."

"If you don't want to help, go back." Bailey pressed on, scanning the path for anything out of the ordinary. "Besides, this path isn't taped off."

"The whole area is off limits, Bailey." Randy watched her pick up a comb with her gloved hands, placing it in a plastic bag. She'd already found a shoestring, a pair of broken sunglasses, a half-used bottle of sunscreen, a compact, three rings, two cigarette lighters, Chap Stick, and a broken watch.

"What are you doing with all that junk?" he asked.

"It could be evidence."

"Then the police should have it."

"They already looked around."

"So it's okay for you to take the stuff without asking?"

"If you're so worried about getting caught, why don't you go back to the café? I'm sure you'd rather spend time with Kelly anyway."

"What? Kelly?" He shook his head. "Where on earth would you get such a crazy idea?"

Bailey turned to face Randy and in a high-pitched voice imitated Kelly, "Randy honey, bring me my usual, and marry me, and make mad passionate love to me."

"What's gotten into you?" Randy rubbed the back of his neck. "There has never been anything between me and Kelly."

"Is that so?" Bailey tried to keep the hurt out of her voice, but wasn't completely successful. "She's very pretty."

"She's a selfish snob. Looks aren't everything in a relationship."

"Is that why you didn't marry her?"

"I have never been interested in Kelly."

"Let's get back to work." Bailey couldn't deal with any more emotional turmoil right now. She had a job to do.

Randy picked up a pop can. "Is this worth anything? Maybe the killer was drinking it before he pushed Ralph over."

"That's not funny." She snatched the can from his hand. "Besides, you don't have gloves on."

"You're still as tenacious as ever."

"And you're still as helpless as ever."

"Maybe I'll be able to help you very soon."

"How?"

"I have a friend who's a lawyer." His eyes moved past her.

She turned to see two police officers headed their way. "Oh, crap!"

Chapter 3

Bailey rolled her eyes and yawned several times while the two officers read her the third degree. She explained her position on the murder case. They, in turn, laughed.

"Old Ralph just got too close to the edge."

"Have you even looked for any other possibilities? Investigated the crime scene? Talked to possible witnesses? Maybe tried to find a motive?" Bailey rubbed her forehead. She hated dealing with know-it-all officers.

"Why would we waste our time tracking down nonexistent leads?" The blond, whose name tag read, P. Mullin, laughed.

"As far as motive goes, just about everybody in town would have one." The older, balding officer's name was D. Davis. "It could take months talking to everyone that had a grudge against Ralph."

"And what about the two of you?" Bailey stood and pounded her fists on the wood table. "The fact that you knew the victim, and that you steadfastly refuse to investigate this properly, puts the police force on the top of my list."

"You think we did it?" Davis asked.

"Why won't you investigate? It's not like you have anything better to do." She plopped back down in the chair. "All those speeding motorists are so much more important than someone's life."

"To be quite honest, those motorists are more important." Officer Mullins leaned closer. "Ralph was a paranoid, self-obsessed loser. He got rich by swindling hard working, honest folks. You can sure bet that there is no love lost for old Ralph."

"But that wouldn't interfere with our jobs," Officer Davis added.

"Right. We don't need any out-of-towners telling us how to do our jobs," Mullins added.

Bailey crossed her arms. "This is my hometown."

"Well now, Miss Rhodes, you moved to New York a long time ago and that doesn't put you in the running for hometown girl. You quit the force and became a private investigator, what prompted that?" Davis sneered. "Police work too grueling for you?"

"Too many rules," Bailey grumbled. "I like the P.I. business better."

"Is that so you don't have to follow the rules?"

Bailey crossed her arms and remained silent.

"We want you to stop nosing around." Mullins informed her.

"Why?" Bailey stared him down.

"Confounded females."

Bailey stiffened and opened her mouth to retort, but a knock interrupted. Another officer poked his head in. "A lawyer is here to see her."

The two officers stepped out in the hall. A few minutes later a tall, dark-haired man carrying a briefcase came in.

"Jeff?"

"Bailey." He was brief and to the point. "I'm only here because Randy asked me as a favor." His green eyes locked with hers. "I don't think it's a coincidence that you come back to town and Randy finds himself trouble again."

"Randy didn't have to go along with me. He made his own choice."

"You don't get it, do you?" The briefcase landed on the table with a thud. "He has always followed your crazy schemes. You were the one with the big ideas and he went along just to be a part of your life. He followed you like a newborn puppy and you just played him for a fool."

"I don't know where all of this is leading, so let's rush past the touchy-feely memories and get me out of here."

"You're free to go, but they want you to promise to leave this case alone."

"Jeff, level with me." She sat forward, arms resting on the table. "Why won't they investigate?"

"This isn't New York, Bailey, it's Grand Ledge. Murderers aren't running loose on the streets. There have been several accidents involving the ledges over the years. Do you remember in high school when that boy, Marty, fell to his death? And, another boy was killed a few years back. Things happen when you test Mother Nature."

"You will notice the pattern of teenagers and young kids that have slipped. Ralph was old enough to know better. I don't believe he would be fooling around by the edge of the ledge." She stood. "And why is the department so intent on me not looking into the case? If it was just an accident, it won't hurt anyone if I look around."

Jeff sighed. "You're making the force feel like idiots. Your imagination is taking a strong turn and the police department doesn't want to look incompetent."

"They don't need me to do that."

"Our police department is one of the best around. Don't underestimate them."

"I'm not working on imagination. I'm going by my gut. This may be a small town, but bad people can live anywhere. Killers aren't confined to the streets of New York."

"Just watch your step," he cautioned. "You alienated a lot of people when you left."

"Including you?"

"Randy is my best friend. He's kind and gentle. I don't want him getting hurt again."

"What about me? Doesn't my broken heart count for something?"

"You're free to go. Randy is waiting for you out front." He picked up his briefcase and left.

Art's office was small and cluttered. It reminded her of her boss's office in New York. She quickly pushed those thoughts away, not wanting to think about Mike or New York.

"So how did you discover the body?" Art got right to the point. He leaned back with arms folded behind his head and propped his feet on the corner of his desk.

After filling him in on all the details, Bailey managed to ask a few questions of her own.

"Did you know Ralph personally?"

"Yeah, we went to school together. Why?"

"I need some background info on him." Bailey took out her notebook and pen. "Was he married?"

"Several times."

"Any kids."

"None that would claim him." Art dropped his feet to the floor with a light thud, and leaned closer. "Leave this alone."

"Why is everyone telling me that?"

"Because you won't listen."

"Is the entire town covering up this murder?"

"It was an accident, according to the police."

"Not according to me." Bailey locked eyes with him. "Do you have an alibi for last night?"

"I don't need one."

"It would ease my mind."

"I don't care about your feelings." His gray eyes bore into her. "But I do care about Randy and his parents. You'd better not do anything to hurt them."

"What do you know about the café?" She'd try a different angle.

"I know that Mick and Linda got shafted by Ralph three years ago. Most people who've rented from him have been cheated. You won't find anyone in this town who is sorry he's dead."

"Why didn't you get along with Ralph?"

"I don't like cheaters." She flinched at the venom in his words.

"Were you cheated by him?"

"I've never rented from him. He couldn't get his grubby hands on the newspaper."

"Thank you for your time." Bailey stood. Putting her notebook into her purse, she made a mental note to check further into his past. The hatred in his tone must be there for some reason.

Randy stood behind the counter when she stopped by the café. As much as she hated thinking it, Randy and his parents were prime suspects.

"Hey." Randy's face lit up. "What can I get you?"

"Just a plain coffee." She handed him the money.

"It's on the house." He winked.

"Thanks." Her heart tightened at the remembrance of him always winking. "Can we talk?"

"Sure. Let's have a seat."

"The place is empty."

"Yeah, things slow down after lunch." Randy sat back in the chair, crossing his arms in front of his wide chest. "So what's on your mind?"

"I need to ask you a few questions about the café."

"Didn't you promise to leave this alone?" He raised a red brow.

"No." She looked him square in the eye. "I believe there is more to this and I'm going to find out what."

"And you think I had something to do with it?" Randy looked appalled.

"Or your parents." She rushed on to explain. "You were arguing over the rent."

"Ralph cheated lots of people." His face tensed.

"I don't like having to ask you this, but it's my job." She didn't like the hurt showing in his eyes.

"It's not your job. You're not in New York."

She ignored that remark. "How did Ralph cheat you guys?"

"When my parents signed the contract, all the equipment was supposed to come with the rental.

Afterwards, they found out that the previous owner had liens on everything. They had to purchase thousands of dollars worth of equipment before they could even open." Randy sighed. "My parents didn't have the money and the loan was a burden. Since the contract stated 'fully furnished,' they asked Ralph for help. But, somehow, he weaseled around a loophole. Instead of helping, he made things worse. He deliberately sabotaged the opening of the café."

"Why would he do that? It seems it would hurt him if the business failed."

"I don't even try to understand how his mind operated. Anyway, it didn't matter. My parents worked hard and made the business successful. So much so that he had other buyers making offers. In the last few months, Ralph was trying to raise the rent. But he had no legal grounds."

"Was he taking you to court?"

"Yes." He looked at her, his face softening. "So if you're looking for a motive, we have one. But we aren't the only ones."

"Do you know if Art had a motive?"

"Art? Not a business related one."

"Are you suggesting he had a personal motive?"

"No. It happened over thirty years ago."

"What?"

"I'm sure this has no bearing on the case, and I'm only going to divulge the information if you agree to let me help."

"That's extortion."

"Seeing as how you've put me at the top of your list of suspects, I feel it's only appropriate to let me clear my name."

Bailey eyed him suspiciously. She wanted to believe in his innocence. The Randy she knew ten years ago would have never been able to kill anyone. But, it had been a long time and people change. After all, he'd lied and cheated on her with another girl. He'd played her for a fool once. *Could he be doing the same thing now?*

"You're a suspect. If I allow you to help, you could destroy the investigation in order to save yourself or your parents."

"Since I think it was just an accident and not murder, there really isn't a case to destroy." He reached across the table and took her hand. His strength and warmth crept along her nerve endings.

"That's a difference of opinion." She pulled her hand away, refusing to let the memories take control. She'd worked too long and too hard burying them. Randy never crossed her thoughts anymore. Well, almost never.

"Then you don't get my information." He stood, walking behind the counter as a customer entered.

She sat contemplating the situation. After the customer left, Bailey went to the counter. "How do I know your information is worth the risk?"

"How do I know my heart is worth the risk?"

"Why would your heart be at risk?"

"Because I could fall in love with you again."

"What is your information on Art?"

"Ralph broke up his marriage."

"He cheated with his wife?"

"Ralph actually married her for a while. She was wife number two."

"They're divorced?"

"It only lasted four or five years. Melinda was institutionalized for a while."

"She went crazy?"

"Being married to Ralph could do that to a person." Randy's tone softened. "I've heard that Ralph was abusive to her."

"Then why did she leave Art for Ralph in the first place?"

"Who knows for sure. Money was always a possible motive. She did get a big settlement in the divorce. The tragic thing was she never got to enjoy it. She left town for a year or so. When she came back, she was never quite right in the head. Six years after she divorced Ralph, she committed suicide."

"She's dead." Bailey had to let that sink in. "Did she have any kids?"

"No."

"Two failed marriages and no children. It sounds like a sad, lonely life."

"Probably why she ended it." Randy reached out and held her hand.

"So if Art truly loved her, he'd not only blame Ralph for the breakup of his marriage, but for the death of his wife, too."

"As I said before, it happened over thirty years ago."

"Heartache and betrayal can live a long time." Bailey pulled her hand away. Marriage had too many emotional entanglements. That's why she stayed far away from it. She had a hard enough time with committed relationships.

"How big was the divorce settlement?"

"I'm not positive about the amount, but from what I hear it was substantial."

"How did she get so much?"

"Ralph gave it to her. He's known for giving expensive gifts when he's through using the girls."

"He didn't fight her at all?"

"No. He just wanted to be rid of her. He already had another girlfriend."

"So old Ralph was a player."

"A big time player. No one could understand why any woman would be with him, but he always managed to snag quite a few. Most were young and good looking, too."

Bailey shivered. "He wasn't anything spectacular to look at."

"Maybe not now, but he was quite good looking in his younger days. Or, so I hear." He winked. "He also had a lot of money. He'd been making shady deals and buying up most of this town for years."

Bailey groaned, realizing this case was going to be hard to narrow down.

"Partners?" He extended his hand.

"For now." She tentatively shook his hand

"How about dinner?"

"Is that part of the contract?"

"Yes. Do you want to meet me here around seven-thirty?"

"Do you want to go home and change first?"

"Changing is left up to you women. I'm fine the way I am."

No arguments there. He looked even better than he did in high school. His hair had darkened from bright orange to a subdued auburn. He'd filled out more and had a few wrinkles around his mouth and eyes, but the overall effect made him incredibly handsome.

When Bailey entered Sweet Linda's café, she gasped in surprise. Randy had set up a romantic table for two. A white tablecloth shimmered in the darkness. A red rose sat in the middle of the table with a taper candle on each side.

"What's all this?" She set her purse down. "I thought we were going out."

"I decided that eating here would give us more privacy."

"Partners working a case don't need privacy." She hated admitting the whole idea had a romantic feel.

"C'mon, Bailey. Let's have dinner like old times." He set two plates of lasagna on the table. "I ordered Italian, your favorite."

"It smells delicious." She sat down. *What could one little dinner hurt?*

They laughed and talked while they ate. When they finished, Randy looked at his watch. "We'd better hurry."

"Hurry?" She furrowed her brow.

"I want to take you somewhere fun." He picked up the plates, carrying them behind the counter to the sink. "And my kind of fun won't land us at the station being interrogated."

They walked past a few businesses and stopped in front of Piece of Mine Pottery. The large window displayed dozens of ceramic figurines.

"I'm not artistic," Bailey protested.

"Neither am I, but it's lots of fun."

Once inside the owner, Jerren Osmar, promptly explained the different techniques of painting, and helped them pick out their pieces of pottery. Bailey chose a coffee mug and Randy selected a new cereal bowl.

They picked out the color paints they wanted and sat at a large wooden table. Randy began sponging blue paint on his bowl.

"Blue was always your favorite color," Bailey laughed.

"And green is still yours, I see." He watched as she added hunter green paint to the dish of soap. "Do you need some help? You picked one of the harder procedures for painting."

"But it sounds so interesting." She put a straw into the bowl and blew air into the mixture, causing bubbles to form. She stopped to catch her breath. "Who knew you could paint using bubbles?" Blowing into the straw again she made the bubbles form high peaks that were tinged green.

"Very good." Jerren stood behind her. "Now, take the cup and gently roll it into the bubbles."

Bailey did as instructed and to her delight when the bubbles burst, splats of green stuck to the cup, making a marbled design.

After she finished the cup, she marked her initials on the bottom.

"I'll glaze them and they'll be ready to pick up next Wednesday," Jerren said.

"Thank you, " Bailey replied.

Randy and Bailey stepped out into the night air. "You were right," she commented as they walked back to her car. "That was fun."

"I'm glad you had a good time."

They stopped at her car and Bailey dug around in her purse for the keys. After locating them she unlocked the door.

"Thanks, Randy." She felt her heart beating faster and mentally yelled at it to stop. He leaned closer. She held her breath. Fear paralyzed her body. No way could she give in to this temptation. Randy was a lifeline to her past, the one place she couldn't be drawn in to. Complications and hurt feelings lay buried there.

"I should be going." She opened the door, creating much needed breathing room. "Goodnight."

Chapter 4

By the time Bailey got to the café the next morning, the four men were seated at their usual table. She ordered a caramel latte and bought a peach scone, then headed to the back table. "Can I join you guys?"

"Art says you're investigating Ralph's accident." Dan sipped his coffee. "Seems like a waste of time to me."

"I don't think it's a waste of time." She scrutinized each man over the lid of her coffee. "Did any of you kill him?"

Art smirked. Dan choked on his coffee. Burt and Jerry exchanged surprised glances.

"You are direct." Art set his coffee down. "Has new evidence come to light?"

"No. But I'm still checking around. Is there anything you want to tell me?"

"Not a thing." His penetrating stare nailed her.

"Are you guys going to give me an alibi?"

"Man! For such a good looking chick with big knockers, you can be annoying." Art smirked.

"You can be as crude as you want, but you can't scare me off." Bailey leaned forward.

"He's not being crude," Burt said. "He's always like that."

"What time are you looking for an alibi?" Art sighed.

"My guess is between six-thirty and seven-thirty."

"Your guess?" Burt arched a brow over the frames of his glasses.

"That is what I deduced from the crime scene. I got to the park around seven- thirty. I found the body at eight. The corpse was still warm, and there wasn't much blood, leading to the conclusion he hadn't been lying there long."

"All this from someone who almost failed English," Burt grunted. "Okay, I'll play along. I was at home with my wife."

"I had football camp," Jerry said.

"I'm afraid I was home alone." Dan looked at her. "But I didn't kill him."

"That leaves you, Art." Bailey crossed her arms and leaned back in the chair, waiting for his answer.

"I was at Hooters having a beer."

She lifted a tapered eyebrow.

"What? There isn't anything wrong with Hooters."

"Does anyone know if Ralph had a girlfriend?"

"There was talk of a new bimbo, but no one had seen her," Dan said.

Art stiffened. "I don't think he had one."

"Do you think he made her up?" Jerry asked.

"Maybe," Art snapped. "It's not unusual for him to lie."

"Yeah, but he's had lots of women over the years. Why make one up?" Dan asked. "Even in high school, he would steal our girlfriends."

Art glowered at that remark. An unspoken hurt coming to the surface. Burt sat silent.

"How do you know he had a girlfriend if you never saw her?" She studied each face.

"He would brag about how young and hot she was," Jerry said.

"Not only that, but she apparently was very amorous." Burt added. "He enjoyed talking about their sex life."

"He didn't just talk about it, he went into explicit detail." Dan laughed and shook his head. "From what he said, she wasn't inhibited at all. She'd do it anywhere."

"She'd been feeding him every aphrodisiac known to man." Burt added. "That's why I agree with Art that the whole story was made up. I don't think any woman could be that wild about Ralph."

"My point exactly," Art grunted.

"Ralph was off his rocker in the first place," muttered Burt. "He often bragged to us about his girlfriends, but he never even gave us her name this time."

"It does seem odd that if he had a girlfriend that beautiful, he wouldn't be showing her off," Bailey said.

"He just liked rubbing our noses in his affairs." Dan sniffed, "He always thought he was better than us. Even in high school."

"Did all of you go to school with him?"

"Unfortunately," Art huffed.

"And, you all hated him?"

"But, we didn't kill him," Dan said.

As Bailey digested the information, she realized she had two more alibis to get, and she wasn't looking forward to it. Mick and Linda had the most to gain by Ralph's death. She'd known them her entire childhood, how could she think of them as suspects? However, in the P.I. business, she'd learned that everyone could be a suspect. She had to remain impartial.

"Hey, Mick." Bailey hadn't noticed him come in. His blond hair was longer, but still pulled into the familiar ponytail.

"Hey. How have you been, young lady?"

"Good, and yourself?" She took out her wallet. "Linda wrote me up a slip."

"Things are going good. We're finally turning a corner on the business." He rang up her order.

"Haven't you learned your name yet?" She noticed his name still tattooed across his fingers; M on his pinky, I on the ring finger, C on his middle finger and K on his index.

"Not yet." He laughed, giving her back the change. "I have it there so people know who's knocking them out." He winked. "So how does it feel being a P.I.?"

"It doesn't always make you the most popular person around."

"It's a lonely business, huh?"

"Sometimes." She averted her gaze and took a deep breath. "Mick, I need to talk to you and Linda."

"Sure. Randy can watch the counter while we talk." His smile seemed a little too good-natured. Or, maybe it was just her conscience.

Bailey entered the back room where she proceeded to interrogate her friends. Mick answered the line of questions with an even temperament, while Linda sounded hurt. However, both understood her position and wanted to help clear their names.

"So, what happened?" Randy asked when she came out of the back.

"They were remodeling the bathroom, and your grandmother called from California and talked with your mom around six-thirty. They chatted for an hour or so."

"Phone records will prove the call was made." Randy crossed his arms.

She hesitated to look him in the eyes. "Your Dad could have done it while your Mom was on the phone. The phone call could be a set up."

"You've become very cynical in your old age."

"I've had to," she defended. "In my line of work, you have people lying to you everyday. I've learned to put aside personal judgment in order to seek the truth."

"And you think my parents are lying?"

She paused. "I don't know."

He stepped closer. "What about me?"

The woodsy scent of his cologne filled her head, making her heart beat faster. She wanted to trust him. "I ... I don't know."

"Obviously your detective skills need more honing." His brown eyes riveted her to the spot. "You know, if it had been anyone else, my parents wouldn't have answered the questions."

"I know."

"Yet their faith in you doesn't mean anything."

"I didn't say that." She crossed her arms. "I can't take someone off the list just because I know them."

"So what does it take?"

"Proof."

"Okay, then let's check the phone records and get your proof." He stormed out the door.

She followed. "There's one problem. How are we going to get to the records?"

"Jeff."

"I don't think he'll be much help."

"Why?"

"Because he told me to stop investigating, for one thing. And, for another, he doesn't like me."

Randy stopped, staring into her blue eyes. "You make it hard to like you, y'know."

"I've never done anything to Jeff. Has he always hated me?"

"No, not always." Randy's tone softened. "But he's my best friend, naturally he's going to stick up for me."

"I haven't done anything to you."

"You're accusing me of murder."

"I said you're a suspect."

"Isn't it the same thing?" Randy rubbed the back of his neck.

"There's more to Jeff's attitude than this investigation."

"You mean besides the fact that you're calling his police friends incompetent? You put his best friend and parents at the top of your suspect list. You keep inventing a crime where it's plain to see that none exists. You're walking around with a chip on your shoulder. And, you broke his best friend's heart ten years ago." Brown eyes locked with blue. "That doesn't exactly put you on his top ten list of favorite people, now does it?"

"I'm not running for any popularity contests."

"No. You're just running away, as usual."

"Screw you." She turned to leave but his grip halted her.

"Why did you leave New York?"

She glared at him.

"And don't give me the excuse about the reunion, or your mother. You're running from something or someone. I want to know what."

"Why does it matter to you?" She jerked her arm away.

"Because you're trying to prove yourself and you're using this case to do it."

She'd forgotten how well he knew her. That kind of open exposure made her jumpy. It had been a long time since anyone had cared about her. She'd learned to depend on her own wit. Trusting other people always left her wounded. "It doesn't matter."

"If I'm going to help with this investigation, I need to know where your head is at."

"It's attached to my neck. Now, let's go see those phone records." She started walking away.

"When are you going to stop running?" He said to her back. "You've got to get tired sometime."

Her steps faltered. Her heart hurt. *No. I can't open up to him. I've been deceived too many times.*

The loud incessant banging intruded on Bailey's sleep. Looking at the clock next to her bed, she groaned, "Seven-thirty. Who's making all the racket?" Rubbing her eyes, she pushed the thoughts of Randy away. She'd managed to ignore him for the past three days.

After pouring a cup of coffee, she went in search of her mother. Tightening the belt on her robe, she headed to the barn.

"Mom," she called. "What's with all the noise?" She stopped suddenly, almost spilling her coffee when she saw Randy.

"Sorry." He swung the hammer again. "I didn't know you were still sleeping."

"What are you doing here?"

"I'm fixing the door to the hen house."

"I mean, why are you on our property?"

"I come over sometimes and help your mom." He stopped hammering.

"Why?"

He shrugged. "She needed help with the farm after your Dad died."

"And since I was the bad daughter and refused to move back, you thought you'd take it upon yourself to fill in." Hurt and anger filled her tone.

"Bailey, why do you always make me the bad guy? I'm just doing the neighborly thing and helping out."

"You're trying to make me feel guilty." She crossed her arms. "I came back for Dad's funeral. What more was I supposed to do?" Tears threatened to fall. She hadn't allowed herself to think about the sudden heart attack that took her dad five years ago.

"I'm not trying to make you feel anything." He wiped the sweat from his brow. "You flew in and out for the funeral so fast, no one had time to talk with you."

"I was in the middle of a big case."

"Why do you always use work as an excuse?"

"Why do you think I'm making excuses?" Her nose elevated with a defiant air. "Can't it simply be the truth?"

"Unlike you, I know the truth when I hear it."

She flinched as if he'd slapped her. "If you'll excuse me, I need to get dressed."

Chapter 5

On her way into town, Bailey stopped at the Grand Ledge Sunoco station to fill up her car's tank before meeting Jeff at Sweet Linda's Café.

"Can you believe the price of gas?" she grumbled as she sat down. "I miss the subway."

"Is that all you miss about New York?" Jeff asked.

"Are you on a fishing expedition?"

"No." He handed her a folder. "Here."

"Are these the phone records?" She opened the folder. "How did you get them so fast?" His willingness to help impressed her.

"I have my sources." Digging through his briefcase he added, "Let's get one thing straight, I only helped because…"

"Randy asked you to." She finished the sentence. "I know."

"I was going to say, because it proves the call was made, so there's no way Mick and Linda were involved."

She looked up from the folder. "Randy is still a suspect."

"Are you really that heartless?" Jeff shook his head. "How can you suspect an old boyfriend?"

"I don't have a choice." Her tone softened. "I have to look at all the evidence. Randy would do anything to protect his parents. We both know that."

"But murder?" He ran an agitated hand through his hair. "Come on, Bailey."

"He fought with Ralph the day he died."

"So did anyone who ran into Ralph. There was no way of having a conversation with that man that didn't lead to an argument."

"Randy has no alibi."

"He was with you."

"He was at the park waiting for me. He could have gotten there early." She looked him in the eyes. "He also tried talking me out of running up there."

"Randy doesn't like running." Jeff leaned closer. "You really are a piece of work." He snorted. "Walking out on him wasn't enough for you. Now you have to come back and break what's left of his heart."

"I'm sick and tired of hearing about poor Randy's broken heart." She tossed the folder down. "What about me?" She pointed to her chest. "He broke my heart first. Why does everybody blame me when he's the one who cheated?"

"Randy never cheated on you. He was head over heels about you."

"Ask Kelly Peterson." Tears unwillingly filled her eyes. "She told me all about their night together."

"And you believed her? Did you bother asking Randy what happened?"

"So he could lie?" She wiped the tears away, feeling disgusted that she'd allowed her emotions to control her.

"So you could get the truth."

"I already knew the truth."

"Just like you know it now." Digging out another file, he tossed it on the table with the other one. "Here's more information for you. Randy thought you might be interested in the autopsy results."

"Thanks." She scanned over the contents. "Were you able to get my bag of evidence back?"

"Don't push your luck."

"I wouldn't be a good investigator if I didn't." Bailey stood. "I'm going to order. Do you want something?"

"Mocha, skinny, decaf. Just tell Linda it's for me, she knows what I like."

"Since when do you worry about caffeine and calories?"

"Since I got married and had children."

Bailey turned and started for the counter when a young woman bumped into her.

"I'm sorry." The blond looked up. "I wasn't paying any attention to where I was going."

"It's fine." Bailey studied the familiar face. "Lindsay, is that you?"

"Bailey! I don't believe it." She gave her a hug. "I didn't know you were in town."

"I've been here for a week. I'm surprised your dad didn't say anything."

"I'm afraid I haven't seen much of him. I went shopping with Mom one day last week, but he wasn't home and I haven't had time to stop by. I get so busy with work and the kids." She glanced at her watch. "I don't have much time. Billy will be out of day-care soon, but I want to catch up before the reunion."

"I'd like that."

"Wait until you see the dress I bought. It was so fun shopping with Mom. It felt like I was back in high school on prom night. Have you got your dress yet? If not, maybe we can shop together. Kohl's and Younker's have the best sales."

"I haven't thought about the reunion or a dress."

"Isn't that why you're in town?"

"Part of the reason." Bailey smiled.

"I wish Dad had told me you were in town. He knows how close we were in school. You were practically my best friend."

"I'm sure he's forgotten. Burt has so many students each year."

"Probably." She gave Bailey a quick hug. "Let's get together soon. The reunion is only a couple days away."

"Okay. By the way, do you happen to remember what night you went shopping?"

"Yes, it was last Friday, the first day of the big weekend sale."

"What time did you leave?"

"Around six. Why?"

"I just wanted to see if the sales were still going on, that's all."

"Well, that one is over, but I'm sure another sale will begin. Those stores are always running some kind of sale. And, I'd recommend getting your hair done at All The Rage hair salon. They do fantastic work."

"Thanks for the info."

The next morning Bailey walked back to the table without even ordering a drink. She slammed her palms down on the table, causing the four men to jump.

"You guys are messing with me and I'm tired of it."

"What seems to be the trouble?" Dan asked.

"I don't like being lied to. So far the only alibi that has checked out is Jerry's." Her eyes met his. "You did have football camp." Her eyes locked onto Burt. "You, however, lied about being home with your wife."

"I didn't lie." His face reddened.

"Your wife was shopping with your daughter."

"They're always shopping. How am I supposed to keep track of which nights I did what?"

"That leaves us back at square one. You have no alibi." Her eyes shifted to Dan. "You already admitted to not having one."

"What about my alibi?" Art asked.

"I haven't had time to check it yet." She knew his would be harder to trace. A place like Hooters has lots of people who never see anything.

"Burt, we need to talk privately."

They took a separate table in the corner.

"Tell me the truth." Her tone softened. "I don't want to think my English teacher and the father of my best friend is a killer. Lindsay said she got to your house around six and you weren't there."

Burt sighed. "I lied because I went to a bar."

"Why would you lie? That gives you an alibi."

"I don't want Debbie to know." He looked down, watching his fingers tap on the table. "I'm a recovering alcoholic." He looked up. "Debbie would flip out if she knew I went there."

"Can anyone ID you?"

"Yes, the bartender knows who I am. But I didn't take a drink. I only had coffee."

"You could have stayed here for coffee." Bailey crossed her arms.

"It's too busy here. I needed to think." He sighed. "Being at The Barn helps me fight the craving."

"I'd think the opposite would be true. Being around alcohol would bring on the craving."

"It's not the craving, so much, as it helps me put my life in focus. I almost lost everything once, I don't want to risk that again."

"Does this trip down memory lane have something to do with Ralph's death?"

"I have a motive that no one knows about." He paused. "Debbie had an affair with Ralph years ago. We separated because of my drinking and he played on her insecurities."

"Was the whole town sleeping with him?"

"No one knows about it. We worked things out. I quit drinking, and when she found out she was pregnant, I never questioned who the father was."

"Did Ralph ever question it?"

"All the time. I'd hoped he'd have his own children someday and forget about Lindsay, but it never happened." Burt continued, his voice so thick with emotion that he could hardly get the words out. "Lindsay is my daughter no matter what."

"Does Lindsay know she might be Ralph's biological child?"

"I hope not." His eyes watered. "Ralph had started threatening us again. Insisting that he wanted a paternity test to prove who her father really was. I'd been afraid that he might say something to her."

"That's a strong motive for murder."

"I know."

"Would Lindsay say anything to you if he had talked with her?" Bailey didn't want to lay this bombshell on her best friend if she didn't have to.

"I'm sure she'd be upset if she knew we'd kept this from her all these years." His brown eyes pleaded with her. "Don't say anything to her, please."

"I can't make any promises. It depends on the investigation, but I won't say anything if I don't have to."

"Thanks."

Bailey picked at her food. Although her mother's fried chicken was still her favorite dish, she couldn't stop thinking about the case. Randy couldn't be guilty. Her heart knew it. However, her head kept reminding her he was the main suspect. The evidence rolled around and around inside her mind until her stomach twisted into a knot.

"What am I going to do?" she sighed.

"How about quit playing with your food and eat it." Martha huffed. "Then you can apologize to Randy and his parents and forget this whole mess."

"This mess is what I do for a living. I find criminals and put them away."

"That's what you did on the police force. Private detectives just run around catching people cheating on their spouses."

"Mom, can we please stop with the third degree." Bailey rubbed her forehead. "You're worse than the police."

Martha's retort was cut short by the ringing of the phone. She reached for the receiver. "Hello, Randy." She shot Bailey a *be good or else* look and handed her the phone.

"Hey, thanks for talking Jeff into getting those reports for me."

"Anything useful in them?" he asked.

"Do you want to come over? We can look through them together." She watched her mother's smile brighten.

"Sure."

"And bring your appetite, Mom made fried chicken for supper."

Bailey found that her appetite improved once Randy got there. Maybe it was watching him devour the food as if he hadn't eaten in weeks, or, maybe he made her feel like a teenager again. The solitude of the country, the home cooked meal and the comfortable company added up to contentment she hadn't expected. It felt good to relax. She never seemed to unwind in New York.

"I have something for you." Randy gave her a wrapped package.

"What's this?" She took it, tearing the paper. "It's not my birthday."

"Do I need a special occasion to give you a present?"

"My cup," she gasped. "It looks even better than when I finished it."

"The pieces always look better after they glaze it."

"What's this?" She looked inside the mug. "I didn't paint a heart on the bottom." She turned the mug upside down and saw her initials. "But it must be mine."

"I put the heart there," Randy confessed. "It's one of the perks of knowing the owner. I asked Jerren to put it there before he glazed it."

"Why?"

"For old times." His voice turned husky. "Do you remember the good times?"

"Yes." Bailey set the mug down on the coffee table. "It was a long time ago." She picked up a folder. "Do you want to look at this?"

Randy slipped on his black-framed glasses and took the folder.

"When did you start wearing glasses?"

"A few years back. I'm a little farsighted and need them for reading."

"I haven't seen you in glasses before." She studied the frames. They looked familiar.

"I lost my other pair, so I had to order new ones. I got these yesterday."

"They make you look like a teacher."

"Thanks." Randy furrowed his brow. "I don't understand any of this."

"The only thing that concerns me is the stomach contents." She slid closer on the couch and pointed to the section she wanted him to read, trying to ignore the magnetic force that pulled her closer to his body.

"This is really gross," Randy moaned. "What are we looking for?"

"You don't have to read the entire list. We are only concerned with his last meal. If you sift through all the words certain ones stand out." She read out loud. "Chili peppers, asparagus, oysters, chocolate, caviar and so much champagne that his blood alcohol content was point one five."

"Sounds like he ate a lot of aphrodisiacs before he died."

"Exactly."

"How does that help prove who killed him?"

"I don't know." She looked him in the eyes. "It's just a gut instinct that somehow this is a piece of the puzzle."

Randy got lost in her blue eyes. He saw a softening that hadn't been there before. "I love how your mind works," he whispered. Without planning to, he wrapped his arm around her and kissed her.

Startled by the sudden intimacy, Bailey tried to pull back, but the familiarity of his kiss overwhelmed her senses. The warmth of his embrace, the hunger of his lips made her feel safe.

Memories flooded back of them laughing and joking. How they played hooky from school. The movies they watched, swimming in Lake Michigan, walks in the park and school dances. She remembered prom and how handsome he looked in a black tuxedo, while she felt like a princess in her blue satin dress.

All these memories had been pushed away, tucked out of sight. As she found herself wrapped in his arms, she could not deny the happiness. She kissed him back with every ounce of passion her body possessed.

Then the bitter memory of his betrayal crept up. The pain and broken trust that she'd buried now stared her in the face. She pushed him away. "We have work to do."

Chapter 6

Hooters was loud and crowded. Sports announcers blared over the noise of chattering customers, while young women in orange shorts and tight white tops served drinks and wings.

Randy got several glances and smiles from the waitresses. Bailey rolled her eyes, grabbed his arm and pulled him to the bar. "Can you stop flirting?"

"I'm not doing anything. I don't even want to be here."

"We're checking Art's alibi and then we're outta here."

They were standing at the counter, waiting for the bartender, when a beautiful blond with curly hair sidled up to Randy. "Did you come to see me?"

"Hey, when did you start working here, Kelly?" he asked, surprised.

"About a year ago." Kelly smiled seductively. "How did you find out?"

"We're checking on something," Bailey answered. "Your shirt seems a little tight. It makes your chest look bigger." Bailey made a surprised face, "Or did you stuff your bra?"

Kelly rolled her eyes and groaned. "The bigger your bra size, the bigger the tips."

"I'm guessing that nine hundred dollars last month came from your tips and not makeup."

"Why don't you shut your crude little mouth," Kelly snapped.

"My mouth may be little but my breasts are big, and real." Bailey smirked. "As for crude, I'm not the one gallivanting around partially nude for money."

"Why you no good ... Why, I oughtta rip your mousey brown hair out by it's boring roots." Kelly tried to push past Randy.

"Hold up a minute." Randy held her back. "I don't think you are allowed to talk to customers that way." Looking at Bailey he added, "Don't we have a job to do?"

"What job?" Kelly glared at Bailey.

"We need to know if your uncle was in here the night Ralph died?" Randy watched Kelly's face darken.

"We're checking out a hunch."

"So you've joined her detective team?"

"We're only trying to find the truth," he defended.

"The truth is, Ralph slipped and fell. Uncle Arty had nothing to do with it. And just to prove it to you, yes he was here that night."

"What time?" Bailey asked.

"Six 'til closing."

"Hey, Kelly, you aren't getting paid to stand around talking all night." The bartender shouted. "Take this drink to table five."

"See ya later, Randy." She tossed a wink over her shoulder and sashayed away.

Bailey snorted and asked the bartender, "Was her Uncle Art in here last Friday between six and seven?"

"Not last Friday. Kelly called off. He only comes in to watch over her."

"Thanks." She grinned at Randy.

The café was quiet the next morning. Except for the group of four men at their usual table the place was vacant. Randy, wiping down the espresso machine, looked up when Bailey walked in. He held his breath, waiting for the explosion. Although thankful to have another suspect besides his parents and himself, he didn't like that it happened to be Art.

Bailey ordered a caramel latte with extra whipped cream.

"Go easy on Art." Randy handed her the cup.

"I'm not saying anything just yet." She paid for her drink. "I want to interview some of the shop owners first."

"What for?"

"To get more information."

"Look." Randy pushed his glasses further up the bridge of his nose. "You can't go nosing around when the police have ruled it an accident."

"They haven't ruled it one way or the other. If it is murder, they will be tight-lipped about it."

"So we shouldn't be asking questions." Randy ran an agitated hand through his unruly hair. "Let the police do their job."

"You sound like Jeff." Bailey snorted. "The police haven't had a murder in how many years?"

"Forty." Dan answered from behind her.

Bailey turned around and started questioning Dan. She followed him to the table. Randy shook his head then went back to cleaning the espresso machine.

Bailey started the interviewing with Dan's antique shop, since he offered during their earlier conversation. The dark and dank Lambs' Gate had the aura of long ago. The selection of old furniture, antiques and clothing impressed her.

"Meet Roxanne and Carol, my landladies," Dan introduced. "Roxanne is going to marry me after she dumps her husband." He laughed, as did Roxanne, obviously being a long-standing joke between good friends.

Lambs' Gate and Miller's pharmacy were just about the only buildings Ralph didn't own, which means he could have been leaning pretty heavy on Dan to get his shop. Although Dan had no alibi, she just couldn't picture this all-around good guy as a killer. *Keep emotions out of the investigation*, she chided herself.

A couple hair salons sat along the strip. Their complaints about their leases involved hot water and electrical issues. Ralph hadn't been good with keeping up the building maintenance. The owners of McDowell's weren't big fans of Ralph's, either, but didn't seem to have any reason to off him. Business was good at Piece of Mine pottery and the owner had never had a problem with Ralph.

The art consignment store, Ledge Craft Lane, were also on good terms with Ralph. Bead Dazzled was the new kid on the block, and so far things had been favorable with the new landlord. After visiting the unique gift shop Four Seasons, and the elegant and sophisticated About The Home, Bailey felt tired.

She ordered a sandwich and drink at the café and avoided Randy's glare. Even though she kept telling herself she was only doing her job, she still felt a twinge of guilt.

"Find out anything?" He finally asked.

"Not much." She took a bite of her sandwich. "People didn't like him, but no one is saying much of anything."

"They don't like strangers asking questions."

"I'm not a stranger."

"You've been gone for years, Bailey." He held back the part about people showing loyalty to him because she'd ripped out his heart when she left.

"This town is something else." She wiped her mouth, tossing the napkin on her empty plate. "You try to better yourself and they forget all about you."

"I never understood why you had to leave to better yourself. You are the one who never thought Grand Ledge was good enough. Things would have been different had you stayed." Randy took the plate. "Maybe people would trust you."

"I don't have time to debate this." She handed him the money. "I still have some shops to interview."

"And the apartments."

"What apartments?"

"The ones above the businesses." Randy looked to the ceiling.

"Great." She sighed. She still had a lot of work to do. "Where did he get all this money? I don't remember him owning all this when I left."

"Businesses fell on hard times and he had the cash flow to buy them out."

"If Ralph owned apartments, why did he live in Lansing?"

"He was a slum lord. The apartments are run down. He was too cheap to put money into them. He charged top dollar and didn't even keep things up to code. I'm surprised he wasn't shut down a long time ago."

"Has anyone ever complained?"

"All the time, but nothing ever got done. He had a top team of lawyers."

"Do you think he paid officials off?"

"Everyone thinks that, but it could never be proved."

"Maybe I can dig up some records."

"How would that prove who killed him?"

"It might not, but you can't overlook anything. Everything is a piece of the puzzle in a homicide."

"Or coincidence if it's an accident."

Something kept needling her, staring her in the face, but she couldn't put her finger on it. Although most of the town had a grudge against Ralph, her gut said it wasn't any business owner, and that included Mick and Linda. Of course, she couldn't think of her English teacher, Burt Wilson, as a killer either, even if he did have motive and had lied about his alibi. Of course, his airtight alibi had him off the hook.

However, she wasn't sure about Art. He had lied about his alibi, and had motive. Could someone hold a grudge for so long? He certainly could have killed Ralph before now. Why wait? This line of questioning kept leading back to Randy. She hated even thinking it. He couldn't kill anyone. Could he?

The problem was, she knew these people, had grown up with them. *It's hard to see things in black and white when you're dealing with people you know and care about.*

She had a hard time keeping those personal feelings from creeping up. She couldn't allow that. Focus is what she needed. "Just stay focused," she sighed.

She entered the grand ballroom of the Opera House, feeling more than a little anxious about this reunion. Round tables were covered with blue tablecloths. Off to the left was the dance floor with bundles of blue and gold balloons surrounding the square.

"Bailey, come sit with us." Lindsay waved.

Bailey smiled uncomfortably, but made her way over to their table. Randy was already there, along with

Jeff and his wife. Lindsay introduced her husband. As dinner progressed, Bailey started to feel more relaxed. Lindsay chattered away, just like old times, and didn't leave room for much conversation from other people. However, between gaps when Lindsay stepped away or left to catch her breath, Bailey slyly asked questions about occupations and marriages of other classmates.

Matt Kingsley won the biggest surprise of the night by showing up with Kelly Peterson as his date. Although, not bad looking, he had a balding head and a pudgy mid-section. Not the type Kelly usually dated. It seemed a strange match indeed.

"How did you manage a date with Kelly?" Jeff asked, when he came over to their table.

"She asked me out. Just walked into the station and asked if I was coming. I wasn't planning on it because of the divorce and all, but how could I turn her down?"

"Doesn't that seem a little forward of her?" Bailey approached the subject. "I mean, why would she just blurt it out like that?"

"Who knows?" He shrugged. "You know what they say about men in uniforms." He winked. "She keeps asking me questions about the police business." He looked over his shoulder and noticed a group of men surrounding Kelly. "I better go. Talk later."

"That must boost his ego," Jeff commented.

"Kelly asking him on a date?" Bailey asked.

"Well, that, and the fact that he's only a dispatcher. It must make him feel important that she's asking questions."

"He is a good guy and deserves some recognition." Lindsay said, then, jumped to her feet. "I feel like dancing." Her husband stood and they joined the other couples on the floor.

Bailey leaned over and asked Jeff, "Is Matt your spy at the station?"

"I have friends. I don't have spies."

"Touchy." She clucked her tongue.

"I'm sorry. Can we just get through the rest of the night without talking about business?"

"I don't have anything else to talk about," Bailey sighed.

"Then let's dance." Jeff led her onto the floor. In the middle of the song, Randy cut in, allowing Jeff to dance with his wife.

"I'd say you two had that planned." Bailey laughed.

"Yes." Randy admitted. "I knew you'd never accept if I asked."

"This feels like prom," Bailey whispered.

"It feels right."

"I think the wine is going to your head."

"No. It's you."

"I'm glad I came," she admitted. "I almost didn't. I wasn't sure I wanted to reconnect with old classmates. But everyone has been terrific. With the exception of being older, everyone seems the same."

"That's small town life. Nothing changes."

"I'm glad. New York is very impersonal, and everything changes so rapidly, you can hardly keep up."

"I find it hard to think of you surviving in a place like that."

"I guess I just learned to adapt."

"You could come back home," Randy suggested.

"There's nothing here for me."

Randy didn't say anything, but she felt his body stiffen. "I don't want to be cruel," she explained. "But we both chose our paths a long time ago."

"Did we?"

"We can't go back and undo the past."

"No, I guess not."

The song ended and a fast tune started. "Do you remember this song?" Bailey laughed.

"Yes." He started dancing like he'd done on prom night, with Bailey joining in. The rest of the night passed by so fast that she could hardly believe it was eleven already and the reunion had ended.

Bailey met Jeff in his office two days later. "The police have uncovered some information you might be interested in." Jeff handed her a folder. "Just so you know, I'm only showing you this so you'll leave the investigation alone."

Bailey read the reports and looked at the photos of the crime scene. "If he was nearsighted, why was he wearing farsighted glasses?"

"That's the million dollar question." Jeff leaned closer. "The autopsy showed he had a cataract. His vision could have been impaired enough that he didn't realize how close to the edge he'd gotten."

"I'm still not buying the accident theory." She studied the pictures again. "It's too tidy."

"Accidents are tidy." Jeff sighed. "Only murders are messy."

"How do you explain the glasses? He wasn't wearing his prescription."

"Maybe he grabbed the wrong pair. His vision had just recently begun to get blurry and the doctor gave him a new prescription."

"Don't they do surgery for cataracts?" Bailey knew something wasn't right.

"Only as the problem gets worse. Ralph's vision seemed okay for now. He complained about blurry vision and sometimes a glare at night, but his nearsighted vision had improved to the point that he didn't need glasses to read any more."

"That doesn't make any sense." She shook her head. "How can vision improve and be blurry at the same time?"

"It's called 'second sight.'" Jeff explained. "Although his vision worsened and got blurry for farsightedness, it improved for nearsightedness."

"How do you know all this?"

"The police interviewed his ophthalmologist." He tossed another folder across the table. "See, they are doing something."

"But they still want to call it an accident?"

"Maybe it was." Jeff sighed.

Suddenly, the needling point that had been eluding her clicked into place like the hammer of a gun. Her heart squeezed and breathing became difficult. She didn't want to believe it. "No." The thought pounded in her head. "He couldn't have done it."

"Who?" Jeff sat straighter.

Her eyes swelled with tears as she pushed the picture across the table. "Take a close look at the glasses."

Chapter 7

"This is crazy." Randy rubbed the back of his neck. "I didn't kill anyone."

"Then why are your glasses on the victim?" The two policemen sat across from Randy. Jeff sat next to him. Bailey watched from behind the two-way mirror.

"I told you, my glasses came up missing weeks ago."

"Did someone take them?" Jeff tried defusing the situation. He knew Randy well enough to know he must have felt ready to explode.

"I don't know." Randy thought a minute. "The last time I remember seeing them was in the café. They just disappeared. I looked everywhere and when I couldn't find them, I ordered new ones."

Bailey entered the room. "Can I talk to him?" Her eyes darted to Jeff. "Alone."

After everyone filed out the door, she sat down. "I didn't do this, Bailey. You have to believe me."

"I believe the evidence." Her voice cracked. "I can't let emotions get in the way."

"You've always been good at that," he sneered. "You left me without feeling one drop of remorse."

"Don't make this personal, Randy." She crossed her arms. "This isn't about me, or us. It's about you." She leaned closer. "They will go easier on you if you confess."

"Is that why you're here?" He stood up. "They sent you in here to get a confession?" He walked over to the mirror. "I didn't do it!" He yelled at the piece of glass.

"Randy, please."

He turned angry eyes on her. "And you." He pointed. "I thought you were my friend. I even hoped we could patch things up. I would never believe anything bad about you." Hurt turned his tone softer. "Even when people said cruel things about you when you left, I still defended you. I never gave up hope that one day you'd change your mind and come back to me." A tear worked its way down his cheek. "When you finally come back, you accuse me of being a murderer and a liar."

"Why should I believe you?" His accusations kindled her fire.

"Because I've never lied to you before."

"Ha!" She stood. "I would never have left if you hadn't cheated on me. I'm tired of defending my actions when you cheated." Her own tears rolled out of her eyes. "You tore my heart out."

"I never cheated!"

"Kelly Peterson told me all about your night together. She rubbed my face in it like a puppy being housebroken."

"And you believed her?" Anger replaced the hurt.

"Not at first." She sank down onto the chair. "But I found proof."

"What proof?" Randy asked, stunned.

"Her compact was in your glove compartment."

"I have no idea how it got there." He shook his head. "It was so long ago, but I assure you there has to be an explanation because I never cheated on you."

"It doesn't matter now."

"Yes, it does. I need you to believe in me." He reached across the table and took her hand. "I remember giving Kelly a lift to the gas station one day. Maybe it fell out of her purse or something."

"Then how did it end up in the glove box?"

"I don't know." His eyes held hers. "Just like I don't know how my lost glasses ended up on Ralph's dead body." He rubbed his thumb across her knuckles. "Use that gut instinct of yours and find out."

Bailey went through every report, picture and piece of evidence for the tenth time. "There has to be something here." She rubbed the bridge of her nose. "Just think." She stood and stretched her aching muscles. "If only I could find out who Ralph's new girlfriend was." That had to be the missing piece of the puzzle.

She decided to talk to Art. Although she had doubts about him as the killer, he was her last attempt at clearing Randy.

She found him in his office. "Can I come in?"

"That depends." He looked up from his computer. "What do you want?"

"I need to talk to you about your alibi."

"I have a deadline to make. I've already told you where I was." He went back to typing.

"You lied." She walked in, shutting the door behind her.

He looked up again.

"Your niece wasn't working that night and you weren't there." She sat down. "You only go to Hooters when she's working."

"Someone has to watch over her." He pulled his glasses off and set them on the desk. "She's gonna get herself in real trouble some day."

"What's your real alibi?"

"I don't have one." He looked defeated. "I was trying to find Kelly. I got worried when she called off work."

"Why would you follow her around town? She's old enough to take care of herself."

"Kelly isn't like you, or most women her age. She doesn't think things through. She's like a little child living in Candy Land. She needs guidance and protection. Since her dad is gone, the responsibility falls to me."

"Maybe she'd grow up if you let her." Bailey arched a brow.

"It isn't me. It's my sister. Betsy and George tried for years to have kids. They'd given up hope of having a family. Then, a miracle happened. A young girl was pregnant and looking for a good home for her baby. My sister and brother-in-law adopted Kelly. My niece was the light of their lives. But they tended to spoil her to the point that Kelly doesn't live in the real world." Art leaned back in his chair. "She has always hooked up with the wrong crowd. Her latest boyfriend was a real snake.

I kept trying to talk some sense into her, but she wouldn't listen."

"Why follow her?"

"She started to suspect that he was cheating on her. She'd been following him, trying to catch him in the act." His gray brows furrowed. "Frankly, she's better off without him."

"Did you ever find her that night?"

He shook his head.

"Did she find out if he was cheating?"

"I don't think so. It would have broken her heart if she'd found out."

"Is she still seeing him?"

"No. The scumbag is out of the picture for good." He put his glasses on and went back to typing.

"I need your help to clear Randy." She leaned forward. "The police are investigating this now and Randy is their prime suspect."

"What!" His head snapped up.

"Do you know the identity of Ralph's last girlfriend? She's the missing link and I need to contact her."

"Even if I did know, I wouldn't tell you."

"Why are you so hostile?"

"I don't like people nosing around things that aren't their business."

"Don't you want the truth?" Bailey crossed her arms.

"Not if it's going to hurt the people I care about." His face turned hard as stone. "I'm warning you to back off."

"I can't. I'm trying to help someone I care about." Bailey took a deep breath. She knew his temper would escalate but she had to dig out the truth. "I know about your wife and Ralph."

"So what." His anger vibrated through her like Jell-O.

"It gives you a motive."

Art removed his glasses and tossed them on top of his desk. "That happened a long time ago."

"Do you know who she left her settlement to?"

"Yes."

"Was it you?"

"No."

"How did she die?"

"What does it matter?" His eyes hardened. "This interview is done. If the police want to talk, they know where to find me." He put his glasses back on.

"Maybe she didn't commit suicide. Maybe someone killed her all those years ago. Someone who'd been hurt by her, someone who waited until the right moment to kill Ralph for revenge."

"Are you suggesting that I killed my wife?" He stood.

"Wasn't she your ex-wife?" Bailey's tone softened.

"I didn't kill anyone."

"Did you love her?"

"I married her, didn't I?"

"And you never remarried?"

"I had my heart ripped out once. That was enough." He sat down. "Melinda had lost both her parents. Her father died when she was three and her mother died of cancer when she turned eighteen. We married not long after that. She always seemed to be this sad, lonely girl looking for love and security. When our marriage hit a rough patch, she chose the easy way out. Her death was the easy way out of life."

"Why did she marry Ralph?"

"I think money had something to do with it. She liked security. But, he also had a very domineering attitude. He treated her like a child. " He took his glasses off and rubbed the bridge of his nose. "In a crazy, twisted way, I think Mindy viewed him as a father figure, even though he was only a few years older than me."

"Kelly sounds a lot like your ex-wife. She needs someone to guide her."

"So what?"

"Why is it your job to be the protector in the family?"

"Why are you so interested in my family? I'd think you have enough problems in your own family to keep you busy."

He'd hit a nerve. "That's the third time you've taken your glasses off since I've come in. Maybe you took them off at the café and set them down, accidentally picking up Randy's instead. You could have figured the time was right to kill your enemy and frame someone else."

"That's a bunch of bull! You have no proof."

"Maybe not, but I'm not about to let Randy take the fall."

"Talk around town is that you've been accusing him all along."

"Talk is cheap. Evidence is what speaks." She leaned closer, staring him down. "I'll get to the bottom of this with or without your help."

"I'm not helping you."

She wanted to continue arguing, but knew she wouldn't change his mind, so she left.

"Hi, I'm Bailey Rhodes, a friend of Randy's. Can I talk with you for a minute?"

Betsy was of average height and slightly overweight, but wore a friendly smile. "Come in." She opened the door and Bailey stepped into the magnificent entryway. The house loomed large and impressive.

"You have a beautiful home."

"Thank you." She led the way to the living room. "My husband designed it."

"Was he an architect?"

"Oh, no. He was an accountant."

"Wow. I didn't know accountants made so much money. I think I'm in the wrong business."

"We had a large inheritance that has enabled us to live above our means."

"Do you mind me asking what kind of inheritance?"

"You should know that my brother called and warned me you would be by." Her kind eyes seemed full of sadness. "He doesn't want me talking to you."

"Are you protecting him?"

"No. He doesn't need protecting." She stood, walking over to the large family portrait that hung above the fireplace. "Kelly was eighteen in this picture. My husband died a year later. Our family seems to be plagued by disasters."

"Are you protecting Kelly or your husband?"

Betsy turned around, arms crossed at her midsection. "We've always protected Kelly. She's our whole world."

"Why does she need your protection now?"

"My husband adored her. After being childless for so many years, you can't imagine the happiness of finally having a daughter of our own. My husband was always afraid that Kelly wouldn't love us if she knew the truth about being adopted. So we never told her." Betsy walked over to the chair and sat down, unable to continue.

"Did Kelly ever find out she was adopted?" Bailey asked, gently.

Betsy nodded, sending her brown hair swirling around her shoulders. "She came back from college at Christmas break. Wanting to help with decorating the house, she went into the attic to get some old decorations that had been stored up there. She happened to start rummaging through some other boxes and found the adoption papers." Betsy's eyes flooded with tears. "She flew into a rage, claiming we were liars and that she was going to find her real birth parents. She stormed out and went back to her dorm for the holidays."

"Did she look for them?"

"Yes. She looked for months and wouldn't even speak to us. She wouldn't take our calls and sent back our letters unopened. There was no way of getting through to her. Finally, she realized she needed our help in locating her parents. She came to us, asking for help. We told her that her birth mother was dead, but she didn't believe us. She wanted money to hire a private investigator. My husband said no and she stormed off again."

"Was her birth mother dead?"

"Yes." She collected her thoughts before continuing. "Anyway, George went charging after her. It was icy outside and he slipped, hitting his head on the cement steps. He died from the blow."

"Did Kelly blame herself for his death?"

"Yes. But it was just a horrible accident."

"So then, did she continue the search for her mother?"

"Yes, it continued for a few years, then one day she just stopped looking. I think she lost hope of ever finding her. The process can be very slow."

"How does your brother fit into all of this?"

"Art stepped in and helped after George died. Kelly adored him and readily transferred the position of Father over to Art. She has always been a handful. He felt she needed a strong hand for guidance. George had always been the strong one. I tend to be a pushover."

"You said earlier that your family was plagued. Is that in reference to Art's marriage?"

"Yes." She sighed. "Poor Mindy. She was a lost soul, searching for love."

"Were you close with her?"

"Yes. We were like sisters. She was an only child and I'd always wanted a sister so we sort of adopted each other. What a blessing the day she and Art married. But the fairy tale didn't last. It broke my heart when she left my brother. I felt like she'd left me, too."

"Did you two ever talk after the divorce?"

"Many times. We had to find a way to still be friends, although I never told Art." She stood and paced around the room. "The marriage to Ralph tore her apart more than anything ever could. She'd realized what a mistake she'd made, but felt trapped. He beat her so severely she'd been hospitalized twice. The second time was when she decided to leave him. George and I helped her leave town."

"Art never knew that you helped her?"

"No. It was a strict secret." She walked back to her chair and sat down again. "You see, Mindy was pregnant."

"What?"

"No one ever knew. She was afraid that Ralph wouldn't give her the divorce, or worse, take the baby. She didn't want her baby being abused. She was desperate to give her child a loving, stable home, the kind of home that she never had and couldn't provide."

"She gave the baby up for adoption?"

"Yes. George and I adopted her daughter."

"Are you sure Kelly never found out that Melinda was her mother?"

"I don't think so. But we never really talked much about it. George's death was hard on me. I think Kelly thought the subject would hurt me even more. She kept her findings to herself. I merely supplied the money."

"Why didn't you just tell her the truth?"

"I honestly don't know." Tears ran down her cheeks. "I thought I was protecting everybody involved."

"Art doesn't know?"

"How could he? Melinda left town after the divorce. She wasn't showing. After the adoption went through, she waited six months before returning. She wanted no one, especially my brother to know. She still feared Ralph."

"Do you think her death was a suicide?"

"What else would it be?" The horrified statement echoed through the house.

"Do you think Ralph could have found out and killed her?" Bailey asked.

"No. The only way he could have known was if Mindy told him."

"If she wasn't in her right frame of mind, maybe she did tell him."

"Never!" Betsy shook her head. "She would never have jeopardized Kelly's life by revealing that secret."

"Did Kelly ever find anything out about her birth father?"

"Not that I recall. But that period in my life was a very anxious time."

"I can imagine." Bailey smiled. "Well, I should be going. Thank you for your help."

Betsy stood and shook her hand. "I hope you realize what a tremendous trust I have placed in your hands. Please use the information with care."

"I will. However, I am curious as to why you have told me all this."

"I'm tired of living with secrets. I want peace, and I want justice. I don't believe Randy killed Ralph."

"Are you strong enough to face the real killer?"

"I'll have to be."

Chapter 8

Bailey's headache intensified and every muscle tensed. She had no desire to see Kelly, but she'd spent too many years thinking the worst about Randy. If Kelly lied, she needed to know.

Kelly opened the door. "What do you want?"

"We need to talk."

"I'm busy."

"It's about Randy."

"You have two minutes." She opened the door. "How did you find me?"

"The bartender. Plus, I had a visit with your mother." Bailey didn't expect such a lavish apartment. "Wow, your tips must be really good. How long have you lived here?"

"Just over a year. What's this about Randy?"

"He's a suspect in Ralph's death."

"That's ridiculous." Kelly walked across the plush Persian carpet and sat down on the Italian leather sofa. "The police said it was an accident. What does this have to do with me anyway?"

"You lied about working that night. The bartender said you called in sick and Art confirmed it."

"Big deal. I wasn't feeling well." She lit a cigarette.

"Why did you lie?"

Kelly's manicured nails tapped a steady rat-a-tat-tat on the black, marble coffee table. "I don't keep track of my every movement. What's it to you anyway?"

"Liars are usually hiding something."

"How dare you." Kelly stood and started walking to the door. "Your two minutes are up."

"You also lied about sleeping with Randy."

Kelly stopped. "Is that what he told you?"

"You planted that compact for me to find." Bailey pinned her with an icy stare.

"It happened a long time ago. Why bring it up now?" She took another puff.

"Because it matters to me."

"I don't care about you." She blew out a slow string of smoke that circled her head.

"But you care about Randy." Bailey held her breath, hoping she'd tell the truth.

"So what? I lied about sleeping with Randy. And, yes I planted my compact when he gave me a ride one day."

"How did you get the compact in his car?"

"Easy, I pretended my car was broken down and he stopped to give me a lift to the gas station. When he went to talk with the man at the station, I slipped it in." She exhaled, slowly. "I knew you'd find it. After all, you were always the jealous type. And, that hot headed temper played right into my hand."

"You are the most hateful, detestable creature I've ever known." Bailey could hardly stand. The room started spinning. All these years, she'd lived a lie. Her world had been turned upside down and Kelly stood there, acting as if nothing happened.

"You don't have to get so nasty." She inhaled again. "You wanted the truth."

"How could you?"

"I wanted Randy. I figured if you were out of the way, we'd have a chance." She shrugged, walking back to the coffee table and flicking the ashes in the ashtray.

"You little whore!" Bailey felt like punching in her pretty, smug little face.

Kelly smiled. "Maybe Randy and I never hooked up, but at least I got rid of you."

"If only your uncle could see this side of you."

"My uncle sees the side I want him to see."

"What about your mom? Does she know this evil side exists?"

"Mom has always been a marshmallow. With dad gone, I get what I want."

"Do you even care that he's dead?"

"Not particularly. He was always stopping me. Always trying to control me. It drove me nuts."

"That's what parents do."

She exhaled again. "Besides, they aren't even my real parents."

"You are one cold fish," Bailey snorted. "No wonder no man has ever loved you."

"I've had more men than you can count."

"Sex isn't love. To be used and tossed away like yesterday's paper must be a sad, lonely feeling."

"Shut up." She stood, walking over to the door. "I've heard enough of your drivel. Just because you can't land a man and keep him doesn't mean you can pick on me."

"I'm not worried about landing my man. After all, he still needs me and has never even looked your way." Bailey sauntered to the door. "From what I hear, your boyfriends are scumbags and you can't even keep them satisfied. Isn't that why you were out tracking your current lover down? Because he was cheating on you?"

Kelly's fist gripped the doorknob so tight that her knuckles turned white. "Good-bye."

As Bailey entered the quiet police station, she realized not much happened in this small town. The most these cops generally dealt with were a few burglaries and a bit of juvenile vandalism. Bailey asked for Officers Mullin or Davis.

The young blond, P. Mullin, came to the front desk. "What do you want?"

"I need a favor." She put on her best smile.

The smile didn't work. "You've caused enough trouble."

"Do this one thing for me and I promise to not interfere any more." She held up her right hand.

He just crossed his arms and said nothing.

"Look, you may not like me or my viewpoints, but you have to admit that my calculations have been right so far."

He still said nothing.

"Do you still have that bag of evidence I picked up in the park?"

"Yes. We keep all evidence."

"Can I see it?"

"Wait here." He sighed, coming back a few minutes later with the bag and plastic gloves.

Bailey dug through the contents, then handed him the item she sought. "If you run the fingerprints on this, I believe you'll have your killer."

Paul looked skeptical.

"I promise it is the last thing I will ever ask."

"We can't run fingerprints without a reason."

Bailey pulled a folded piece of paper from her purse. "Look at this."

"It's a lease for a condo."

"Look whose name is on it."

"Ralph's." The officer looked puzzled.

"He transferred the deed over to his girlfriend two weeks before he died."

"What does that mean?"

"Ralph frequently gave expensive gifts when he was ready to break up with his girlfriends," Bailey said. "Sort of a severance package."

"And you think his girlfriend killed him."

"We'll know after you check the fingerprints."

The police sirens pierced through the night like a howling dog. The sound wasn't uncommon for this part of Lansing, however, having police burst through the door of the Hooters and arrest a pretty blond for murder was a definite twist.

"I didn't do anything," Kelly insisted as the police read her, her rights.

"Call my uncle," she yelled to the bartender as they placed the handcuffs on her wrists. "Owww. That hurts."

Randy and Bailey walked in during the commotion.

"This is all her doing." Kelly stopped in front of Bailey. "You're just mad because I broke you guys up and now you're trying to get even."

"There is evidence, Kelly. The police don't arrest people for revenge."

"You think you have this all figured out, don't you?"

"You lost your compact on the ledge, probably while struggling with Ralph. Your fingerprints are all over it."

"So I lost my compact on one of my many walks. My lawyer will tear that evidence apart in court."

"They're on Randy's glasses as well. You stole them to frame him, just in case the police didn't buy the suicide or accident angle."

"Or maybe we're lovers, and I put my hands all over everything, including his glasses." Kelly licked her lips seductively.

"You know, I almost feel sorry for you." Bailey stepped closer. "But, I know how appalling you really are."

"You can't prove anything."

"One thing bothered me at the reunion. Why were you with Matt?" Bailey asked. "Although he's a nice guy, he's not your type. When he told me you kept asking questions about his work, I figured you were fishing for information."

"Why would she kill Ralph?" Randy asked.

"Because she thought he was cheating on her."

"That's ridiculous." Kelly's face reddened. "You have no idea what you're talking about."

"He transferred the condo to you." Bailey crossed her arms. "Your uncle finally verified that point."

"Uncle Arty wouldn't say anything. He swore us to secrecy. He didn't want anyone knowing I was living with Ralph. He thought my reputation would be ruined."

"You didn't need Ralph for that," Bailey scoffed.

Kelly spit in her face. "You're a vindictive liar."

Randy handed Bailey a napkin.

"Kelly." Betsy pushed through the crowd. "Kelly, what's going on?"

Art stood next to her. "Don't worry about a thing. Our lawyer will meet you at the station."

Bailey wiped her face, then looked at Art. "Don't you think it's odd that she slept with the man that stole your wife?"

"What?" Betsy's face paled. "You knew she was sleeping with Ralph and didn't say anything to me?"

"I wanted to protect you."

"She's my child. I'm the one who needs to make those decisions." Betsy looked at Kelly. "Do you have any idea what you've done?"

"Yes." Kelly stepped forward, staring at Betsy. "I killed my mother's killer."

Betsy gasped. Art folded his arms. Bailey stood emotionless and Randy didn't blink.

"I found out a long time ago that Aunt Mindy was my real mother."

"What are you talking about?" Art barked.

"How?" Betsy trembled.

"My mother gave you every penny she had so you could raise me right. She wanted what was best for me. She died of a broken heart. Ralph did that to her. I waited and plotted for years. Finally, the time was right."

"And you knowingly slept with your father?" Betsy felt sick to her stomach.

"Ralph wasn't my father." Kelly shifted her eyes to Art. "Uncle Arty is."

Art stood transfixed.

"What?" Betsy swayed.

"Aunt Mindy wrote a letter explaining everything. Her lawyer sent it to me when I turned twenty-one. She had gone to Uncle Art one night for protection. One thing led to another and, well, they ended up having me."

"No." Betsy shook her head. "She told me Ralph was the father."

"She had a paternity test done. She sent the results along with the letter. My DNA matched Art's." Kelly's blue eyes bore into her mother's. "She ended up snagging some hair from Uncle Arty one day. They used that to run the test." Kelly's scornful, hysterical laugh bounced off the televisions still broadcasting the various sports games. "And to think I killed daddy for nothing."

Betsy froze. "You ... you killed George."

"I had to. He wouldn't give me the money I needed to find my parents. I knew once he was out of the way, you'd give in." She shrugged. "It worked, although no leads ever came out of the investigation. But a few years later, I got all the answers I needed. Mindy explained that she was out of her mind and couldn't live with the guilt of giving me up. She'd also never told Uncle Arty, for fear he'd never understand or forgive her." Kelly's eyes misted up. "Ralph caused all of this and had to pay. I made him pay." She shouted. "I wasn't about to be played for a fool like my parents had been." She stared right at Bailey. "He was the fool. He died like one, too."

Kelly smiled at the memory. "I coaxed him to the park with a picnic of all his favorite foods and champagne. After we ate, I led him through the park by playing strip hide-and-seek."

"How did you get the glasses on him?" Bailey asked.

"We used the glasses in place of the blindfold. I had him put the glasses on when it was his turn to find me." She shrugged her shoulders. "I knew his vision was blurry and he wouldn't know how close he was to the edge."

Her smile turned wicked. "He came searching for me and I jumped out from behind the tree. I gave him a long, slow kiss. His sense of balance was off, then, I simply pushed him over the edge."

She licked her lips as a surge of adrenaline pumped through her body. "He died with my kiss on his lips. How's that for poetic justice?"

"You're going to serve life in prison." Bailey stared her down. "How's that for justice?"

"I'll get out of this. No one messes with me. I wasn't about to let him break my heart. I watched what he did to my aunt and uncle. You can sure bet I wasn't going through that."

"You know what?" Bailey stepped closer. "I actually feel sorry for you."

"I don't need your pity."

"You've destroyed your entire family. Pushed away everyone who loved you. Killed your own father, all for what? Revenge."

"Isn't that why you're after me, Bailey? Revenge for breaking up you and Randy. You should understand the feeling. The need."

"I'm not after revenge. I'm after justice. There's a difference." Bailey watched the officers lead Kelly away, then watched Betsy collapse in Art's shaky arms.

Bailey was packing her suitcase when Martha came in.

"You're really leaving?"

"Mom, you knew this was just a visit. The reunion is over. The killer is caught and my vacation is up. I have no more reasons to stay."

"What about Randy?"

"He's not even speaking to me."

"You two can work this out if you wanted."

She took her mom's hands. "My life is in New York."

"I'm going to miss you." Martha hugged her tight.

"I promise to come visit more often."

"I suppose I could come see New York sometime." The battle lines needed to disappear if she wanted a relationship with her daughter. "I don't want to wait another five years to see you again."

"I don't want that either." She hugged her mom. "Just because I choose to live somewhere else besides here doesn't mean I'm choosing to leave you. I love you."

"I love you, too. And I'm sorry I let the distance between here and New York put distance in our relationship."

Bailey stood by the large window, watching the planes land. Her flight would be leaving soon. She wrestled with her feelings. How had she let her life get so mixed up?

"Bailey."

She turned, stunned. "Randy. What are you doing here?" Her heart beat faster than the jets taking off.

"I wanted to say good-bye."

She held her breath. Would he ask her to stay? Try to work things out?

An awkward silence stretched between them.

"I'm sorry, Randy. I never meant to hurt you."

"I know." He rubbed the back of his neck. "I just can't believe we let Kelly mess things up between us."

"I let her." She couldn't hold the emotions back anymore. Tears filled her eyes. "If I'd only trusted you. If only I'd come to you instead of believing her lies."

"We can't go back now." He stepped closer. "Anyway, thank you. If it weren't for you, I'd be in prison."

"But I suspected you in the first place."

"Not really. I know that. When it came right down to it, you were on my side." He pulled her into a tight embrace.

She let the warmth of his body seep into her soul. "Can you ever forgive me?"

"If you'll forgive me."

She pulled back, looking into his eyes. "For what?"

"For not coming after you when you left. I could have tracked you down and asked why you left. But I was too hurt and didn't care enough to find the answer."

"I was hurting too."

"We were both stubborn." He smiled. "If only we could go back."

"But we can't." She shook her head.

He kissed her. "For old time's sake."

She put her arms around his neck. "I miss the old days. Back then, we would have kissed and made up."

"Life is more complicated as adults."

"My life is in New York." She didn't know if she was trying to convince him or her own heart. She knew, deep down, she had no ties in New York.

"I didn't ask you to stay." He touched her cheek and traced the outline of her jaw. "My life is here. We both know you never wanted to settle down in this town. Your dreams were always bigger than Grand Ledge."

"I would have stayed for you."

"And you would have been miserable. It would never have worked."

"Guess we'll never know." This time, she kissed him. "Good-bye, Randy." She felt her heart break as she walked away. All the missed years, all the could-have-beens played in her mind.

Bailey sat by the window, looking out over the city. Her dinky, ratty apartment was filled with stale air. The noises from the streets below drifted up through the closed window: car horns blaring, people yelling, kids crying. There never seemed to be quiet or solitude here. Not like back home.

Then again, maybe homesickness and a heavy heart colored her world in shades of gray. In these desolate moments, she relived the past, condemning her behavior. Bailey drank the last sip of her coffee, the red heart on the bottom peeking through the last remains of the dark liquid. She ran her finger around the rim, remembering the night she'd painted the mug. The memories of that night turned into a string of other memories.

She'd walked out on her best friend and the love of her life ten years ago without once looking back. He'd waited all these years, hoping she'd come back someday. When she finally did, she accused him of murder.

"No wonder he wants me as far away as possible." She would have stayed if he'd asked her. But he hadn't.

The doorbell brought her out of the reverie. "Who could that be?" She asked the goldfish sitting on the table. "Probably Mike."

In the two weeks since she'd been back, she'd been looking for another agency to work for. Mike had tried talking her into staying at his agency several times, but catching him with the new secretary was more than she could handle. Unlike with Randy, she had more than enough proof that he'd been cheating.

"What do you want now?" She jerked the door open. "I told you …" She stopped, mouth open, eyes wide.

"I wanted to see New York." Randy smiled.

"What about school?" Tears filled her blue eyes, making them shimmer like a lake on a sunny day.

"It doesn't start for a few more weeks. I figured I'd better get my vacation now. Is that okay?"

"Yes." She threw her arms around his neck. "It's fantastic."

He hugged her tight. "I made the mistake of not following you years ago. I don't want to make that same mistake again." As they kissed, she felt her broken heart die a quick, painless death.

Country Roads

Have you ever walked down a long, winding road, feeling the sun bathe your skin in its warm embrace? Or taken a scenic drive through the country, inhaling the scent of hot sunshine on freshly turned hay, driven over an old covered bridge, or, maybe, just stopped to walk in a field redolent with the scent of sweet clover?

Time seems to slow down. The colors look more vivid. Life lessons are much simpler. Perhaps you've picked a bouquet of wild flowers, enjoyed the crunching of the autumn leaves under your feet or noticed the beauty of a sunset. Maybe you've stopped and petted a cow meandering along the fence, or listened to the bullfrogs croaking in the pond. Whatever the case may be, one thing is certain; Nature is always at her most vibrant when traveling through the country.

We hope you'll slow down, take a deep breath and savor the stories and poems in this chapter.

Can I Go To The Woods?

Diane Bonofiglio

I love long, lazy rides through the countryside, especially early in the morning, with the radio turned off and the windows rolled down. The aroma is almost as good as the smell of chocolate. The fields, the trees, the old farmhouse with its weathered barn and mended fences, they all combine to make me feel like God created this time and this place just for my pleasure. If I were the only one in charge of my life, I would live in a remote forest somewhere in the world, where my only neighbors were the four-footed kind. I truly like being alone. That's my mantra.

I once wrote a poem, titled "Yours Forever," about a trip I took to the Canadian wilderness. After a good friend of mine read the poem, she thought I had taken a lover. In my mind, that was the only way I knew how to express the deep emotional experience I had encountered.

I like uncluttered, unhurried and all natural. I like the sounds and sights, the feelings that filter through me when it's just me and the squirrels. I see myself as a great conservationist, a second Henry David Thoreau. I always wanted to be like him. I keep a copy of one of his quotes in the front of my daily calendar, to remind me of the life I dream of leading. *"I went to the woods because I wished to live deliberately, to front only the essential facts of life, and see if I could not learn what it had to teach, and not when I came to die, discover that I had not lived."*

Over the past several years, I've watched the phone towers go up in fields once planted with soybeans. I feel I should stand at attention and salute every time I pass a lineup of power towers, the ones that look like they were built by a giant, with a super-sized erector set. My stomach does little flip-flops when I see a field of wheat give way to a new subdivision.

New roads, bigger and better cars, more power, more, and more. There is quite a large chasm between my mantra and my life. I keep trying to close the gap, but most times, it's one step forward and two steps back. I recycle newspaper, but use paper towel instead of an old cut up T-shirt. I turn off the lights when I leave a room, but I turn up the central air a couple more notches when the temperature inches toward 90 degrees. I buy birdfeed for my feathered friends while at the same time I throw away the stale bread ends left in the back of the refrigerator. I drive when I could walk, I pay to go to the gym, but I mow my lawn with the riding mower. It makes me uncomfortable to admit to such gross consumerism. Have I become one of the spoiled masses I love to hate?

Is it too late for me to live the life I imagined? Can I go to the woods?

The Old Barn

Diane Bonofiglio

Your tired eyes gaze out over barren fields,
where once an explosion of gold
spread endless light.

Your mouth lies agape and empty.
The backs that kept your belly full,
long since gone in search of their fortunes.

You bore the years with dignity and grace.
Sharing the laughter of children, remembering
the passions of first love, and the fulfillment of bountiful
harvests.

Your silhouette against the early morning sky,
brings comfort to those who once knew you.
You are their connection to Mother Earth.

Your heart has seen much, and only memories remain,
to keep you company. You may stand alone, fighting age
and the elements, but you stand in stately grandeur.

Ghost Shoes

Kerry Tietsort

Standing in the middle of a long, abandoned road.

Who has passed here before, yet to cross, or return again?
Traveled the here and thereafter.

Footprints missing or engraved in time.
Wispy apparition, there and gone, sometimes forgotten.

Faintly treading through earth and ages.
Gone too soon or lingering on.

Like echoing footsteps in an empty hall.
Whisper a name to remember forever.

Whose ghost shoes have gone walking?

Red Bird

Diane Bonofiglio

Red bird so beautiful,
flitting from branch to branch.
spread your regal crimson wings in flight.

So bright against the newly fallen snow,
your golden beak searching for morsels
to fill the emptiness left by winter's icy breath.

Thankful Hearts

Diane Bonofiglio

The junipers were laden with heavy mounds
of snow the color of alabaster, looking like
chandeliers all covered up for the season.
The cardinals growing exasperated
looking for the passage into the feeders,
flitted around the trees until the flapping
of their wings shook the snow to the ground.
Song abounded everywhere as they
called out the good news and once again
could commune with full bellies and thankful hearts.

A Hay-Day

Jan Sykes

The dusty red tractor chugged along rhythmically, row by row, in the twenty-acre field. Attached to the tractor was a rattling hay baler followed by a large, flat, wooden wagon, slatted up the back. It was a parade of vehicles and a cacophony of sounds, jostling and bumping along the rutted field.

Standing balanced, with his feet firmly planted, seventeen-year-old Mike jammed the hay hook into the crisp bale of moss green hay, pulling it from the baler. Sweat ran down his tanned face and darkened his blond hair, just visible under his farm hat, as he struggled to lift the bale and put it in its place. He heaved the bale onto the stack in a brick-like fashion.

Ninety degrees would normally feel hot, but with the high humidity the heat was stifling, visible in waves over the horizon. Despite this, Mike was dressed in a heavy long-sleeved shirt and blue jeans. As he lifted the bales they scratched across his arms and legs, leaving hay on his clothing.

By two o'clock the heat was unbearable as the humidity continued to rise. The clouds had darkened and there was an ominous stillness hinting at an incoming storm. Even the birds were quiet. The only sounds to be heard were the rustling of the hay and the methodical rattling of the machinery. Occasionally, a voice shouted instructions over the noise of the farm equipment. The sweet smell of hay became stronger in the heat. Chaff clung to the sweat on Mike's neck.

Visible in the distance was a dark sheet of rain. It would be approaching soon and they still had two rows to go. The tractor moved along at a quicker pace and Mike stacked the bales as fast as they came through the baler, knowing a rainstorm could ruin the hay.

Watching from the barn at the edge of the field, sixteen-year-old Anna saw Mike's dilemma. Moving quickly, and not oblivious to his good looks, she put the horse she'd been riding back in its stall and ran to help. Her brown, permed hair bounced as she sped across the field. With a running jump, she landed on the still-moving wagon beside Mike. Mike glanced at Anna with a sparkle in his eye, being careful not to fall off the bounding wagon. With two of them working, the tractor was able to move along at a faster pace. Mike hauled up the bales and Anna stacked them in place, flinching as they scratched at her bare arms, leaving thin, red welts.

After the last bale was in place, Mike and Anna jumped up on top of the stack of hay and clung to the bales as the tractor raced against nature across the field. Mike looked at Anna, noting how cute she was with hay stuck in her tousled hair. She gave him a coy smile as he watched her. They balanced precariously as they grabbed at the bales bouncing around, threatening to tumble off the wagon.

Streaks of light flashed in the sky and thunder rumbled in the distance. A few drops of rain fell. The tractor putted along as fast as a tractor could go.

Within yards of the barn, Mike and Anna began to laugh. It had been quite a ride, but they had made it. No rain could damage the hay now.

They made it to the barn just as the downpour came, closing off the entrance with a rain door. Mike and Anna flopped back on the hay, out of breath, sweating and grinning.

Winter Forest

Diane Bonofiglio

Winter forest, feet buried in snow,
stripped naked by cool October winds.

Standing tall and slender, limbs, like arms,
stretching toward the warmth of the sun.

All huddled together, bent by the wind,
fighting to stay winter's icy fingers.

Biding time, 'til warm April showers,
bring budding leaves to fashion regal coats.

Now standing straight and proud,
in the glory of summer's green finery.

A Wondrous Winter Scene

Diane Bonofiglio

On a journey through the countryside
on an icy January day,
I stopped to gaze upon a wondrous winter scene.

Shadows and sun were playing,
brisk breezes sang an aria as
barren frosty branches reached toward heaven
with beckoning arms awaiting God's gift.
As if on cue, rays of sunshine, like shooting stars
fell to earth, embracing every pine, oak, and maple
slowly and softly,
like a mother stroking her child's hair.

Time ceased to be.
An eternity passed in a moment.
A moment seemed an eternity.
A cocoon surrounded this place, protecting it.

Before me, magic filled the crystal air,
as if a fairy passed her wand.
From each little branch, from every bough,
snowflakes burst, spilling like gold dust everywhere.
Twinkling and glimmering,
until the soft gentle sounds of tiny bells sang,
an aria that only I could feel.

My Gravel Road

Alta C. Reed

There are few gravel roads left in Mason County. Maybe, because my farm homestead is the only home on this mile between the old country store on Tyndall Road and the closed two-story school building on Maston Road, my road will remain gravel, the way I prefer it.

I can count the number of deer that cross the road each night between my woods and the winter wheat field on the other side. Telltale tracks, some big ones with splayed hooves and some little ones denoting the spring fawns that have joined the herd, let me know the upcoming deer season will be successful.

Road commission trucks keep the gravel base smooth and level. Brine keeps the dust under control. If any soft spots develop after a rainstorm, fresh gravel is brought in to correct the base.

Middle-sized stones mixed with the gravel make outlines for my flower beds. Some smooth, round stones, I have painted with bright red stripes to resemble ladybugs. I hope the Road Commission will forgive me for using some of their gravel stones.

A single car going by provides excitement for the entire day. There is peace and quiet beyond compare here on my gravel road.

Main Street

From the hubbub of businesses to the quiet tranquility of the front porch of houses sitting adjacent to Main Street, you will be entranced with the tales in this chapter.

Every town, large or small, has a street running through it that attracts the most attention. The road is the busiest traveled. Businesses inhabit the old buildings, and the town's people can be found milling around during dusk hours.

Main Street is the heart and soul of a city. It speaks of the community's commitment, spirit, values and even their work ethics. Shall we take a stroll down Main Street and see what we find?

Childhood of Yesteryear

Alta C. Reed

Having been blessed with the good fortune to be born and raised in Custer, almost one half century ago, I would like to take a minute to remember some of the experiences of that child I once was.

First, the whole town was our playground. We had complete freedom from the fear of being harmed or getting hurt. We were acquainted with everyone, William Fisher, John Roach, Hjalmar-Smedberg, Howard Howe, Joe Sanders, Mrs. Woodhead, Mrs. McKenzie; the list goes on.

Mrs. Jesse Barrett always gave us a nickel for a bouquet of myrtle that grew in profusion up in the orchard. Eileen and I sat on the steps in front of Joe Howard's barbershop and each licked one side of an ice cream cone. Nothing will ever taste that good again.

Every May Day was special, as May baskets were hung on doorways all over the area. Adder tongues, violets, mayflowers and trillium were picked in Chisholm's woods and down in Steven's gully. To go to the gully, we had to pass Steven's beehives which we achieved by running as fast as our young legs would allow.

We played hopscotch by the hour; hide and go seek. We would shout, "Oley, oley outside comes in free." Three youngsters made a ball game, but it was always more enjoyable when Mrs. Howe, now Mrs. Joe Laiskonis, came out to catch for us.

Our imagination worked overtime. We hid make believe items for the Yellow gang, Vic and Duane, to find, which they always managed, somehow. We buried brightly colored stones inside tobacco tins, and made treasure maps so we could find our loot again someday.

Only two of the youngsters disappeared long enough to worry the neighborhood parents. Leonard Green decided to find his dad one day and walked up the railroad tracks, almost to Walhalla. A train crew picked him up and brought him back home. Another day, Victor Sanders went to sleep in the open space under his house. After a long nap, he crawled out and wanted to know who everyone was looking for.

We roller-skated in the summer and slid down Sanders' hill in the winter. We played house on a blanket under the shade trees and fed sugar to the ants living in the cracks of the sidewalks. One never stepped on a crack, as it broke your mother's back.

We stamped every horse we saw which meant we put a thumb to our tongue, then pushed the thumb into the opposite palm and hit it with the other fist. It was important to do that, but I couldn't explain why.

We played in the old Lampman building and caught baby mice. We climbed all over the Squire-Dingee pickle factory, in and out of the vats like squirrels; we hid in the old jail; we went to the top of the abandoned elevator by the railway tracks.

Eileen, Duane, Mable Ann, Vic, Jimmy, Mary Agnes, Charles, Dick, do you remember too?

Don't Mess with Tradition

Randy D. Pearson

I sighed when I heard the front door slam. Putting the bookmark in my science fiction magazine and closing it slowly, I sat on my bed and waited for the commotion to begin. My roommate Bill could never simply enter the house and go about his business. For some reason, his life always had to involve me.

"Hey Dan," Bill bellowed from somewhere beyond the other side of my closed door, "come out here a sec!"

Having an obnoxious persistence about him, I knew he'd only continue his caterwauling until I emerged. So I hauled myself out of bed, pushed my door open and ambled into the living room.

His justification for my attention became immediately apparent. His hair, for starters, had been dyed a bright purple. The majority of it shot upward in three large spikes, standing nearly six inches above his skull, while the remaining strands drooped haphazardly around his angular face. He had an awful lot of makeup on his face and neck, in various shades of pink, baby blue and purple. To me, it appeared as if a circus clown had attacked him. Clad mostly in leather, the vest and chaps offset the pink, neon tank top and cowboy boots quite hideously. He completed the ensemble with a clip-on hoop nose ring and large, dangling earrings. He was certainly dressed to kill... Or be killed. He looked at me through his badly applied mascara, smiled through his smeared lipstick, and spoke, in his usual manly tone, "I'm a punker! Cool, huh?"

Like he really needed to tell me this. This should've been the most humorous, ludicrous thing I had ever seen. But instead, every fiber of my being demanded that I run, screaming, from the house. Fighting the urge and with no expression on my face, I calmly replied, "I don't think the lipstick goes well with your chaps."

"It's the only color I liked," he said through a smile. "Besides, it tastes like strawberry."

This statement worried me. A lot. I almost released the words, *Excuse me, but I really have to leave now* when he said, "Do you think I'll win? I think I will."

With a furrowed brow, I asked, "Win what, top freak of the campus award?"

"No," he laughed, "at the frat Halloween party, stupid!"

He must have seen the relief rush through me like a lake escaping its dam. I finally cracked a smile as I giggled, "Oh! Man, I thought you had gone completely mental!"

As I slapped my hand on my forehead, Bill answered, "Nah, I know what I'm doing. But you obviously don't. You completely forgot about Halloween, didn't ya?"

"Yeah. Well, I've been busy."

"Haven't we all." Bill glanced at the kitchen, then headed toward it as he talked. "I'm gonna be gone most of the night, so I guess it's up to you to hand out candy to the li'l gremlins."

I spun to stare at the back of his spiked head. "What?! Oh man, that's right! Kids. Crap! Do we have any candy?"

"Beats me," he shrugged, "I don't buy the groceries here. The question is, did YOU buy any candy?"

Sometimes, I really hated that dude. "No, I never buy that garbage."

He shrugged and turned to leave. "Well, you'd best buy something. Don't want angry kids burning down our pine trees."

I gave him one of my best evil glares, but he wasn't paying attention anyway. *Another wasted glare*, I thought. "What, are they really all that crazy around here?"

"The children of Main Street take Halloween pretty darned seriously. You remember those trees down by the end of the street? The charred ones?"

"Whoa! Kids did that?"

"Yeah," he nodded. "We've got vicious little scoundrels around here. They've destroyed yards, shaved pets and even torched an entire white picket fence once, all because they didn't get good enough junk. Or so the rumors go."

Even though I really didn't believe Bill, as he did tend to lean toward exaggeration, I felt apprehension creep into me. "Really?" I drawled.

He shrugged, grabbing at the doorknob. "I dunno. But I will say one thing. Go Trick-or-Treating around here. You'll get the best grub you've ever seen."

He opened the door as he yelled his good-byes. But I interjected with, "Hey, how many kids we got around here?"

He shrugged again. "Dunno. Not many, really. Couple bags oughta do it. Well, catch ya later!"

I smiled, even though I didn't really feel happy enough to do so. "Sure. Have fun." I waved, but he didn't look back to see it as he yanked the door closed.

"Crap," I breathed to no one. I grabbed my keys and coat and headed for the door, the car and eventually the store. It was just past 5pm, so I still had time before the little monsters came out.

Entering the ThriftoMart, I came to the realization that I should've prepared for this sooner. Slim pickings, to be sure. I had to settle for a sack of suckers, but I managed to find a bag of Milk Duds as well. As a child, I used to hate the houses that gave out those tiny Dum-Dum suckers and wads of gum. At the end of the run, I'd be stuck with 35 suckers of varying sizes and textures; 23 gum configurations, be they balls, wads or Bazooka Joe and his weird friends; and maybe, if lucky, about 10 miniature candy bars.

Oh well, I decided, *I'm the adult now. I have every right to make them suffer just like I had to when I was their age. It's a right of passage, after all. What do they expect for free, anyway?* I wasn't going to be scared off by juvenile hoodlums wielding matches and electric razors.

When I returned home, darkness had crept into the evening sky, so I knew I'd have to get ready for the little tykes. I dumped the Milk Duds and suckers into a ceramic bowl, and stared at it for a while. "Man, it looked like a lot more candy in the bags." So I jogged into the kitchen, and dumped everything into a smaller bowl. "There! That's better." I smiled as I sat the bowl next to the door and walked into the living room, flopping in front of the TV.

As I sat there ignoring the program in front of me, I thought back to my Trick-or-Treating days. One year in particular, I wore a Snoopy costume, complete with the thin, plastic mask. No one in the neighborhood recognized me and I loved that feeling of stealth. Another year, for some bizarre reason, I donned one of Mom's dresses and, complete with tennis-balls in the appropriate region, I went as a girl. I recall getting laughed at, but I got some great candy that year.

At nearly 6:00pm, I heard the doorbell ring. Springing out of my seat, I rushed toward the door. I was actually beginning to look forward to this.

I flung the door open, looking down to greet the little ones with a broad grin. However, I quickly realized I had to look up to be witness to three gargantuan teens, tall and thick, dressed as football players with their helmets in hand.

"Gimme!" One of them said, and the other two grunted in unison.

I smirked as I pushed the bowl closer to them. One of the grunters grabbed a handful, while the other two picked a few Milk Duds boxes from among the suckers.

"This blows," the verbalist of the bunch said. The others grunted. They all turned and vacated, mumbling something about toilet paper.

I slammed the door, grumbling, "Well, that pretty much killed my enjoyment."

A few minutes later, the bell rang again. I stared down at four smaller children dressed as Iron Man, the Incredible Hulk, a witch and a homicidal maniac, complete with a bloodstained hockey mask and plastic hatchet.

None of them said anything, so I uttered, in a typical *I am an adult and you are kids* tone of voice, "What do we say?"

The kid in the mask raised his hatchet and yelled, "Be hasty with your candy, sir!" The others laughed.

I shrugged my shoulders. *Seemed reasonable enough to me.* I handed the bowl out to them and again they mostly dug out the Milk Duds. They thanked me in an insincere tone as they left, which probably occurred only because their parents stood out front within earshot.

The same scenario continued for maybe a half hour, until all of the Milk Duds had vanished. Finally, when the children had no choice, the suckers started dwindling as well. When only eight suckers remained, I started handing them out one to a customer, which really irked them. I believe one little girl, dressed as a princess, even whispered a vile word under her breath. In retaliation I yelled, "Princesses don't use such language, y'know!"

Finally, when the doorbell rang at a bit after seven o'clock, I stood with my last sucker in hand. My sweat glands kicked in as I stared down at three small tykes standing at my door. I dropped the sucker into one of the bags, but what to give the other two? I quickly dashed toward my kitchen after yelping, "Hold on just a minute, you two!" Flinging open the fridge, I cursed myself for procrastinating on my grocery shopping. I could hear them grumbling impatiently at the door, so I pulled open the fruit tray and grabbed a couple apples. Smiling as wide as my face would allow, I said, "Sorry, this is all I have."

As I dropped the fruit into their bags, it occurred to me that one of these apples was actually a tomato. The boy, dressed as a Zorro-type character, saw this and looked up at me with wide, disbelieving eyes. But not more so than the other kid, a gorilla, with his apple who said, in a deep, eerie tone, "No candy left? This is very bad."

Zorro muttered, "You shouldn't oughta mess with tradition, mister," and with that, they both spun and hopped off the porch.

Moments later, I heard a gooey sounding splat against the side of the house. I didn't even have to look to figure out where that tomato ended up. I made a mental note not to give out anything that could be used as ammo against me.

When the bell rang again, my heart began pounding like Neil Peart working a drum solo! What to give them? I dashed around, flinging open cupboards like a hungry old woman searching for her teeth. I heard the bell ring again and I knew I needed to find something right now. My vision landed upon a box of ChocoDucks cereal. (I never said I ate healthily!) Lunging at the box, I dashed for the door. I flung it open to be stared at by a Bart Simpson clone and an Indiana Jones. Indy snarled, "'Bout time!"

"Yea yea, sure," I mumbled as I poured about two seconds worth of cereal into both children's bags.

They looked stunned, believe me. Bart reached in his bag and pulled out a ChocoMarshmellow, and held it at arm's length between us. "Whazzis," he drawled, "some kind of joke?"

"Hey," I yelled, "ya want some milk with that, too? It can be arranged!"

Bart dropped the ChocoMarshmellow and I watched it descend to the porch. "Dude'll pay," he said to his partner.

Turning to Bart, Indy asked, "You got the eggs, right?" I didn't hear the answer as they walked off my porch and into my side yard.

The next hour brought a lot of anxiety. The bell rang too fast for me to think about my next move, so I had to constantly think on my feet. And my feet were pretty darned stupid, let me tell you. I handed the kids things like cough drops and antacid tablets stolen from the medicine cabinet at work, as well as ketchup and taco sauce packets collected over the years from various restaurants. Oh, it got worse. I gave them small bars of soap and bottles of shampoo from previous hotel stays, dusty packets of Ramen soup and cans of tuna fish from the top shelf, even packages of bologna and other crappy lunchmeat that I saved for times of severe gastro-desperation. Why, I even gave a little boy a frozen burrito. Although, in my defense, he did have on a homemade Bandito outfit. He seemed grateful enough, but his father gave me one heckuva look.

While still digesting the father's evil glare, I thought I heard a noise across the room. As I turned, I heard it again. It sounded like scratching. I cautiously crept down the hall toward the dining room. As I rounded the corner, and caught a glimpse of the bay window, the doorbell rang, startling me.

Running into the kitchen, I grabbed a box of macaroni and cheese. I continued to hear the scratching noise, which worried me, but since I couldn't see anything on my cursory glimpse while touring the kitchen for goodies, I decided to deal with the problem at hand.

When I opened the door, no one stood there to view my friendly, albeit fake smile. *Another good emotion wasted*, I thought. Now, the scratching noise sounded an awful lot like an opening window, so I bolted toward the dining room.

Upon arrival, I saw a small window had indeed been pushed open. As I stood there, brandishing the box of macaroni and cheese like it was some medieval club, I had to release a quick chuckle at the absurdity of it all. Since the window hadn't been opened far enough for anyone to enter, I shrugged before shutting and locking it.

The doorbell rang once again. As I walked toward it, I heard a couple dull thuds against the window I had just shut. I turned, but from my vantage point in the hallway I couldn't see the windows. Breathing a heavy sigh, I decided to deal with the door.

Again I stood alone at the front door, but at least this time the brats left a treat of their own, a burning lunch sack. *Well, at least the pine trees are still intact*, I thought, as I stomped on the bag. My first big strike caused a bunch of red stuff to spit out and onto my left shoe and pant leg. Kicking the bag, I shook my head slowly when out rolled a few packets of the ketchup and taco sauce I had handed out. "I'm gonna get you, Cartman and Harry Potter!" I screamed, directing it at the only two characters I could remember who received such treats from me. "In my day, we used dog crap!"

As I slammed the door, cursing about the mess, I heard a couple more splats on the other side of the house. I hurried to the back and saw all the rear windows dripping with egg goo. Immediately after that, I heard more rustling on the front porch.

Now, anger rushed through me. Grabbing a frying pan from the cupboard, I bolted toward the door. I flung it open, and nearly plowed into the cutest pixie I had ever seen. The pixie, a woman probably in her early 20s, had a small child with her, dressed as a ballerina. They both let out screams, which sent me sprawling back inside, tumbling down and landing on my butt. The skillet skittered from my grasp and bounced into the wall, but I hardly noticed. The pixie costume looked fine on this woman, with her petite, shapely body and long, blonde hair. "Oh jeez," she said with a breezy tone, "you startled me! Sorry!"

"Um, yea, me too. Sorry, I mean."

"Twick or Tweet!" the little ballerina mumbled, with the biggest grin on her adorable little face.

The pixie giggled, then said, "She tries awfully hard, you know? Ya got something for her, for the effort?"

My smile faded. What to give this cute child? Mac and cheese just didn't seem appropriate. Having no choice, I mumbled, "Uh, yea, um..." as I pulled out my wallet. I had nothing smaller than a twenty, so I pulled it out and handed it to the child.

Both of their eyes got huge. "Wow!" the ballerina shouted.

"Wow!" the pixie echoed. "That's awfully generous of you!"

"Gee, twirn't nuthin. Say, you want anything?" I asked as I pointed the business end of my wallet toward her.

"Oh gee, uh, no thanks sir. But thanks," she quickly added. As they turned to leave, she said to her little partner, "What do you say to this nice man?"

She looked up at me, and gave me an even bigger, even cuter grin, and exclaimed, "Wow! Money!"

The pixie laughed, "I mean, what ELSE do you say?"

"Tank yew!"

"Chur welcum," I slurred back. "Bye," I said to both of them as they walked toward the street.

Standing there watching them leave, I actually felt some joy. The look on both of their faces might've just made this day worth it. I continued to grin, with the door open, until I heard the kid yell, "Look whut dat guy gave me! Money!" When I heard what sounded like twenty kids exclaiming their delight, my smile quickly failed. I knew I was in trouble when I not only heard but actually felt the trampling, like a thousand bulls stampeding toward my porch. I let out an involuntary scream as I slammed the door shut, to protect myself from the Running of the Children.

"Gah!" I exclaimed, imagining a zombie movie, or the frantic scratching on the doors of a full fallout shelter after the big one's dropped.

Hearing the horde chanting 'Trick or Treat' only made things worse. By the time I had run into the kitchen, grabbed the bag of in-the-shell peanuts and made it back to the door, I had nearly lost it. Part of me wanted to grab the frying pan and dive into the crowd, swinging maniacally. Instead, I flung the door open and yelled, "Treats!!! Yaaaaa!!" as I ripped open the bag and started whipping handfuls of peanuts at the throng of children outside my door. It felt kinda like trying to appease some irrational god in my mind, with the peanut sacrifice, but it came across more along the lines of an angry old coot feeding the pigeons with a vengeance. Clearly, I had lost complete control. Hearing all of the moans of disappointment and shouts of hatred only made me whiz the peanuts harder. I even nailed that Indiana Jones kid in the back of his little head as he turned to leave. As he bent over to pick up his fedora, I pegged him on his backside. When he spouted something about shaving cream, I knew I had made a tactical error, but I still smiled at my accurate toss.

Shutting the door, I felt a tiny bit better. Somehow, I managed to save myself a peanut. I popped it open and downed the two nuts as I walked back into the living room.

After a couple minutes, I thought I heard more rustling. But this time it sounded like it came from the basement. At this point, I wasn't scared, only upset. I reaffirmed my grip on the frying pan, and flung open the basement door.

I took all of three steps before my ears picked up the sound of hundreds of peanuts bouncing off the house's aluminum siding. Furious, I let loose a primal scream as I turned and attempted to jump all three steps back up. I cleared the first two with ease, but the bottom of my left shoe caught the edge of the last step. I nearly regained my balance before bounding into and bouncing off of the opposing wall, my weapon tumbling out of reach. I got up, cursed and ran outside.

Once I arrived out there and looked around, my jaw dropped. I was flabbergasted. The little cretins had done an extremely thorough job. Most of the trees had toilet paper or other noticeably unnatural items hanging from them and nearly all the windows were either caked with egg goo, tomato paste or had been heavily soaped. Even the tiny basement windows had nasty words etched on them with soap. I found a couple wrappers from the soap bars I had given out, and sighed as I said to myself, "Another stupid treat, Dan!"

I felt a tap on my shoulder. My adrenaline still near maximum, I spun around like a jaguar on Mountain Dew. Bill was rather lucky I no longer brandished that frying pan, because he would have been retrieving his pierced nose from across the yard. Giving me his very best shocked and startled expression, he screamed, "Geez Dan! What'd ya give the kids, suckers?"

"Yeah," I spoke softly and deliberately. "Suckers, Milk Duds, little bars of soap, tomatoes, packets of ketchup, money, lighter fluid, tuna fish and frozen burritos. Just trying to be unique."

Bill stared blankly at me for a spell, before he shook his head slowly and asked, "Um, dude, why didn't you simply turn off the porch light?"

If my brain had its own porch light, it would've popped on at that moment. I smacked my forehead and replied, "Lordy. That thought never entered my mind. It all happened so fast." I lowered my head.

After chuckling softly, Bill sat down on the lawn. He just finished saying, "Dude, I'm not helping you clean this up, y'know," when he looked between his feet and noticed the ground was covered with in-the-shell peanuts.

"What's up with this?" He extracted one from the grass and held it in front of me.

I dislodged it from his hand, cracked it, and ate one of the nuts. As I handed the other peanut to him, I said, "Oh yea. Forgot about these."

He sighed, then allowed his spiked head to fall back on the damp grass. As he hit, we both heard another peanut crack. Then we both started snickering under our breaths. "I don't suppose there'd be any full beer cans out here, would there?" Bill asked.

"No, but I think I saw some pretzels over by the pine tree."

"The tree with the underwear and balloons hanging on it?"

"No, the one covered in shaving cream."

"Next to the one painted purple?"

"Yeah."

"Cool."

After a long pause, I said, "Bill?"

"Yeah, Dan?"

"I really hate Halloween. What about you?"

"Nah," Bill told me as he finished another peanut, "Halloween is cool. You just have to remember one important fact."

"Let me guess. Don't mess with tradition, right?"

"No," Bill replied, "buy chocolate bars, stupid."

He laughed, and eventually, so did I.

Eye O' the Storm

C. J. Tody

Summer refused to introduce itself. The unfortunate weather remained bleak, damp and sunless. *Without summer, autumn will forever remain a fantasy, for how can autumn follow without first having a summer?* I hypothesized, unrealistically, faced with an uncooperative Mother Nature.

I dreamed of Autumn – of warm breezes, cooling breezes, any breezes at all tickling the edges of my maternity shirt, edging its way underneath, saying, "...it's OK, nothing to fear. You can come out now!"
Summer arrived late the year I was pregnant with my first child. So late, in fact, I feared that my baby's anticipated autumn birth had propelled itself into the abyss of some endless future. I couldn't wait for infinity to pass to realize my baby dream.
Why don't I just bypass summer and slide right into fall? I connived, subconsciously plotting ways to control Mother Nature. Excited and eager to hold my baby, my arms trembled with impatience which stretched into a void that threatened to turn eternal.
For weeks, I drifted like a candle on water, in need of the flame growing inside of me for guidance to navigate the undulating waves of pregnancy. With Nature refusing to cooperate, only the endless, unsaid love between wishful mother and growing infant encouraged me to persevere.
How I wanted to talk with my child. I finally found the right tone for communication... "Come...stop your crying, it'll be alright. Here, take my finger and hold on tight, we'll keep you warm and safe tonight, help you

smile and keep your dreams in sight." This singsong chant grew into a constant and ever-present litany.

Meanwhile, outside my window, spring buds held their blossoms tightly furled and kept their secrets from the world almost as well as my child held onto its own secret.

Will it be a girl? I reflected every time I lumbered up the stairs to our second floor apartment, a few ounces heavier each trip. *Shall I knit a pink blanket to bring her home from the hospital?*

...Or will it be a boy? I stopped the ascent, foot dangling midair.

A boy! That's a possibility, I realized, thinking, *how many times I've wished that I'd had a kindly big brother to share the love of life and laughter, and protect me when I'd arrived in the world the oldest of five children on an increasingly tough life journey.* Novel to me, the prospect of having a boy as my first child raised my spirits. *Perhaps, later in life, he'd protect any daughters I have.*

Quietly I decided. *Guess I'll knit a blue gown for Baby's homecoming!* I turned and ran back down the stairs, heading for the store to buy blue yarn.

Finally, the first May flowers erupted in bloom and spread across the lawn. A veritable cacophony of color surrounded our house like a multicolored umbrella, breathing into the air rainbow-flavored fragrances and the promise of coming warmth.

Frigid, raw northern winds ushered in the month of June. Wet cyclones blew backyards ragged until blossom-laden trees lost their spring quality and fallen petals blanketed the ground with a colorful carpet that was only a shadow of what was once a beautiful canopy.

Just as quickly as the cold winds arrived, they departed again, leaving cloudless skies in their place.

Summer's palette of flowering perennials blossomed in a sultry heat wave that left us wishing the cold winds would return. Thermometers reached 95^0 in paved portions of town.

With my clothes tightening around a burgeoning belly, I sweltered, sweated, and sizzled every time I ventured out of my air-conditioned downtown office building with oh so many questions on my mind.

When autumn finally arrives, will my child arrive too? I issued a silent plea heavenward, ...*Healthy? Happy? Ready for life?*

The weather remained sizzling hot, humid, and blisteringly bright. Could it possibly be any worse?

That, of course, is strictly a matter of personal taste.

Though I was hot and bored, while waiting, waiting, waiting for my child, I was also a bit uneasy. My life had not been uneventful or easy since I turned ten years old. For the past twelve years, the storms of my personal life had regularly interspersed with Michigan's dramatic atmosphere until I became a battering ram of issues. I felt like I was in the eye of a storm, waiting for a catastrophe to occur, but hoping instead for the ecstasy of new motherhood.

One Saturday that summer, my husband Roarke and I were at home, dreaming together in the living room over the prospect of nursery furniture. Muted sirens stirred the distant humidity and mixed with televised music. This created enough confusion inside that it nearly masked the telephone when it began to ring insistently in the bedroom.

"Roarkie, would you get that?" I begged.

"Alright." Roarke unfurled his six-foot-two frame from the couch where we sat side by side, and asked me as he rose, "Do you want the phone on speaker so you can hear, too?"

"Sure thing, hon," I agreed.

He followed his usual casual greeting with a series of expletives strong enough to sink a ship, not to mention a five-foot-two pregnant lady. I cringed in anticipation.

"Look outside – quickly!" the caller warned.

Roarke caught his breath, held it while he took the phone off speaker, then exhaled and uttered a muted response. "What? No, it can't be, can it?" He turned to me, this doubting, daunting husband of mine who was still adjusting to marriage several months after being wed.

"Stay inside, Caryl!" he ordered, once again my best friend. He looked back at me sternly over his powerful football quarterback champion shoulder as he stepped over the threshold to adventure.

Seconds later, he was back again, gesturing wildly toward the stairway. Taut as a violin string, his posture signaled urgency even before he regained the power to speak. He resonated anxiety from every pore. "Get down below – now!" he burst aloud through his frenzied bubble. Then he turned to leave again.

Propelled by renewed urgency in his dilated eyes, which were now wide and agitated like mine, my own adrenaline rose to a new high.

"What...?" I started to ask. But already I found myself alone and not quite sure what to do.

I watched him sail down the lower stairs three at a time, heard the outside door slam.

Anxiously, I obeyed his edict. Because he rarely issued orders, I knew this could be serious. I took only a book and purse when I reluctantly descended into the black gloom of damp, musty cinder block known to occupants of the aging townhouse as a basement. Murky, subterranean windows blocked light. I tried to engage myself in a story but reading became impossible. With safe movement curtailed by darkness, I sat underground for twenty minutes without music, paper, pen or any other kind of entertainment to pass the time. Despite becoming outrageously bored, I waited another twenty-five minutes by plumbing the depths of my own imagination.

What could be happening to cause such danger? I wondered, visualizing a fractured list of impossibly fragmented scenarios. *...Attack? Invasion? Body snatchers? "War of the Worlds?" Alien aviators? Movie filming? Train wreck? Fifty-car pileup? Earthquake chasm? Airplane crash? Storms? Aha! Bet that's it - it's a storm.*

Finally convinced that Roarke forgot about me, I stomped defiantly up the stairs muttering things that a young wife might better keep private, and swaggered outside under a full head of steam.

It was eerily quiet. Outdoors, a copper haze dulled the midday atmosphere. High in the western sky, floated the longest, blackest funnel cloud I've ever seen. It was nearly overhead now. The twister had been hovering above our historic old townscape close to the heart of Michigan state government for nearly three quarters of an hour while I crouched underground!

I watched the spectacle riveted in place by astounded, wide-eyed wonder while a memory tape ran on a parallel track inside my mind. I remembered another midsummer afternoon several years earlier and morphed virtually into the student I once was...

I was nearly twelve that long ago season, a 'tween' living with my family on a country estate surrounded by the diverse Michigan topography of evergreens and hills, which closely neighbored a seven-mile long glacial esker. My mother was away while my father planted wheat in a nearby field. I was trying to act domestic by staying close to home, instead of wandering to where life held more interesting social venues. Since my dad was usually away tending career and business matters, I often had a relatively large amount of freedom and had to restrain that habit when he was home. Later, I realized it was lucky that events turned out as they did.

I'd been lying on a cozy patchwork blanket in the shade of a giant oak tree.

Overhead, lazy cloud formations entertained me, pushed by strong winds into shifting shapes backlit by a brilliant sun.

Unaware of the approaching front, I daydreamed on and on. I watched the wisps of cloud pouf into sheep, dragons, and then full-sheeted sailing ships so real I wished I could board and travel far, far away.

Fluffy abstract shapes in the nearby heavens soon transformed into dense, darkening clouds passing by in a line so straight that it seemed to be a picture drawn by a celestial yardstick.

Suddenly, wind whipped my shirt and tore away the blanket from under me, wrapping it around the trunk of the tree. I jumped up fast enough to hit my head on a low branch. My spooked feet were in motion, running to our nearby ranch house for cover, even as I touched the bump on my skull. The wind died around me and the air turned a sickly grey shade of yellow. I thought I heard a train coming, though I knew no railroad track was in range.

When I arrived at the house, I was relieved to find my family already inside. Most of them were already in the basement, where I joined them under cover by sliding down the stairs on my behind in one long bumpy chain of panicky moves.

Shortly after, Dad ran down the old wooden basement steps, almost flying at times, screaming at us as if demons pursued him. He raced into the southwest corner where I huddled with my younger brother and sisters.

"Get back!" he'd said protectively, "Stay away from the windows! Over there, everyone." He motioned to the southwest corner. "Get under the table and throw this blanket over you."

Outside, the deadly, silent, coppery sky had broken into gusty, rushing wind. Freight train noises roared directly overhead now. We held our breath almost collectively as the building creaked and screamed in the two-hundred-fifty-plus mile an hour windstorm. Our hair raised into the air as if suctioned by an enormous vacuum cleaner as we cringed in each other's arms. Rain, wind and hail pelted the house like Hadean banshees.

Then, silence engulfed us. Almost as suddenly as it began, all had become quiet again. The house shuddered and settled back in place with a hundred creaks and groans. We couldn't see further than the basement rafters, but we'd been pretty sure the house still stood above our heads.

The five of us looked at each other. Stunned into shocked silence and disbelief, nobody said a word.

Only one thought had survived the stunned silence of my otherwise blank mind at that moment: *Wow! We're still alive.*

Unsure what to say to the others at such a time, I'd said nothing. This had been my first experience with a truly violent storm. In fact, most worldly violence had managed to escape my protected awareness until that moment. I'd been raised in lovely wild areas around books, art, campers, and a loving extended family, as well as on a working ranch with cattle, sheep, poultry, and horses for playmates. I had gardens, fields, barns, lakes, and a vineyard as playgrounds.

Back to the present, the black funnel waved its tail to us from high over the Capitol building. I watched, clutching my burgeoning baby belly and fearing what could happen if it touched the ground, for I remembered the aftermath of that other storm so long ago.

Father beckoned us upward from the cellar. One by one we'd climbed, guardedly expecting we knew not what. He emerged first, followed closely by my younger brother and sister. Then I stepped out into the fresh backyard air, just in time to see the children collect softball-sized hailstones and ensconce them in the Back Porch Freezer Hall of Fame as marvelous proof for posterity.

Just as the fierce wind returned, the last of us made it back inside. We'd entered the house this time by tumbling over each other with an almost reluctant rush that revealed our penchant for testing Mother Nature. Until the storm passed completely, we sheltered in the basement.

Once we felt safe enough to do so, we'd emerged again to survey for damage. The cyclone had ravaged a ravine that lay north of the house below an evergreen forest, which cut it even deeper than ever with a new funnel-excavated trench.

Other evidence of the twister bisected the densely forested wetland across the road from our house, where its path traced a zigzagging swath of downed trees. The same trail of destruction crisscrossed the road, continued through our front yard, and left a generalized path of leafy debris a hundred yards wide. It nearly reached our southwest basement corner, below which we crouched holding our breath during the tornado.

A third path revealed itself more subtly in the field immediately behind our backyard. Miraculously, the funnel jumped our two-story frame house, dropped to the ground a few feet behind it, picked up an A-frame field house, and whirled it 180^0 mid-air. Incredibly, the field house settled back down on its foundation precisely backward, so that its previously front-facing door now opened to the back woods!

Wind-driven straw from the horse barn pierced the trunks of fruit trees in an orchard slightly offset from the side of the house.

Vines, with their quivering grapes still clinging to them, wrapped the metal uprights of our tall, wildly spinning windmill.

Fortunately for us, the tornado spun off into the distance. With its powerful tail whirling and jumping around between heaven and earth, it attacked the unsuspecting ravine and cleared new patches on the hillside for us to skate and toboggan the following winter. The fierce storm then pushed east until it crashed headlong into an urban Flint neighborhood with such violence that the National Guard activated troops to restore order and curtail looting. Our grandparents who lived there were displaced for several days, until construction crews completed necessary repairs.

My family was amazingly lucky to survive such a direct confrontation with a powerful tornado. When the storm departed eastward, it never returned. Our house and contents remained intact. Mere days of cleanup stood as an icon to remind us of our ordeal.

We found it easy enough to recognize the fragility imposed on us, after having our peril shoved right into our faces. Our short lives might have ended if the tornado hadn't lifted its tail seconds before impact and shone good fortune on both the house and its occupants.

My father deserved a great deal of the credit, too. He risked his own life by staying outside to watch the storm behavior before joining us undercover. By that time, he knew the house was almost certain to be obliterated because he'd tracked the trajectory of the funnel until it was almost inside the front door.

My humility-stirred relief mixed together with some 'what ifs' and other residual concerns about our encounter, until it eventually wove a pattern of cyclonic superstorms into my indelible young cybernetic memory. I cringed during every severe thunderstorm for a year or two afterward. Occasional nightmares crept into my sleep, bearing lightning bolts that blasted out furiously from an ethereal, celestial realm to obliterate everything in their path.

The dreams subsided by the time I finished school, and they disappeared entirely as I faced adulthood with its daunting mixture of parenthood and career.

Spared any serious damage, I was filled with a waking sensation that we have purposes to fulfill, gifts to give, and guardians to protect our dreams. The storm left behind a sort of legacy, sharing its lessons amid chaos. I just hoped my protectors and lessons learned would be accessible in the future when I need to fulfill those bigger needs that lurked beyond the storms of the day.

Reflecting back to the present from my earlier tornadic episode, a notion came into my mind with a wham, blam, full-force realization of the new spectacle unfolding over my head. It arrived as a fully hatched, ponderously heavy thought: *Can I really protect my own unborn child as well as my father protected us?*

I knew the giant black hole whirling overhead wielded the potential for mass destruction. *I have to do something*, I thought. *It's hovered now for nearly an hour without dropping, but the tail can whip around instantly and drop to the ground, causing damage or loss of life.*

My reverie concluded with an inner declaration of our independence: *You can't destroy us! I'm about to give birth, bringing the next generation of new life into the world.*

"I am a SACRED VESSEL! I'm carrying a child; our shared time, and this new life itself, are precious gifts to the world," I insisted.

What surfaced then was instantaneous. The resurrected memory of a long-ago triumph over the wild forces of nature resurged. My defiance rose to new heights.

I confronted the funnel squarely. "I've faced you before and I'm not afraid." I shook my fist at the sky. "Pregnancy represents the highest level of creativity. New life is forming and you simply can't have it. Move on now, you big bully, go back upstairs where you came from and quit scaring these people!"

About that time, the giant black funnel paused its relentless tail whipping briefly, as if to decide whether or not to possess. Light rain twinkled in midair, then descended on the cyclone. Its momentum lost, the funnel slowly vaporized. What remained of the storm moved into the east. All signs of rotation ceased, replaced by a brilliant double helix rainbow, which lit the far reaches of the cloudy metro area for another half hour as the storm edged its damp way out of town.

I could have puzzled over the hidden significance and symbolism of the storm's departure endlessly, because the whole situation was so unusual. For instance, a direct tornadic touchdown has to date avoided our town. Meteorologically speaking, we rarely experienced catastrophic storm damage other than blown around signs and downed power lines. Usually, damage consisted mostly of lifted roof shingles and ceiling leaks from rain driven horizontally underneath, during the passing low-pressure system. Most cyclonic activity occurs to the north and south, east and west. So far, it has been as if we exist in the bottom of a great bowl, with cloud rotation rimming our outer edges like a golf ball circles around the hole on a green.

That, of course, encouraged other explanations to surface that were more related to quantum physics and metaphysics than to meteorology. I chose to explore them later.

For the time being, I decided to recognize that our power to attract is amazing, and that our power to alter our circumstances to meet our needs may be equally amazing.

As an added benefit, I no longer feared storms in that abstract, global, universal, "War of the Worlds" phenomenon that choreographed my childhood nightmares. I began to enjoy storms as naturally refreshing, even exciting events.

With this growing sense of personal power, I grew to respect the fragility of life and developed a responsible mindset that enhanced my ability to protect and nurture the coming generation. I was entering parenthood courageously, with a little more wisdom and a little less baggage.

Soon, the cold early season winds gave way to intense midsummer heat, which mixed with vapid, vaporous, overheated air from the Gulf of Mexico and descended upon us as humidity made thick and visible.

By then, my belly had outgrown even my stretchy maternity wardrobe. Humidity and extra body heat drove me inside.

In a ridiculously ironic twist of fate, installers had added an arctic air conditioning system to my office building upside-down, so that the basement became a deep freezer while the upstairs remained an overheated oven. So, while most of the office crew sweated upstairs, my own rather frosty staff working out of the lower level developed arthritis. For me, this meant entering the ripe old age of twenty-three about to give birth with creaky knees that threatened to become arthritic!

I took partial leave of the office a few weeks before Baby's scheduled arrival.

Meanwhile, back at the townhouse, our upstairs sizzled in stifling, near-deadly temperatures that caused me to long for the cold workplace. We installed bedroom air conditioning and I endured the rest of the summer lying on our big old bed watching classic movies and knitting a soft blue blanket. I was desperate for relief: outdoors a cool-down, indoors a birth. Would autumn ever arrive?

Finally, baby's expected birth date approached. Glory be, I was excited! "Will we have a boy or a girl?" we commiserated, clueless.

In early September, my mother arrived at the townhouse on a two-week leave of absence, expecting soon to care for Baby. Pressure to birth this baby grew exponentially from that point forward.

My due date passed uneventfully into history. Days passed, then weeks. Soon Baby was four weeks past due. Yet no sign arrived of Baby, autumn, or any other significant happening.

It was, in fact, much too quiet. "Surely," I thought, "the eye of the storm draws near."

My wait began to take on the proportions of the tornadoes and twisters I'd encountered and survived. As

I realized that illness, pressure and atmospheric aberration could create an inner storm just as powerful and threatening as cyclones that overhung my dwellings promising to touch down. I knew I had to change something. Then I recalled the onset of personal power experienced when the storms abated. I latched onto that sense of power and rode the wild storm pony with a loose rein.

Summer temperatures still raged outside, and we already anticipated that the ravages of a cold northern winter would follow a shortened autumn – if indeed any autumn at all.

September passed into a sizzling October. Colleagues and friends called frequently for status updates.

At this point, new nightmares began to interrupt my uncomfortable sleep, this time populated by strange, hairy, deformed, one-eyed babies. With my peace discouraged this way, I knew that another course correction was in sight.

I practiced thinking positive thoughts until I became motivated to adapt to my new circumstance.

Soon, I managed to shrug the nightmares from my conscious thoughts and instead chose to dwell on the joy I would experience holding my baby. Even so, I floundered in a state of hapless wonder: "Will relief ever come? Is Baby's birth ever going to happen?"

My stomach grew so large that comfort became a thing of the past and I could neither sit nor stand comfortably. Clothes refused to fit and I found myself reduced to only two choices of attire: gusseted smocks and wide-panel slacks. Bathroom frequency increased to every few minutes and I thought I might as well just live in there. Finally, I gave in to the soft bed and turned myself over to knitting and classic movies. Pretty soon I had a nice layette consisting of tiny blue embroidered sweaters, bonnets, booties, onesies, and blankets.

I was ready!

Sure, *I* was ready, but was Baby?

To make matters worse, daily callers posed the question, "Has anything happened yet?" My stress level increased infinitely every time the phone rang.

Fatefully, just before taking this maternity rest, my employer promoted me to head a newly formed unit, with an offer in place to hold the position until my return from maternity leave, if it didn't take too long. That meant I could manage only two scant weeks of leave after baby's birth before the managerial position would be released. My overdue situation had prolonged my return-to-work timeframe and Administration was getting nervous.

Anxiety accompanied the baby in the pit of my stomach. "No," I continually answered the daily "anything yet?" inquiry, "...no, we're still waiting."

Mother extended her leave of absence another month. She suggested giving Baby a little encouragement to make its worldly entry.

My personal storm cloud grew a little darker and started to build its inner winds.

Frustrated by so frequently answering "no," I committed to try mother's inducement techniques. While my practical side questioned the validity of her ideas, my desperate side decided they deserved consideration.

Old wives' tales, I'd reflected, *are a mythological way to take power over nature. At the same time, the inherent 'shaking Baby up' principle survived through history, probably because midwives still found it effective. In any case, with Baby and I healthy enough to try new things, doing so seems harmless when compared to the hopelessness of my month-overdue situation.* My belief level moved up a notch. *Besides,* I rationalized, keeping this thought strictly to myself, *...if there was any reality to the influence I felt when the hovering tornado threatened my little corner of the world, maybe I could now advance that sense of power to a sense of being influential, step outside the dugout of traditional thought and place some emphasis on unproven holistic techniques to see what might happen.*

For the sake of mother's job and my own, I vowed to give her ideas a try.

Dawn the next day found me mopping the kitchen floor on my hands and knees with Mom directing. I supported my unwieldy belly so Baby wouldn't do all the mopping. Waves of activity swamped my underbelly. I collapsed into an easy chair, willing the magical labor to start. Hours later, Baby still clung tightly to its vine.

"Castor oil," proclaimed Mother next.

"What am I trying to do...slick the approach lane?" I lamented, "OK, I'll try." Three teaspoons that appeared as big as soup ladles later, I became queasy and nearly threw Baby into acrobatic spasms.

"Drinking oil is a failure!" I declared, swearing never to venture there again.

What happened next I found even harder to believe.

"Sometimes," Mom cajoled, "people try sliding down the stairway on their b..."

"This is beginning to sound a bit crazy!" I steamed, patience forgotten, "my doctor is a loon to let it go this far! Self-inducement is insane."

"I have other ideas..." Mom pounced, her opportunity close at hand.

But I had other ideas, too. I changed directions entirely.

"I'm grateful," I told her, vowing to be patient a bit longer. "Grateful for Baby's health, for yours, for mine and for the gender mystery that's about to reveal itself. I'm claiming the right to be patient a bit longer. In other words, I accept the wait."

That's when the miracle happened! Later that day, I ventured out to fry an egg on the badly melting car hood to protest the prolonged heat wave. On the way there, a cooling breeze whirled the summer dust, tickled the edges of my bulging maternity shirt, edged its way underneath, and drove the message deep inside: "Autumn is coming...it's OK. You can come out now!"

Around midnight that night, my 'storm' accelerated when strong labor began. Bag in hand and with three hopeful smiles prominently displayed, we raced to the hospital.

Nurses settled us into a labor room, probed, prepared and coached.

About an hour later, labor ceased completely.

"Braxton-Hicks again, oh no!" I wailed. Twice before, false labor propelled us to the hospital then sent us back home again, temporarily defeated. Four weeks overdue, though, is getting very risky for an outside birth. This time, the staff detained us with suggestions similar to those my mother made.

"Walk the hall until it starts again!" came their edict.

"Oh no, what if it doesn't start again?" I muttered as Roarke and I shuffled down hall after hall and fluttered back again trying to restart labor, trying to get the 'storm' cloud hanging over us to rotate a bit.

When it finally resumed hours later, however, I simply wasn't prepared for the sheer magnitude of pain and gave myself over to rhythmic breathing as best as I could, refusing medication that might affect Baby.

Forty hours...that is how long it lasted. Cramp force multiplied by forty hours of natural, intensifying, unmedicated labor is not for the feeble of heart. I no longer felt the least bit courageous in the face of debilitating pain, but managed to keep my 'no meds' resolve firmly in place.

To make it more interesting, the medical staff announced the imminent arrival of twins halfway through the extended labor, because there were two 'bumps.' Our doctor had only blessed us with the anticipation of only one child.

"I am so thrilled!" I prayed between contractions. "Please let it be true." That prospect excited me, as I would have been happy to have twins, perhaps a boy *and* a girl. But a punishing ride down the hall for hasty x-rays interrupted by contractions disproved that theory, and the hovering 'cloud' really began to whirl.

"One very large child," they explained, replacing their expectation. Overwhelming disappointment shrouded me. Grief faded quickly, though, as the next cramp reminded me that I still had one very large baby trying to enter my life.

By that time, it had been nearly a day after contractions began and all three of us neared exhaustion. Nurses sent Mother and Roarke out to rest and recover and insisted that I, too, rest.

But I was not about to try to sleep amid severe pain and roared my disapproval.

"Impossible," I screamed. Nurses prepared a sedative that diminished the contractions briefly, so I slept mere minutes until it wore off.

Labor then progressed robustly, with my somewhat refreshed dual coaches alternating at my side.

Wave after wave of squeezing cramps weakened my resolve not to medicate the baby to save myself pain, and I became vulnerable to the prospect of a spinal injection. Cramping muscles clamped my belly and back, constricted me from head to toe like the python-like coils of a black hole trying to suck me into oblivion.

It was too late for spinal relief now, even if I had agreed.

At that moment, I remembered the terrible cyclone hovering over my childhood house and, more recently, the one over our city townhouse, both of which wavered at the brink of sucking a cowering me into the vacuum at its center. These tornadoes were like gigantic drama queens! Each stopped just short of annihilating us after putting on a big show.

Wasn't incessant labor just another kind of tornado, trying to draw me into surrender? The instant after I realized these parallels, I stopped resisting and breathed long and deep. I reset my thoughts on the joy of a healthy Baby about to finally reveal its mystery and introduce his or her self to us.

Instead of fighting the contractions, I breathed rhythmically and allowed my compressed spirit free rein to romp and roll along the labor coaster. I rode the waves with all my might much as one would while riding a bucking bronco atop a roller coaster with one hand aloft, one clamped on for dear life. Somehow, this carried me through two long days and nights of relentless, gritty, unmedicated contractions that weren't quite strong enough to fully dilate and deliver.

Barely gaining control of my senses during a rare few seconds spent alone long enough to center myself, I asked nurses to break the water. They refused. A little while later, the birth water released naturally. Baby's head crowned at the same time and pushed into the open air as nurses hastily pushed us to the delivery room.

Finally! Forty hours later, my beautiful daughter arrived. Nurses delivered her, while our doubting doctor hid in some mysterious, never-revealed lower reaches of the hospital. I realized the truth of the rumor that nurses really deliver our children most of the time.

Weighing in at nine pounds, Jasmine greeted us with eyes wide open and a sustaining purr on her lips as she looked from one of us to the next in wide-eyed wonder.

"Well, hello! Look at you!" we chimed in unison, afraid to let her out of sight for even a second.

"Here, let's have a little squeeze." I took her in my shaking arms to unwrap the blanket and expose a bit of bare skin.

"Oh, look what we made," we said as mother ushered herself into the room. "And she's perfect!"

Baby Jazz introduced us to the gentle nature in her deep blue eyes, providing a window into an ancient soul as deep as a silver well. Much of her weight shone in her face. Her plump, rounded cheeks reminded me of nuts-tucked-in-chipmunk-cheeks and provided a good impression of the Roman Emperor Nero after eating too many grapes. Around the crest of her rosebud mouth radiated a rainbow of tiny scars carved by fingernails already grown long before birth.

It became clear that Jasmine had been in no hurry to face the summer heat those last four foul summer weeks, and soon grew too large to move. Languishing in her protective space, she entertained herself during long, lazy weeks by sucking her thumb, listening to my imagination, and developing her own creative skills for that time in the future when she chose to carve out and claim her independence!

Once more I relaxed into the eye of the storm, this time with a full heart, while learning how to care for Jazz. Both day and night carried their own lessons on feeding, self care and follow up as I welcomed a few precious assisted hours of strength-building sleep.

At last we found that we were ready to end our hospital incarceration, dress Jasmine and venture into the world on our own.

Opening my suitcase anxiously, I exhaled a sigh of relief...there they lay. The sight of soft fibers in several shades of blue rose to meet my gaze and I dove my hands wrist-deep into fragrant gowns, booties, a blanket and miniature hat, lifting the items I'd knitted for the baby to hold them close to my warm cheek.

"Here, Jazz, we're going to put on your own clothes now. This blue gown'll keep you cozy during the nap I know you'll take on the way home. I'm taking you out dressed in blue, but I have lots of pink clothes waiting at home, too. As soon as I can shop again, I'll buy you the prettiest, fluffiest dress available. I love you just as you are. In fact, I'm mad about you! Soon as you're a little older, I'll dress you in every single outfit you have and take photographs."

I sat on the side of the bed holding Jasmine for a moment, waiting for an aide to wheel us to the exit where proud new daddy Roarke impatiently revved his engine.

It's starting again, I thought. *The next round of the storm is about to begin.* At that moment, I realized the full impact of the fallow zone that lies in the eye of the storm. Waited on for days by helpful nurses, I existed in a free zone, a recovery zone free of the tiring conflict and struggle that lie ahead during our adaptation to life with baby Jazz.

Seems to me that the fallow zone in the eye of the storm is where my dream often comes true, I reflected, *...after a long period of effort, dodging lightning bolts and twisters, and waiting, waiting, waiting to claim the reward.*

The new daddy chauffeured Caryl and baby Jasmine away from the hospital toward their little townhouse. Suddenly, it seemed more like a palace complete with its own princesses.

Driving home, we heard the radio broadcaster say, "Know what, folks? Looks like cool weather is finally here to stay. Autumn has arrived at last."

And when autumn finally came into the dreamy eye of our personal storm, it found me with the precious Jasmine cooing in my arms and my greatest dream finally realized.

Fairy Touch

Alta C. Reed

It was a typical spring morning, but somehow the fact that I had watched and marveled at it enhanced its indefinable beauty.

Billows of pure, velvety clouds, white as seafoam, were strewn about like little stray ships across the clear blue sky.

The lawn sprinkled here and there with dashes of dandelions; the cherry trees in full bloom, scattering tiny, white flowers like snowflakes hither and yon; the apple trees with buds pink unto bursting; the elms and maples dress parading in spring finery. The bright morning sunlight shining through everything added carefree life and shimmering gaiety to every object.

A brown mother wren, holding within her a promise of tiny nestlings, broke the silence, peace and solitude with trilling sounds of musical refrain. From a distance, I hear and then see a little old Ford rambling down the street. At the wheel sits— but I think you know the rest.

Note: I wrote this when I was fourteen years old. I was married to him for 63 years.

For Sale: Americana

Alta C. Reed

Whose pulse hasn't quickened at the sign on the corner? GIGANTIC YARD SALE, TODAY, ONE BLOCK AHEAD. Saturday garage sales have become the American pastime, the last entrepreneurial spirit not regulated and taxed by the powers that be.

Garage sale finds abound in my home, from the peach colored curtains in the bathroom to the three goose cookie jars in the kitchen that are never empty. Outside, plants are standing on wire formed tables and large ceramic ladybugs guard the petunia patch.

We're at it again today! Whether it's a garage sale, yard sale, porch sale or moving sale, we must find a parking spot, sometimes on the driveway to the home and sometimes several cars down the street. And, guess what? There's Mary! I haven't seen her in ages. We rehash all the news and nonsense of the summer while examining china plates and boxes of old Valentines. My find for this sale is a corner cupboard for $25.00. I have to go back home for the pickup. It will not fit in the car.

We go on. Another sign. HUGE, THREE FAMILY YARD SALE, 124 STATE STREET, 9 TO 5. We stop. Most of the merchandise is for pre-schoolers, lots of clothes and plastic toys. A paradise for someone with a young family.

In the upscale side of town, prices are out of our reach, so we back track toward home. At our last stop, I purchase several embroidery pieces and enough quilt panels for a full-size spread. I am told the lady who was making the quilt became ill before she could finish it. So now, it will be mine, a treasure to help me remember a wonderful Saturday afternoon in summer.

The Heart and Center

Kerry Tietsort

Seen it all through the years
Hailed real heroes, caught drops of tears
As enduring as Rushmore and the tallest trees
With similar names along your streets

Felt the rumble of all-sized wheels
The click and clack of everyman heels
Tree-lined pathway through their town
Sharing deep-night with hidden sound

The faces and seasons rearrange
Yet, despite wear, you never change
Right-angled stability,
Providing for their mobility

Catching snowflakes or sunny rays
Ticking minutes turn into days
Many weeks and then a year
Silently reflecting all you hear

First daylight brings hustle and bustle
By evening lives slow to a shuffle
Little children safely tucked in
While you wait for it to begin again

Ice cream treats with jingly bells
Sunday service chimed with echoing swells
Various faces greeting one another
Taking for granted your support down under

Holidays bringing joy and glee
Lined streets as far as we can see
Etching memories hand in hand
Hearts and lives all intertwined

Some will stay their whole lives through
While restless others seek something new
Few return from time to time
Perhaps reminiscent of the Five & Dime

Bloodied knee and scraped shin
Cheerful laughter, happily ever after
Pitter-patter of rain and tears,
Windswept leaves and passing years

Children and flowers, always growing
Quietly marking their coming and going.

Message From Max

Donnalee Pontius

The town looked deserted. The shops were all dark with the occasional SORRY WE'RE CLOSED sign hanging in the window. I saw no other cars, not even parked along the sides of the road. I sat dazed at the four-way stop on the corners of Fifth and Main and stared down at the clock on the dash.

"Hmm, Wednesday afternoon. What's up?"

Max laid sprawled across the back seat, his tail thumping against the car door, oblivious to my unusual findings. I glanced to the left, then the right and continued down Main. Even the homes appeared deserted. No kids playing in the front yards, no one relaxing on a porch swing.

"This is too weird." I whispered half to myself and half to Max.

He sat up and laid his big, red head over the seat.

"There's not even a squirrel around."

His ears perked up at the word 'squirrel'; chasing them was one of his favorite hobbies. As we neared the school, I caught sight of something out of the corner of my eye. I braked hard and heard Max slide off the back seat onto the floor.

"Sorry, buddy."

Was it a kid, a plastic bag? What was it and where did it go? I strained my eyes and rolled the window down to get a better look. Everything was still and deathly quiet. A shiver ran down my back. Max had climbed back up onto the seat and was trying to wedge his head between the seatbelt and the door so he could catch a sniff outside. Maybe my eyes had been playing tricks on me. After all, it had been a long drive from South Bend. I sat a couple more minutes then rolled up the window, gave Max a pat on the head and hit the accelerator.

"Let's just get up to Mom and Dad's."

Max settled back down and for the next few miles I tried to focus on the road straight ahead of me. After we left the city limits, I let my gaze drift up to the rearview mirror.

"Still no cars." I looked back to the road. "Ahh, there's the house, Max."

He sat up again. This time he put his paws on top of the front seat; his tail thumping wildly, anxious to get out of the car.

"Let me stop first." I laughed.

I pulled into my usual parking spot and jammed the car into park. Then, I grabbed my purse and opened the door. Max bolted out in a flash and began running laps around me. I couldn't help but laugh at him. I felt safe. Everything looked the same as it had when I left for college six months ago. Max ran up the porch in front of me and started barking and pawing at the door.

"I'm coming, silly. Let me get my suitcase." Suddenly, Max jumped up on the door, flattened his ears and began growling. No one had come to the door to investigate the racket he was making.

"That's not right...Max..."

I dropped my suitcase in the driveway and ran up the steps. I grabbed the door knob, pushing Max out of the way. It was locked, so I dug around in my purse for a second and found my spare key. As soon as I got the door open Max charged in past me, barking and growling.

"Mom! Dad!"

When no answer came, I felt a wave of panic fall over me. Max had never acted like this before. He raced back and forth between the kitchen and the living room, barking and whining. I dropped my purse on the counter and followed him into the living room.

"Mom! Dad!" I called louder. Still no answer.

Max sat in front of me and continued to whine. I headed upstairs, taking two steps at a time. When I reached the top, Max pushed past me and began to pace back and forth in the hall.

"Mom! Dad! C'mon, this isn't funny!"

I grabbed the knob on the bedroom door, hesitated a second, then pushed it open. Empty. The bed was neatly made, as usual. Nothing appeared out of place. The same went for the bathroom and my room. Max continued to pace around and investigate each room with me, occasionally growling. I hurried downstairs with him at my heels and ran into the office, my heart pounding in my chest.

"Neat and tidy, just like everything else." My voice cracked.

I stood in the middle of the room. Tears began to sting my eyes. Max bumped my hand with his nose and whined.

"What do you know, buddy?"

I looked down into his soft, brown eyes and somehow felt safe again.

"Maybe they just went out for a minute and we're just overreacting."

Suddenly tired and weak, I collapsed into the overstuffed chair in the corner of the office.

"Maybe I'm just a little stressed right now. Finals were kinda tough and I haven't slept much, you know."

Max whined again and pushed his head up under my arm. The room grew foggy; I could hardly keep my eyes open. I ran my fingers around the long hairs on Max's ear. Just when I began to relax, the phone started ringing. I jumped up and lunged for the desk. I grabbed for the phone, pausing briefly to catch my breath before I picked it up.

"Hello...hello...Who is this? Hello!"

No one answered, yet I was sure I could hear voices. I clicked the receiver, once...twice...still nothing. I slammed it down. Instantly, it began to ring again. I ran to the kitchen. Maybe the office phone wasn't working right. My hand shaking, I grabbed the kitchen phone.

Hello...Hello!" Nothing. "This isn't funny! I can hear you!"

Tears began to stream down my cheeks and the room began to spin. My heart was pounding so hard my chest began to hurt. I reached down to pet Max, but he wasn't there.

"Max...Max!!" I screamed "Where are you...Max!"

Panic was taking over. I couldn't catch my breath, my throat was tight. I leaned against the wall and stumbled back into the living room.

"Max." My voice hoarse. "Max..."

Everything was spinning and blurry. I dropped to my knees and tried to pull myself up to the couch. I felt a warm, soft touch on my arm.

"Max." I whispered. Then all went dark.

"Christine...Christine." A soft female voice called out. "Jim, get the doctor. She's moving. Open your eyes. Please, open your eyes."

The voice sounded familiar, but I was so tired. Again the voice called out my name and I could feel that soft, warm touch on my arm.

"Max." I whispered.

The woman's voice became more excited and insisting.

"Open your eyes...Do it now Christine. It's time to wake up."

The room was overwhelming, so bright and white, yet foggy. I could hear several voices now; the same woman as well as two men. There were people shuffling around me, touching and pulling at me. I couldn't quite make out their faces or words. Was I caught in a dream? Several painful minutes passed before I tried to open my eyes again.

"Christine."

Slowly the woman's face cleared, her silver streaked hair somewhat mussed, but familiar.

"Mom?" My voice didn't come out right, only a harsh whisper. My throat felt as if it were on fire.

"Christine, oh my God, finally, you've come back."

Tears were streaming down her face.

"Come back?" I didn't understand. "Where's Max, he..."

"Shh..." she stroked my arm, "don't try to talk. You've been in a terrible accident."

"You've been in a coma for several weeks." A male voice said. "It will take some time."

I turned to look, but something restricted me from doing so.

"It's Dad, Christine. Just relax; it's going to be okay now."

I closed my eyes and let myself fall asleep.

The next day I felt stronger. I could sit up and some of the monitors and IVs had been removed. I kept asking about Max. We had always been inseparable since I was five. I was worried that he wouldn't understand what had happened to me. I was still confused about the accident and couldn't remember even driving home that day.

"You need to tell me about Max, Mom." I insisted. "Was he in the accident too? Was he killed?" I whispered, closing my eyes tight and trying to remember.

"Christine." She said softly, taking my hand in hers. "Honey, Max died three years ago."

"But he was there...in the car with me and in the house."

She squeezed my hand. "It's okay. It's hard to remember everything right now."

"But I followed him through the house, then I lost him. I wanted to follow him."

"He made sure you were safe, Christine. Just like he always did. Then he had to go on." Mom kissed my forehead. "They weren't ready for you yet and Max led you back to us."

Letter from a Small Town

Rosalie Sanara Petrouske

Dear Friend,
It's been many years since we saw each other.
You write, "Tell me about your daughter."

My daughter is all long-legged child,
graceful tap dancer in a blue feather boa.
She is a flash of sunlight
spinning across the morning fence
touching hyacinth, you'd never recognize her,
almost to my shoulder, string-bean girl.
Everyone tells me she has my eyes.
She is up north for the summer, at the big lake,
    I miss her.

Dear Friend,
You write, "Tell me about your home."

We live near a river,
sooty and green even in mid-afternoon.
How can rivers not be clear and blue?
I don't know for sure the poetry of rivers.
They are noisy at sunset when geese fly over
and mallards honk love tunes to their mates.
The racket echoes past the carwash
all the way to higher ground.
Moon puddles over treetops and when wind rises,
the river remains calm, only a fish splashing,
leaving small ripples behind.

Our house is old, built in 1910.
It hunches like a stunted sunflower
in the center of our block.
Up and down Jefferson Street
flags unfurl from every porch,
a cacophony of red, white and blue.
When this house was new,
children wore white cotton,
played hoop games in the dirt road,
fathers worked at the chair factory,
and mothers sewed gloves,
took in laundry from lawyers' wives.
It was the "Age of Optimism."
Mothers dreamt of owning an Alexandrovna Hat,
having a butterfly tattoo painted on a bare shoulder,
dancing until midnight at the Island Hotel.
This used to be a grand resort town.
Back then, men talked about motorcars,
and their young sons imagined walking on their hands
from Vienna to Paris, setting world records.

Dear Friend,
You ask, "Is there anything new in your life?"

Our street rarely changes.
Yesterday, city workers came by
to cut down a maple tree struck by lightning.
The garden club ladies planted tulips
and daffodil bulbs in front of our town hall.
Time passes slowly,
yet babies once pushed in strollers
soon ride past on their bicycles
down to Lick-ity Split.
When my daughter comes home in August,
we will rollerblade to the river,

and buy sugar cones filled with Mackinac Island
Fudge.

Dear Friend,
You ask, "Do you ever miss me?"

I miss you, far away near the Atlantic Ocean.
Do you often think of me?
I know you kept the picture of me in a green dress,
tanned and laughing by Superior.
I gave that dress away, worn and stained,
it fell reluctantly into the Goodwill box.

Dear Friend,
You ask, "Are you happy now?"

When I see light curl out from undersides of leaves
or hear the Mourning Dove coo
as mist rises from the lawn,
I sit out on my porch with hot tea and honey,
then walk down to the river,
embrace each morning like a lover,
breathe in neck smells of Magnolia blossom,
damp mud, sodden leaves mulching into earth.
And, yes, then I'm happy to bless each coming day.

Main Street

K. L. Marsh

I grew up on Main Street among the tourists and the boaters, the busy housewives and the businessmen. I loved them all for the stories they told me through what they wore, where they went, and what they said. I was probably six or seven when I ventured downtown by myself without my brother and without my mother's consent. I wanted to go to the Woolworth store and visit the lunch counter where my grandmother took us for Tulip sundaes. I thought I might take my birthday money and buy one for myself.

The store was a wonderland with birds and fish, candy of all kinds and ladies in mint green smocks who smiled at me and asked where my mother was. I drifted through the Notions department, looked at the Butterick patterns, and fingered the materials by the yard. I looked over the purses and picked out a pink one. When I was older I spent hours in the record department lingering over Bobby Goldsborough and the Beatles. Alva was the clerk there and she always kept an eagle eye out for the kids who would try to take the records out of their jackets.

It was years later when I came home from New York for the first time that I felt the need to visit Woolworth's. It had such an anti-New York feel with the wood floors and candy counter. I wandered from Notions to the record department and then I saw her. I stopped in my tracks and stared. I couldn't believe it; she hadn't changed at all. She still had the same flat brown hair and cat eye glasses. She wore the same green smock and orange lipstick. Her nameplate said, 'Alva,' but I already knew that.

She had waited on me wordlessly throughout my childhood spent on Main Street.

Her loud counterpart Shayda always shooed us away from the parrot who screamed, "Merry Christmas" and, "Pretty Bird" when the store was noisy. Shayda measured out my favorite chocolate covered peanuts and inquired about my mother, but Alva never did. Alva dusted around us. She returned patterns to their drawers after we messed them up while looking for the dresses we saw in the *Ladies Home Journal.* All the while, she never said a word.

Now returning to Woolworth's as an adult, Alva, more than anyone else, was the one that I wanted to talk to. It was on her blank face I wanted to write my story. I wanted to tell her about my life in New York City. How much as a child I longed for something other than a town that stretched from the river to the fairground in one short street. I spent my young life waiting to leave, but now that I had returned I wanted to see everything, and I wanted to take Alva with me so I could witness my life through her eyes. I never did work up my courage to ask her, but I thought she would be my narrator, and review the girl I had been, comparing her to the woman I became. She could tell me where I had changed.

Next to the Woolworth store was the Gold Dust Ballroom, which in my parents' day had hosted Paul Whiteman and Harry James. Older people still talked about our town during the war, when visitors bought drinks in paper cups at Spike's Keg 'O' Nails. How they wandered Main Street, going from one show bar to the next, listening to the big bands, dancing in the street and smoking.

When I was a teenager, I snuck into the Gold Dust with my girlfriends to see if we could get served a drink.

None of us were old enough but we thought we could pass. The waitress was so pale she looked like she had never seen the light of day and we knew she wouldn't know us. We ordered Bacardi cocktails and tried not to choke when she brought us straight rum. Later, we learned that no one ever ordered anything but bottled beer there.

Kretchman's Donuts stood across the street from the Gold Dust at the corner of State and Main. It was there that the early business crowd gathered to hear the latest gossip. The girls poured steaming cups of coffee and knew everyone in town by their first name. Kretchman's was to breakfast what the Riverside was to lunch and Pappas' was to dinner. A husband and wife team ran the place and I came to know them well over the course of my childhood Saturdays spent in pursuit of a treat to start the day. My parents sent my brother and me with a five-dollar bill to order and we wandered and skipped, petting the stray dogs, stopping to watch the Bois Blanc boats on the river.

We stood in front of the doughnut case with our eyes wide, trying to decide which one to pick that week. Saturday was a big deal as our mother was strict with our diets. Until we were old enough to go to other kids' homes, raisins were the only candy we knew. As we stood there placing our order, we would see Mr. Wadsworth, the mailman, and Larry, the barber. We spoke to Mrs. Hermanson, who cut my hair and gave our sister permanents and, finally, we always talked to Mr. McArthur from the Bank, who asked after our mother. My uncles told us that she had been quite a looker in her day. As I grew older, I could see our banker admired our mother in that way, not only because of our disabled sister, as most people did, but also for her beauty, her French twist, and her ready smile.

Also, ever present at Kretchman's was Mary Lois Farthing, who was a cleaning lady long before everyone had one. We were warned never to talk to her, as it was said she was a gossip and we heard she would "bring a bone and take one away." It was about Mary Lois that my Grandmother said her mouth went like a "whippoorwill's ass in huckleberry season."

South down the street was the J.C.Penney store where my mother worked when she was in high school, earning a quarter an hour. She dressed the mannequins and did inventory, rang up sales and chased the neighborhood dogs out of the store. The Penney store sat next to the Citizen's Bank, where everyone in my family had an account. Mr. McArthur had been president for years and wore a grey Chesterfield coat with a velvet collar. I liked him; he shone like a new penny and smiled at everyone he met.

Every day at four, you could see Horsehead Shipley sitting with her two retarded sons on the bench under the bank clock. She wore old housedresses, ankle socks, and Olaf Daughter clogs, remnants of better times. She chewed tobacco and with a crazy smile on her face, she looked through her thick glasses up and down Main Street, her sons waiting quietly beside her.

Kitty-corner across the street was Leonall's Drugstore where we went after school to do our free reading. They had all of the good comic books there and the clerk couldn't see us from behind the counter so we were safe by the hour. The pharmacist looked like the Charmin Man with his pencil mustache. He spoke in muffled tones with the customers, giving them directions for their heart medication and their childrens' earaches.

Main Street was my teacher, as well as my trainer. It was there I could find out the time and the tone of the season, the last from Mitt McDonald who always changed from a wool chuke to a straw boater on Easter Sunday. I loved it when I was younger and I loved it when I was older, but it was the in between years that made me yearn for larger climes. But that is another story for another time.

The Perfect Ride

Rosalie Sanara Petrouske

When I was about four years old, my father worked the night shift in a sawmill. My mother woke me and carried me down to the car so we could pick him up when his shift ended at 11:00 p.m. What do I remember most about those nights? The smell of my father's clothes; the black lunch pail he carried. When he scooped me out of the car, I buried my face into the shoulder of his jacket and breathed in the loamy, warm fragrance of sawdust.

On the ride home, we always stopped at a little restaurant, The Nod Inn. My parents drank thick, black coffee out of heavy white mugs. Sometimes my dad let me take a sip. He put cream and sugar in his. Most kids hated coffee, but I loved its taste. It made me think of the stories my dad told me about the swamps he saw in Louisiana, steamy, dark, and slightly sweet smelling. I watched the waitress refill my parents' cups, her smooth white hands with silver rings, her white dress and white Ked sneakers. I wanted to be that waitress when I grew up, pouring coffee at midnight and wearing silver rings on my fingers, smelling like the oranges at Nagelkirk's Farm Market where my mother bought peaches Saturday mornings.

The Nod Inn was by the railroad station when the last passenger trains still ran, cutting their swathe through the Upper Peninsula from places farther south: the Chicago Northwestern midnight special. Something still feels mysterious about a railroad crossing sign at night, the bars shaped like a large X, the flashing red lights, and clangs of the signals to warn drivers the gate will come down. *Danger, danger*...they seemed to toll out. My father knew I loved trains, so he walked down to the depot with me so we could watch the '400' make its entrance. My heartbeat raced in tempo to the rumble of the tracks as the big engine pulled into view, steam rising up like a dragon from my picture books, the brakes squealing as it slowed to a stop. By then I was wide awake and for the burgeoning writer in me, my thoughts circled with descriptions, my senses filled with the delight of sound, taste, touch; the burnt smell of hot steam, the beautiful, dark-skinned conductor in his smart uniform directing people through the doors and down the narrow stairways.

I twisted my head, right and left, to see the people stepping from the train. There were men in pinstriped suits toting large leather bags with their wares, always in a hurry even so late at night. Tall handsome soldiers coming from places that were on maps I did not know the names of yet, pretty ladies in high-heeled shoes, families hugging, and girlfriends with tears on their pale night faces clinging to the arms of those young men. They were a blur of faces and I loved watching all of them.

It was even more exhilarating to me when my father took me into the depot and bought me a Hershey bar from the vending machine. There were little sandwiches in the machines cut into perfect triangles and cold, foamy bottles of Coca Cola. The dark wood benches were scuffed, and the ticket master stood behind a black-gated window selling the most delightful tokens: paper tickets that you gave to the conductor to enter the magic train and travel far away into the dark, starry night. I begged my father to buy a ticket, to take us on the train. He said, "Maybe, someday." And I said, "Now, please. Let's buy one now."

"Someday, we will, I promise."

And it was one promise he kept.

When I turned six years old, two years before the '400' quit running forever, before the tracks were torn up and the depot became a derelict with graffiti painted on its red bricks, nailed boards across its shattered windows, my parents took me on the Chicago '400' all the way to Milwaukee to visit my sister and her husband. I wore a white linen dress, navy blue coat, and new black patent leather shoes. My matching black patent purse was decorated with a white silk rose, and snapped shut with a delicious click. I don't remember every detail of that trip, although it seems I should. I do know my heart beat in time to the wheels while the voices of the conductors drifted through the aisles as they stopped to assist those who needed a pillow or a cup of coffee from the dining car. I know my father got off at Green Bay and brought back ham sandwiches from a vending machine, the ones cut in perfect triangles and I was so hungry by then, they tasted like ambrosia, or at least that's what my father said. I was not sure what 'ambrosia' was, but I knew it was something good.

There are perhaps only a dozen perfect events in a person's lifetime, and my ride on the '400' was the first one I counted. The first time I really wanted something and my wish came true. I know I fell asleep with my face pressed to the window watching the small winking lights of farmhouses pass by, cars waiting at crossroads, and when I looked up, stars scattered across a clear, black sky. I have always loved traveling at night. In the small town where I live now, on the edge of a bigger city, a freight train is still in use. Occasionally, when I am up late writing, I hear its rumble on the tracks down by the fire station, the mournful whistle faintly echoing and stop to listen. I remember my mother's warm shoulder, my father lifting me up to carry me off the train at Milwaukee; my sister in her pretty yellow dress waiting to meet us at the end of our journey.

Where Are You?

C. J. Tody

Where are you, O my love, my one,
Who comes a friend and never leaves?
Are you figment or do you breathe,
A vulnerable soul in warm solid flesh?

I know you deep inside, you know,
You can't elude unconscious flow,
You mean too much to me to forget,
Way deep, where I sense you yet.

Hidden under sparkling, image-rich sleep,
I touch your temple, remove its tension,
Transform a sparkle, brush it into your eye,
Do you still know where to find me?

I see your closeness, so touchingly open,
Your secrets like cells, your cycles elastic,
Liquid, deepening, fresh and e'erchanging,
Lining your foundations, towers, and turrets.

Healing cocoon, wrap my impenetrable soul,
Out fly cherished childhood memories,
No small treasure, these linking renewals,
Freeing my soul to dream a fresh world.

Hopes of lost childhood are skipping a'round,
Finding dreams come true in magic wonderlands.
Are you there, on the bridge to the sun?
Holding twinkling doors open, my love?

Where are you, in my childhood remembered?
Perhaps part of myself is back there still,
Amid clouds shrouding talents, promises hiding,
Perceptions, viewpoints differ from yours.

A lifetime later...finds clouds separating,
The sun burning through to claim all a'mist,
Uneasy changes bring new paradigm, wonder,
Do I hide, turn away? Find me betwixt!

Play to me, Cello, you inspire strange moods,
Rich and provocative, inviting and deep,
I sense my lover concealed there within,
Your waves undulating, my hunger to pique.

Must I break code, solve mystery for you?
What, think I now, if I'm hidden in costume?
A bridge spans Cello's waves out open window,
Transports my heart o'er battered old moat.

Weary feet start gliding together to follow,
Opening once again the weathered old door,
I say heartfelt wishes and Castle winks open,
Where are you there, my love, O beloved?

Over the Garden Gate

"Hey Mary, did ya hear about Agnes?" Oh, the gossip that once spilled over the Garden Gate! Two neighbors, whether old friends or newly acquainted, have often met at the dividing line of their adjoining properties. They discuss everything from politics to the goings-on of their community, or simply chat about the day's events.

Much information has been shared over the white picket fences or low-cut hedges of a small town. But more than that, this section explores how neighbors in a tight-knit community interact with one another, how they will go out of their way to be kind and to do what's right.

In this section, you will find neighbors being neighborly and mothers tending gardens with care, as well as what one can find blowing in the wind.

An Act of Kindness

Lori Hudson

The world had tilted, Addie thought. Everything was off-center, out of focus, unsteady.

She ran her hands along the arms of her wicker chair, feeling notches where the wood had chipped, places where the padding had peeled away. The floorboards on the old porch sighed when she moved. Paint had bubbled along the eaves. Droplets of water, condensation from the air conditioner rattling in an upstairs window, ran down one of the porch columns. Moisture had collected by the railing and a small puddle formed underneath. Addie watched as a new drop landed in the puddle, then another and another.

There were no miracles. Death would not be deterred by the sheer force of her unshakable resolve. She had put her shoulder to Carl's illness, thrusting against it with all her strength, refusing to give in, to admit that she might lose, but it had overtaken him anyway. And at the end, she had not been able to buy an extra moment, even with her boundless guilt that she had not heeded his early whispers of fear.

Now, alone in their house, in *his* house, the family home where he grew up, the house that echoed him, sang him, breathed him, Addie sat alone on the porch and cocked her head at the street, trying to remember if it had always curved in that odd, uneven way. Was it part of everything that was slowly becoming unraveled, and would it soon go blurry around the edges like the railroad tracks and the post office on the corner? Once this little town had seemed confining, but now the world outside it had disappeared.

Caroline wiped her hands on a kitchen towel, gazing out her window at the woman sitting motionless on the porch next door.

Addie Prince, thought Caroline, Carl's widow. Carl met Addie at a college football outing. When they married, they moved to the east coast, returning for holidays and short visits with Carl's parents, and the kids spent a week with their grandparents each summer, but no one knew Addie very well. Caroline remembered her at Carl Senior's funeral, dressed in a crisp dark suit, pleats ironed in her sleeves, a handkerchief folded perfectly in her hands. She had always seemed unapproachable, but Carl doted on her. You could tell by the way he watched her with that half smile, always a touch on her shoulder when she drew close. After he died she opened up the old house and the children quietly helped her move in. It was hard to imagine her and Carl not together.

She hadn't aged much over the years, but now, seated nearly motionless in her mother-in-law's old chair, she seemed to have gone slightly transparent, like a feather or a bit of cloth. Caroline blinked and glanced over at her stove. A pot simmered on the back burner. She had always liked fresh tomato soup, made with a small pinch of basil, and a thick chunk of French bread. The weather was never too warm for tomato soup and fresh bread. She reached for a clean bowl and her ladle.

Addie tried moving her head the other way to see if the road looked any different. With her head cocked to the right, the chicory growing along the shoulder looked blue rather than purple. Was chicory blue or purple? The question puzzled her. She turned it over several times in her mind, wondering at its significance. Why did her thoughts seem to swoop toward inconsequential details, then stick there, refusing to budge? Addie pulled her eyes away from the flowers, glanced down again. The puddle by the post was growing larger, despite the sun that wept down on the floorboards.

Something moved by the fence, and Addie turned her head slowly in that direction. A woman made her way across the yard, carrying something wrapped in a towel. In a few moments she had climbed the steps of the porch and was standing before Addie, smiling.

"I'm Caroline Westerfield," she said, balancing her burden in her left arm and holding out her right hand for Addie to shake.

"I remember," Addie answered. "Yours is the blue house. Your husband is Bill."

"That's right," Caroline answered. "No, don't get up!" she added when Addie shifted in her chair. "I've brought you some tomato soup and a loaf of bread. I'll just put them in the kitchen for you. I picked up your newspaper, too. Here it is."

She handed the paper to Addie and Addie laid it in her lap unopened, lacing her hands across the dusty folds.

"Thank you." Addie squinted into the sunlit yard. She looked up at the ruined paint, then down at the widening puddle on the floor.

"I haven't been here for a while, probably not since Carl's dad died. But I used to come over a lot," Caroline called.

She was in the kitchen, Addie noticed with mild surprise. She had been staring down at the floorboards and hadn't heard her go inside.

"I loved Carl's folks," Caroline went on. "When I was a little girl, my dad and his dad played horseshoes at the park every Thursday, and Carl's mom helped hang the wallpaper in my Sarah's room when she was born.

We didn't know if she would be a boy or a girl, and if she was a girl I wanted butterfly paper. My mother was fit to be tied." Caroline laughed. "She told everyone I'd lost my mind. 'What's wrong with some nice daisies?' she said. 'Or kittens?' But I wanted butterflies. You know how it is with your firstborn. Pretty soon folks began looking for butterfly wallpaper when they went to the city. Arlene and Tom Olson found the pattern I ended up choosing. Tom came running over with the sample, all excited. I saved a little piece and put it in Sarah's scrapbook. Funny how the whole town got fired up about that wallpaper."

She's talking, Addie thought. Talking about everyday things. Talking about her youth and her own children. Had she ever put her shoulder against death and found it unyielding, like the water dripping steadily from the air conditioner? There were no miracles.

"When it gets a little cooler, I'll send Bill over to mow your grass," Caroline called from the kitchen. Addie could hear dishes clinking. "I'm washing this teapot, okay? It's actually better to keep the grass short when it's so hot," she went on. "That's what my father always did. Helps it green up better once the rain comes, he said. I put the soup on the back burner and turned it on low. It tastes better when the basil has been simmering all day. One of these oranges has a bad spot. Mind if I throw it away?"

Caroline walked back out on the porch and put her hands on her hips. The sun looked reddish orange and the clouds hazy. She wiped her forehead.

"I can't believe how hot it is," she commented. "But your kitchen stays real cool. I noticed the Queen Anne's lace on the windowsill. Did your daughter pick them? Her name is Chloe, right?"

"Yes," answered Addie. "Chloe picked them."

Caroline grinned. "My Sarah picks wildflowers, too. Drives her husband crazy. He says it makes his allergies kick up. Would you like me to fold that laundry on the stairs? I'd like to help, but I don't want to interfere."

Addie made her mouth curve up. She hoped Caroline would see it as a smile. "Thank you," she said. "You're very kind."

She looked down when the screen door slammed again. The puddle was still growing, creeping toward her like a dark shadow. Soon it would touch the toe of her left sandal. It would be a miracle if her shoe didn't get wet.

Caroline went back into the cool darkness of the foyer. She picked up the pile of laundry and glanced over her shoulder at the woman on the porch. Addie was staring at something on the floor, her head bowed and the sun bright on the back of her neck. Her hands were still clasped on the newspaper. Caroline shook out a blouse and hung it over the back of a chair, folded a flowered pillowcase and some underthings.

The house looked much as it did when Carl's parents had lived here. Would Addie find it odd to live in this quiet place, in this town where Carl had been a little boy and where everyone's lives were intertwined, like the morning glories Caroline planted each year around her mailbox?

The laundry was done. Caroline went back to the kitchen and pulled down some paper towels to wipe the counter. Addie still sat silently on the porch, staring down toward her feet. Caroline stood on her tiptoes trying to see what she was looking at. Finally she walked out to stand behind her, the towels in her hand.

"Is there anything else..." she began, gazing down at the nape of Addie's neck. Addie was watching a little pool of water fed by the dripping air conditioner.

Caroline knelt next to Addie's chair. "Shall I wipe that up for you Addie? I have a towel right here. Shall I?"

Addie didn't answer, but Caroline saw her blink slowly. She frowned slightly, and one of her hands tightened around the newspaper.

Caroline leaned forward and dropped the paper towels into the puddle. She soaked up the water until there was nothing left, and then squeezed the toweling over the railing into the flower bed. She saw Addie curl her toes in her sandal, and the spot where the moisture had been shrank slowly in the sun. Another drop fell from the air conditioner, but Addie was looking at the morning glories.

Birds of a Feather

K. L. Marsh

The warbler and sparrow, side by side, faces to the sun.
Preening, beady eyes waiting to be fed. Cheeping.
Young, green and clever, chubby faced and confident.
Wise, old, tired and wondering.
Birds of a feather.

Flocked together to migrate south with the teacher.
Rummaging through their memories from last night or last year.
Offering up for review, their stories raw and ruminative.
Wise, young, and fired.
Birds of a feather.

Chewing their stories first, like a mother feeding her young.
Explaining their motifs with shy eyes and hope.
Learning the ropes like prize fighters in the ring,
    egged on by applause and praise.
Up and out of the nest.

My Mother's Garden

K. L. Marsh

My mother's petunias bloomed from April through October.
They bloomed through broken bones and cut knees,
through problems and solutions,
through my grandfather's funeral and past my father's job.
She could make them look like a picture
and no one asked her how.

My mother's flowers were her couch,
her chair,
her mirror,
her confessor.
Some day people will ask me how I stood it,
how I could possibly bear it
and I'll tell them about my mother's flowers.

When her heart cracked with each new diagnosis,
with false hope and faith that must have worn thin,
her flowers bloomed.
There were never any weeds or stray papers.
She never cried or told us what the closed doors meant.
She protected us against crabgrass and boll weevils,
against too much rain.

There were always red petunias and white,
purple and occasionally stripes.
From her kitchen window, she looked at them often.
I asked her later how she did it. How she kept us and
    them.
She said that she didn't know but she did.
She had to.

Neighborhood Watch

Randy D. Pearson

Looking out my bay window, I shook my head and frowned. I really hoped this year would be different, but no such luck. Every autumn, without fail, there has been at least one extremely windy day that rips the leaves from the mighty oak trees that line my street, flinging them into my yard. It's even worse when it happens overnight, waking to such a large mess. I sighed as I trudged outside, rake in hand.

I had assembled the wayward leaves into a large pile, filling several bags, when Ralph leaned over the garden gate. As one of the leaders of the Neighborhood Watch program, he always took the time to converse with me. I certainly didn't mind, but I wish he'd stop asking me to join. I don't know anyone on this street but him.

"Howdy Bill," the pudgy man said with a wave and a smile. "The eternal cycle, eh?"

"Yeah, autumn's a messy season," I said, leaning against my rake. "Whose bright idea was it to create plants that litter?"

He shrugged and replied, "Certainly not mine. But, it is kinda neat to see what the wind'll bring into the yard."

I grunted. "Just leaves and garbage, my friend."

"Not always!" Ralph grinned as he brandished a ten-dollar bill. "Not only did I find this, but I ended up with a paperback and a pair of panties."

"Must've been quite a gust, huh?" After a chuckle, I said, "Well, I best get back to it. Maybe the rest of the girl is in this pile!"

"Trust me," he spoke as he walked away, "if you'd seen the size of these bloomers, you wouldn't be in such a hurry to uncover her."

I raked and bagged for another hour, until a good share of my upper body screamed in pain. I had made good progress, but the only non-tree items I discovered were junk food wrappers and cup lids. Just as I decided to call it a day, my rake uncovered a white piece of paper with writing on it. I lit up a cigarette while snatching it off the ground. The handwriting had an obvious feminine touch. Pretty and neat, it had lots of loops and swoops. I almost crumpled it up, but then my curiosity kicked in and I changed my mind. I could afford to waste a couple of minutes. The note had the feel of a carefully thought out poem, celebrating the beauty all around us. It spoke of trees *with leaves of majestic fire* and the *coming brilliant luminescence of the full autumn moon*. I assumed this had been written yesterday, since the moon looked almost full last night. I grinned, feeling just the slightest bit naughty reading someone's personal thoughts. But then, the tone changed dramatically.

Oh, dearest Monty, how I love you...how I loathe you. I gave you my all... my trust, my love, my heart, my very soul, and in return, you have given me your anger, your grief, your infidelity. You have injured my soul; you have wounded my pride. Your betrayal has cut me to the quick. I can take no more. You can surely live without me, but I have come to realize that I cannot live without you. You were my first, and you will be my last.
By the time you read this, I will be gone. By the light of the full autumn moon, I will be no more. My death will come quickly and painlessly.

Will your pain linger? Will you even notice? If you are as selfish as I truly believe you are, you will not even mourn my passing. My death is on your hands, but I fear you will only wash them, dry them and be clean once more.

If this is the case, all I ask is you think of me on occasion and smile. Remember the good, for we were truly happy once.

In death, I will be happy once more.

Daisy

As I read it, my mouth dropped open. She clearly went to a lot of trouble concocting this letter, even taking the time to draw a little flower above the 'I' in Daisy.

I stood there, utterly dumbfounded. My initial reaction told me this had to be a hoax. Maybe Ralph planted it in my yard, as a joke. I doubted it, though. We didn't know each other nearly well enough for a prank like this. But still, why would a completed suicide note be blowing in the wind? It made no sense.

Again, I contemplated tossing the letter, it being none of my business, after all. I've never even met the girl, so why should I interfere?

But no, I knew it would haunt me all of my days. Besides, I love a good mystery.

I decided to take the note next door to Ralph and Lauren's house. Even though I had lived in this neighborhood for a few years, I kept to myself. I jokingly told my friends that when I finally snapped and went on a murderous rampage, the neighbors would describe me to the press as, "that quiet, unassuming guy down the street... I knew he was trouble, keeping to himself like that." However, Ralph had the gift of gab. He would know Monty and Daisy.

"I don't know Monty or Daisy," said Ralph with sympathy in his voice. "I've never heard of them, and Lauren's in Buffalo, visiting her Mom." He stood quiet for a moment, staring at the note in his hand. "Man…" he said softly and trailed off in thought. After a while, he looked up at me. "You're not just messing with me, are ya?"

"Oddly enough," I replied, "I was hoping the same thing of you."

"What're we gonna do, Bill?" The genuine concern plastered across his mustached face gave me pause. I really thought Ralph would have the answers.

"Okay, let's think this through logically," I said as I started walking toward the door. "Follow me." Once outside, we stood on the sidewalk. "The wind had been blowing from the east, so it came from down there," I said, pointing. "There are, what, a dozen houses in that direction?"

"More like sixteen, but at least it gives us a place to…" He paused, then his brown eyes lit up. "Oh, I know! Let's ask Margaret! C'mon!" He started jogging down the street, but he slowed pretty quickly. Apparently, Ralph really needed to jog more often. "Margaret's lived in the neighborhood all her life," he wheezed. "If anyone'll know this girl, Margaret will."

We knocked on a door four houses to the west of mine. Moving westward did not feel like the best of plans, but as soon as the door opened, I felt a wave of hope flutter through me. Margaret had the appearance, to me at least, of the quintessential neighborhood gossip. It could have been her pear-shaped body, or maybe the inquisitive furrowing of her brow gave me optimism. Of course, it might simply have been the fact that her ears were just a bit oversized. I smiled politely as Ralph introduced us. "Oh yeah," she said with a country-girl twang to her nasally voice, "I've seen you a few times. You keep to yourself, don't ya?"

"Yeah," I grinned as I said, "that's me. The quiet, unassuming guy from down the street." I paused, but when I didn't get the laugh I anticipated, I continued, "Say, we were wondering, do you know a Monty or Daisy?"

She quickly nodded her head. "Oh sure, well, I know Monty Turkel pretty well. Only met his wife a couple of times." She moved her head closer to us and lowered her voice to a murmur. "She's kinda flaky. She's one of them artsy-fartsy types. Prone to emotion, from what I've heard. But, of course, so's Monty. Got a temper, that one does. I hear he punched a hole in a wall once." She returned her head to its original position and asked, "So, why ya askin'?"

I hesitated, then looked over at Ralph. I didn't feel it prudent to be blabbing any more gossip to this lady, but before I even finished turning my head, he had already yanked the letter from my grasp, handing it to her.

Once she read it, she desperately wanted to tag along.

So, we had a little convoy, walking down the sidewalk with a purpose to our stride. I had to keep slowing down, however. Apparently, this neighborhood needed an exercise regimen.

When we reached the Turkel residence, three houses east of mine, I felt increased trepidation, but having a posse with me helped to assuage my uneasiness somewhat. I rather doubted I could have done this on my own. I let Margaret ring the bell, but no one came to the door. We all looked at each other, not knowing what to do next. "Should we bust in?" asked Ralph.

"Um, no, I don't…" I started.

"That would be stupid," Margaret loudly blurted. "Forget it! This is probably someone's idea of a bad joke. I mean really, who loses a suicide note?" She turned and walked away without saying another word to us.

I looked at Ralph and shrugged. "Maybe we can keep an eye out," I said quietly. "If one of us sees either of them come home…"

"Yeah, Bill, good idea." He looked at me for a long moment, before adding, "I hope everything's okay." Then, he turned and walked toward home.

"Me too…" I whispered.

I could not sleep, so I sat on my porch, staring up at the full moon. If I craned my neck, I could just barely see their deck from mine. Every so often, I would stand up and walk out to the street, look at their driveway for a moment, then walk back. I had to wonder what the rest of my neighbors thought of my late-night pacing.

After a while of sitting on my deck, I must have dozed off. When I jolted awake at around 1:00 am, I saw a faint light coming from their patio. I jumped off my porch and started marching, my heart punching my chest like a boxer working over a speedbag.

As I advanced, I could see a single candlelight. There sat a woman with long, blonde hair, her back to me. She wore a full-length white robe, hunched over a small table.

Good Lord, what am I doing? Only lunatics would be out at this hour, skulking in the shadows. Her neighbors had not raked, so the rustling of leaves announced my approach. The figure turned sharply and shouted, "Who's there?"

"Oh, um, don't be startled," I stammered, "I'm your neighbor…Bill. Something of yours blew into my yard yesterday."

"Oh," she replied before turning her back again. As I rustled closer, I could see her hard at work. Her head hung down and her pen moved rapidly across a piece of paper. I reached the deck, and said softly, "Um, Daisy? May I come up?"

She continued scribbling for a few moments then paused and turned slowly. " Okay," she said softly, then, clearly as an afterthought, asked, "How...how do you..." but she trailed off before completing her thought, her concentration back upon her work.

I eased up the stairs. Though difficult to see, the candle tossed enough light on her paper for me to notice similar loops and swoops on the page in front of her. I walked up beside her and laid her letter on the desk. "This blew into my yard."

She stared at it for several seconds before looking up at me through glassy eyes. She flashed me a weak smile. "Oh. I wondered..." and said, very softly, "Now I can stop rewriting..." and laid her head on the table.

At that moment, her predicament became apparent to me. She did not even flinch as I placed my fingers on her neck. Her pulse felt very weak. I pulled out my cell phone and dialed 9-1-1.

After disconnecting, I asked, "Is Monty home, Daisy?"

With considerable effort, she looked up at me. "No idea where... which woman he's... the bastard..."

As the sirens began wailing in the distance, I pulled up a lawn chair and sat down beside her. "Don't worry, Daisy," I whispered as I rested my hand upon her head, gently petting her like a puppy in a lap. "The Neighborhood Watch is here."

Steeples

From morning chimes to the bells tolling midnight, from the cheerful announcement of weddings to the solemn pealing of a funeral, from Sunday church service to baptisms, steeples have been a large part of our lives.

Although many churches don't have steeples anymore, the sentiment still holds a place in our hearts. They represented the ordinary daily activities that brought comfort, along with the excitement of special events.

Within the pages of this chapter, you will encounter stories and poems of people living their daily life, overcoming tragedy and looking to God.

Call Waiting

Lori Hudson

The rain turned to hail as I spied the first sign for the freeway.

"Gary?" My cell phone crackled, and my colleague's voice faded for a moment.

"Gary?" I said again, tucking the phone under my shoulder and trying to wipe condensation off the windshield with my free hand.

"...schedule a meeting...client..." Gary sounded as if he were speaking inside a giant tunnel, echoing and remote.

"I can't hear you, and the driving is getting really bad!" I said, more sharply than I meant to, hoping he could hear me better than I could hear him. My tires slid alarmingly toward the edge of the narrow paved road.

"Let's pick this up later," I said breathlessly.

I snapped the little phone closed and wiped at my windshield again. The hail was coming down harder now, pounding deafeningly on the roof. My car plowed forward, but it was getting harder and harder to drive and I feared I would skid into the ditch if the visibility got any worse. Squinting, I tried to see what was up ahead. I couldn't drive in this. I had to find somewhere to pull over until the storm let up.

Then I saw it—a white country church, its steeple an admonishing finger pointed at the angry, churning clouds. With a quiver of relief, I pulled into the gravel parking lot, rolling my car to a stop next to a beige sedan with a layer of ice on the hood.

Dim light shone through the sanctuary's stained glass, glowing purple and golden and teal. I stared at the window for a moment, weighing its beckoning against a cold, wet dash across the parking lot. Then I grabbed my purse and cell phone, held a newspaper over my head, and opened my car door.

Icy water splashed against my legs as I sprinted toward the church, while rain and hail pelted my makeshift umbrella. I burst, shivering and soaked, into the quiet safety of the foyer, wiped my feet on a carefully-placed mat and looked around me. I saw a bulletin board, bright with children's drawings, an announcement about an upcoming potluck, a coat rack with a plaid jacket and a scarf folded on an upper shelf. A plaque next to the door listed the names of soldiers killed during World War I. A basket overflowing with canned goods stood underneath.

The air inside the old church felt dry and cool against my wet skin. A soft light illuminated the altar, shining down on a vase of purple and yellow chrysanthemums and an old Bible. The sanctuary was small, with wooden pews that could seat perhaps a hundred people. A rack on the back of each bench held a blue hymnal.

I slid the sodden newspaper into a nearby trash bucket and walked a few steps inside, listening and wondering if I should call out to whomever was here. Would it be the pastor, or perhaps a maintenance worker?

Quiet footsteps sounded, and a woman appeared in a door near the front of the church. She wore slacks and a long sweater, and her brown hair was pulled up in a barrette.

She smiled.

"Good day to be inside!" she said. "May I help you with something?"

"No, I guess not. The roads are just really bad, and I wanted to stop for a minute. May I sit here 'til the weather clears?"

"Of course," she replied. "Help yourself to something to read, if you'd like."

She pointed to the coffee table, where magazines were spread in an inviting fan. I looked at the magazines and then at my cell phone.

"Thank you," I said. "But I also have some calls to make." Gary would be waiting. The deal I was working on might fall through. I would miss my three o'clock meeting.

"Of course," she said. "Make yourself at home."

She checked the thermostat on the wall and turned the heat up a little for me.

"Fresh coffee on the table there." She pointed, smiled and turned back down the darkened hallway.

Slipping onto one of the pews, I rubbed my chilled hands together and felt the tension begin to slide out of my muscles.

I took out my cell phone and ran my finger reluctantly over the buttons, then stuffed it back in my pocket. A few minutes of quiet wouldn't hurt. I took a deep breath, sat back and looked around me.

How many aunts and uncles, children, grandparents, friends, pastors, mothers and fathers had passed through this little place? The air here felt full, somehow, so thick with souls that I fancied I felt someone brush my shoulder, heard a child's laughter in the balcony.

I imagined the sanctuary filled with people singing, sunlight streaming inside through amethyst and jade glass to caress the faces of the faithful. I imagined a slender woman holding an aromatic tray of freshly-baked muffins, steam rising upward, placing it on the table in a fellowship hall. A grandmother wearing a white orchid corsage sitting quietly in a pew, hands folded across her Bible, feet crossed at the ankles. A small woman with gnarled hands at the piano, playing, playing, playing, and singing to the music of her church. A boy carrying an Easter banner down the aisle. A father helping his tiny daughter light the altar candles. A pastor looking out over his flock, his eyes crinkling at the corners.

Perhaps I dozed a little in the warm comfort of the little church, for suddenly I realized the muted rumble of hail hitting the roof had turned into a placid swish. As I sat musing, the hail had turned to rain, just a gentle spring spray that would feed the daffodils and turn the new leaves silver when the sun emerged from the clouds.

It was time to go.

I got to my feet and walked slowly to the door to let myself back out into the moist world. When I had climbed behind the wheel of my car once more, I took my cell phone out of my pocket and laid it on the seat next to me.

It rang a moment later, but I let the call go to voicemail.

French Sunday

K. L. Marsh

St. Charles Borromeo Church was the French Catholic Church in Cheboygan and that was our church. It was just down Ball Street from my Grandmother's house. There was also an Irish Catholic church and at one time, two Polish churches, one of which was way out in the farm country called Riggsville. Every Sunday after my father read us the comics we dressed in our best; my sister and I in our lace hats and matching Circus Shoppe coats, my brothers in caps and bow ties, and paraded off to St. Charles.

My parents were like New York models to me on those long ago Sundays. My father took down his Dobbs hatbox and put on a suit. My mother did her hair up in a French twist and wore a fox stole and gloves. She had a good story about the French and Irish churches. Her grandmother went to the Irish Church on the east side of town and her grandfather to St. Charles on the west. When she was a little girl it was said that she used to pray for his conversion.

The church was dark on the inside. The many stained glass windows, with family names etched on them, did not let in much sunlight. My great-grandfather, Theodore Rapin, had a window and we always tried to sit close in homage. Dr. Dickinson, everyone's favorite dentist, led the congregation that attempted to follow the choir. Anyone could join the choir; Catholics are like that and so the music was more often enthusiasm than melody.

I remember Father Imbault. He, like the church, was dark and foreign. He spoke with a heavy Romanian accent, and every sermon seemed to include talk about giving more money to fix the school furnace. I don't remember the Latin Mass, as Vatican II came early in my life but I do remember wondering about all of the formality, all the pomp and circumstance. Despite the fact that I went to Catechism every Saturday of my life and won prizes, I didn't feel like a Catholic. When the Canadian girls dropped to their knees with the appearance of the priest, I always hesitated for a minute and wondered about my fealty.

    I think my grandmother also wondered and I liked her the more for it. She was Theodore Rapin's French daughter and I would have expected her to be at Mass every Sunday. I don't know if she stopped going after my grandfather died or if she had always been like that but I loved her. We used to go to her house, nicknamed the Hitching Post Cottage, every Sunday for dinner. Marie Rapin Green was short, plush and bosomy. She had deep-set blue eyes and a Roman nose and she wore a wig always a little off kilter. To give her a little height she was never without her Naturalizer heels and a pillbox hat. I will never lose the memory of that familiar smell of hers, of powdered rouge, Estee Lauder and bowel gas.

    Grandma Green often served lamb with mint jelly for Sunday dinner. She liked pickled beets and favored gherkins made by a local farmer's wife. She was handy with desserts and served lemon meringue pie or divinity with strawberry sauce. Her house was warm and inviting. The kitchen smelled like marmalade and toast made fresh from the oven. Knotty pine covered the walls and gingham framed the windows. She was an antiques dealer and sold them from a shop in the garage. There were antiques everywhere.

    A long high Mass with hours of kneeling was always made bearable by the knowledge that we could go to Grandma Green's. After the itchy clothes and the off-key hymns, the request for more money for the school, and the long looks from my parents for talking too much to my brother, it was all made better by a visit to Ball Street and the Hitching Post Cottage.

Snowflakes

Candy-Ann Little

I watch the snowflakes falling down
   Silently gathering on the ground.
Wrapping the world in a blanket of white
   With crystal drops shining so bright.
The only disturbance that I can see
   Is the trail of footprints in front of me.
Whose they are, and where do they go?
   These answers I may never know.
But one thought stands strong and true.
   In this life your choices are but two.
You can either forge your own way,
   Down a trail that's unsure, leading to decay.
Or, follow the path that Jesus made.
   With love was this strong foundation laid.
A life of blessings, or a life that's hollow.
   Which path will you follow?

Second Tuesday of Next Week

Donnalee Pontius

An eight-foot bridge and a ten-foot van.
Pontius shortcuts with the kids.
Mint fields and morels; Pepsi and peanuts.

A world full of memories; a father lost.

Dark purple lilacs for a daughter-in-law.
Bright red cherry tomatoes for little ones to steal.
Gentle words and strong hugs.

A world full of memories; a friend lost.

Potato soup from hand-peeled spuds.
A table too small for all the family.
The lazy boy rocker to fall asleep in.

A world full of memories; a grandfather lost.

The strong, gentle hand of Jesus.
A path without pain.
His son, brought back home.

A world full of memories; a soul found.

Sunshine Again

Candy-Ann Little

Looking across the lush lawn, I notice some yellow and orange mums; their bright, cheery colors are a strong contrast to the cold, gray stone they surround. In the distance is a white fence, with four bushes strategically planted in front. The fence and flowers provide stark contrast to the greens of the grass and trees.

In the thick patch of trees at the edge of the property, I hear birds, tree frogs, locusts and crickets chirping their songs, lifting their tune in unison to their Creator. I also listen to the happy humming of bees as they flit around the flower bed.

The rustling of leaves, produced by a gentle wind, soothes my soul. Amazed, I watch as the branches dance, stretching their arms toward the sun in a gesture of praise. The large yellow ball brightens the cloudless, blue sky, reaching down with its warm glow to gently caress my skin.

This inspiring, peaceful afternoon brings a song to my heart and praise to my God. My spirit dances with joy as I delight in another beautiful summer day. Strange how my feelings differ greatly from the first time I set foot here.

Although it has been seven years, I can still feel the bitter wind whipping about, chilling me to the bone. The dreary fog not only settled around the cemetery but also rooted itself deep into my heart. Bitterness and sorrow whirled inside of me like the storm clouds swirling in the sky that day. Raindrops pelted against my face as if nature herself grieved. These physical indications served only to reinforce the misery I felt while burying my baby girl.

As I stood in this very spot saying good-bye to a daughter I never got to know – her life taken away even before her tiny body entered the world, I wondered if there would ever be sunshine in my life again.

Thankfully, as I sit here all these years later, the pain and sorrow dimmed, I can answer with certainty — yes!

Town Hall Meeting

Town halls are an important symbol of communities. They house more than government officials. They are the meeting place for the members of the town.

People gathering in a town hall celebrate more than just politics. They celebrate life. This is the place where communities come together. Within those walls people have debated issues and voiced their concerns. They've voted, laughed, cried, talked and sometimes even danced.

No building. No town. No community. No city is anything without the people living there. So, in this chapter, you will read about people, their trials and their triumphs. You will grow with the people living within these pages.

He Loved Me
My Daddy, My Dad, My Father

Diane Bonofiglio

My daddy used to take care of me when my mommy
 was away.
Sometimes he would fall asleep and I would play with
 the pens and pencils in his shirt pocket.
Once I ate his Camels.
His advice: don't eat cigarettes, don't smoke cigarettes,
 don't tell your mother.
My daddy told me he loved me.

My arms wrapped around daddy's neck from behind.
I stood on the back rung of his chair, my chin on his
 left shoulder.
My mouth, wide open, like a little bird
waiting to be filled with something delicious.
His words to me, "*Mange cara mia.*"
My daddy told me he loved me.

My daddy used to walk to and from work.
Every night I would run up the drive to meet him.
He would pick me up and carry me back home.
He said I was as light as a feather.
My daddy told me he loved me.

I went to work with my dad.
He let me sit at his light table.
He told me I could make maps just like he did.
I made a map of my back yard.
He said: "You do great work, you should be an artist."

My dad told me he loved me.

I was supposed to wait for an adult,
to help me slice my orange.
My dad took me to the doctor to get stitches in my
    hand.
His advice to me: there are reasons for rules.
Don't play with sharp objects.
My dad told me he loved me.

I took my dog for a walk in the park.
I didn't tell anyone where I was going.
When my dad found me, he gave me a spanking.
His advice to me: always let your parents know where
    you are.
My grandmother told me my dad loved me.

Ron wanted to walk me to the seventh grade dance
I said yes, my father said no.
I argued and I cried.
My father said: it's better that I cry now, than he cries
    later
My father told me he loved me.

I'm fat, everybody thinks so. I'm ugly, I hate myself.
My father told me I was not fat. He said I was *safdig*.
He told me his mother was a very beautiful woman.
He told me I looked just like my grandmother.
My father told me he loved me.

My friends used to come to my house.
They spent time talking to my father.
I was jealous. I hated my father.
My father said I had very nice friends.
My father told me he loved me.

I had six weeks left in Nursing School.
I wanted to quit.
I could never work with old people.
My father told me, you can do anything if you want to.
Always finish what you start.
My father told me he loved me.

I told my father I was getting married.
He said he was happy for me.
He told me he liked my husband to be.
He danced with me at our wedding.
He said I would always be his baby.
My father told me he loved me.

From being my daddy through being my father
He always loved me every day in so many ways
Before he left me, I told him how special he
always made me feel, all through my life.
I told him how special he was.
I told my daddy, my dad, my father
I love you.

One Sided

K. L. Marsh

"Wait a minute"
"I'm trying to get outside."
"There, now I can hear you."

"Where are you?"
"I'm at West Campus."
"You haven't? It's grand."

"What did your therapist say?"
"Do you feel better now?"
"I know codependency is *so* hard."

"What are you doing there?"
"Kristin can eat Indian food now, not to worry, she is
 over that phase."
"Give her my love."

"I know, her parents will never get over it."
"At least the ceremony will help Linda's daughter."
"I know it's not the same thing."

"I'm wearing your socks. Yes, the ones with the birds."
"What are they doing? Speak up, I can't hear you."
"I know they are so charming."

"Don't worry about that!"
"Once you turn fifty you don't care what people think."
"You mean you've never been to a psychic?"

"You should see 'In Bruges'."
"He's not like that in this."
"What did you say?"

"Sitting shouldn't do that."
"Are you drinking lots of water?"
"Try Miralax. M-I-R-A-L-A-X."

"If you say so…"
"I'm enjoying this seminar."
"Some people write well and some people talk well."

So Much Mess

Rosalie Sanara Petrouske

Today, nothing but clouds,
and a brackish river like
coffee muddied at the bottom of a cup.

A girl whose little brother died,
drops a question into the box.
"Am I still a big sister?" she asks.

When I come home, it is already night,
the dog has not been walked for a week.
He bounds to the door, jumping and
scattering clumps of loose hair.

There are socks dropped carelessly
on steps where shoes stand in
levels, often tumbling down
with a loud thump when dog
catapults over them.

So much mess to clean, dull stainless
steel, mirrors speckled with fingerprints,
dabs of toothpaste. Popcorn kernels
crunch when I step on them. I am tired
of keeping order.

On my desk, a tin cup overflows
with broken pencils, capless pens—a
Map of Kansas —Coronado, Leoti, Utica,
towns no one knows exist.

We lived there once, drove to the
Topeka Zoo, past landscapes dotted with wheat
fields, windmills, silos—November earth, color
of burnt toast.

March is always a sloppy month,
days growing longer, still a probability for snow.
Even nature can't keep her house clean;
last autumn's leaves a soggy mess,
clumped in gutters, rotting in flower
beds, smothering the first crocus shoot.
Where is a sign of spring?

Someone says a robin hopped
across their porch, our state bird
can't possibly be the sign we are looking
for—surely they would migrate to warmer
climates, proclaim themselves Florida's
sweethearts.

The biopsy comes back negative,
another checkup in six months.
My earlier complaints seem small and petty
when life can be so fragile.

The Philadelphia Six

Diane Bonofiglio

We stood at attention against the wall. The Philadelphia Six, as we had become known among the in-crowd, heads bowed in proper contrition, were about to be publicly castigated for the benefit of the masses. Sister Maximus, the Prefect of Discipline, glared at us with obvious disdain. She paced back and forth, stopping in front of each of us for added effect. Her riding crop slapped the palm of her hand with each word, keeping a beat, a rhythm of sorts. It helped her to remember all the lyrics racing through her head, to give us the full and complete version of the sentence about to befall us.

Barely above a whisper came the dreaded decree, "You have brought shame to yourselves and your families."

Doing an about-face at the end of the line, she continued, "You have dishonored your fellow students, not to mention the staff."

Half way down the line she stopped, centering herself for our benefit, so we could all see her face, and her body language. At a pitch that could have broken every test tube in chem lab, she boomed. "And brought disgrace to the uniform of this holy institution."

Continuing her tirade, singling out each one of us by name, she began doling out our penance one Hail Mary at a time, so to speak. The pronouncement came: "You shall be banned from all extra curricular activities for one month."

"You will appear in my office every day after school where you will be assigned various chores to be performed for the benefit of this school."

Gasps, tears and "oh no's" could be heard from some of the accused.

Taking her crop and slowly moving it across the front of us like a maestro, she smiled, for she was about to bring down on us the *coup de grâce*, the penance she could revel in, the penance that made her the winner. There was a prolonged silence to give her next proclamation added weight, as we hung on to her every word.

Then it came, like a gut punch: "Each one of you will write a letter of apology to the staff and your fellow students, to be read at a full school assembly."

There was stunned silence. The emotional pain was almost audible as we were left standing alone in front of that firing wall, our bodies trying to repel the bullets of consequence.

The stage was set, the actors lined up in the wings in order of their appearance and the director/emcee was basking in the limelight, so proud of her ability to bring all who had sinned to their knees. The auditorium was filled with a captive audience and the acts of contrition began, most gushing with remorse and begging forgiveness. Nancy and Florence shed the required tears. Vicky, Mary and Alice competed for the award in shortest apology on record. That left me to uphold the freedom of expression and the pursuit of happiness, rights guaranteed to us in the Declaration of Independence, even if we were Catholic.

Paper in hand, I stepped up to the mic and began, "Principal Mary Robert, Sr. Maximus, staff and students. I would like to extend to you my sincerest apology, because Sr. Maximus told me I have brought shame to the school, the staff and my fellow students. She says I have disgraced the uniform and myself. If what I have done is sinful and you truly feel I have caused you shame,

I am deeply sorry. I, however, feel no shame. I do not feel I have disgraced myself by my behavior."

Taking a long deep breath, as if it were my last, I caught sight of an extremely agitated Sr. Maximus, standing in the wings. She was staring at me, willing me to go mute or die. But I did neither and continued my death march:

"I now see that my only sin was a lack of good judgment. I should not have worn my uniform while attending such a public function. I have learned my lesson well. In the future I will wear my street clothes whenever I appear on American Bandstand."

Snowballs

Lori Hudson

It's morning and it has snowed and my husband is cranky. He is upstairs muttering his litany about Michigan winters and rummaging for his thick socks.

The front porch needs shoveling and the screen door is frozen shut. The dogs go out the back, but in moments are shivering, miserable and scratching forlornly to get back in. I hope they've been brave enough to do their business in the sleety mess that is our back yard.

My daughter is in the bathroom upstairs, engaged in her daily ritual of making her lovely face lovelier—applying foundation, eyeliner and blush, curling her hair, then flat-ironing it because the curls won't work, washing off all her makeup and starting again. She's annoyed because she hoped the schools would be closed today and they aren't, despite the fact she absolutely did *not* wish for it the night before when she saw the weather forecast.

I force the screen door open and slog out to scrape the ice and snow off my car. Looking up, I can see the yellow glow of the bathroom light in the dark of the winter dawn. I know my daughter is usually up there for at least another half an hour—parked in front of the mirror finishing her makeup while I'm driving to work, putting away the curling iron and spritzing perfume on her wrists as I'm walking to my office from the parking ramp. I think of how yesterday she was crying because her boyfriend hadn't called, and how she has a math exam on Tuesday and we need to turn in the paperwork for her to take the ACT.

On impulse, I bend to scoop up a handful of snow and form it into a soft ball. I lob it at the bathroom window, not too hard, but just so that it will make a satisfying splat. It goes wide and hits the wall to the right. I try again. This snowball hits to the left. I overcompensate, and again my snowball thuds to the right.

The bathroom window slides open and my daughter's astonished face appears behind the screen. She stares down at me while I patiently retrieve another measure of snow, pat it carefully and chuck it, missing still again. She keeps watching while I keep at it, throwing over and over. I toss one onto the roof, squelch one against the eave, another hooks left. Finally, I hit the window frame. I'm getting closer, and she's beginning to grin.

A half dozen more tries, and at last, a bull's-eye. My snowball hits the screen and snow spatters inside. My daughter screams, dodges, and laughs.

"You're so weird!" she yells out to me as I climb in my car. "You got me all snowy!

"Weird yourself!" I call back. "How come you didn't move away from the window?"

She returns to her ritual while I drive to work, humming. I may be weird, but no one can convince me I don't have a darned good arm.

Tired

K. L. Marsh

I was so tired of listening.
I heard diagnoses every place I went.
Heard it in the shop girl's tired voice.
Heard it at the wine bar in my coworker's stories.
Heard them in my lover's lament.
I wanted to step out of my clothes,
change the lock on my door
and put a 'gone fishin' sign out for all to see.

People wore me out.
I wanted someone to ask after me
with the same solicitous concern
that had always been my calling card.
"Ask for her, she's the best," they would say.
That used to make me proud.
Often, in my youth, I dined out on that.
Now, I just wanted time.
Time to rethink my life and change gears.

People's stories, their problems and their peccadilloes,
their hopes or dreams,
their gripes and groans.
I was no longer interested in diagnoses and test scores.
They only took you so far.
I wanted to talk about myself now
until their eyes crossed,
or they grew tired of me.

Somebody's Hero

Rosalie Sanara Petrouske

The loud whoosh of air brakes and pungent smell of diesel fuel filled the terminal as another Greyhound bus pulled in. I hopped excitedly on my right foot, and then switched over to my left. "Settle down," my mother scolded. "You're bouncing around like a Mexican jumping bean. Act your age. You're almost ten years old!"

Everyone was here; my grandmother, father, and mother waiting for my cousin Merritt's bus to arrive from Green Bay. This was the last stop on his journey from Fort Bragg, North Carolina, where he'd just finished basic training. His leave would last about three weeks before he shipped out to Germany, or possibly Vietnam.

The Greyhound finally came to a stop after nosing its way into the parking lot at the front of the station's large plate glass window. The bus's folding door opened like an accordion and people began spilling off, some dragging carry-on bags and other paraphernalia. I began jumping on both feet, trying to see over the head of a woman with puffy, teased hair, who was blocking my view of the exiting passengers.

"There he is," my grandmother said. I bobbed up and down, trying for a better look. The puffy-haired lady finally moved out of my way and then I saw him. I almost didn't recognize the young man in the perfectly pressed uniform, with creased trousers and cap to match, a duffel bag slung over one shoulder. My grandmother pushed through the exit door and enveloped her grandson in a huge hug. The rest of the family followed. Suddenly, feeling very shy, I dawdled behind, staring down at my pink Keds, my long dark hair falling over my eyes.

Merritt spotted me and stepped forward to ruffle my straight Chinese bangs with one large hand. "Hey, kiddo," he teased. "You've grown about a foot. When I left, you were still just knee high to a grasshopper." He laughed. "So, are ya ready to beat me at Crazy Eights?"

My shyness suddenly gone, I pulled excitedly on his sleeve. "I've been playing everyday," I told him. "I've been beating everybody. I'm the Crazy Eights queen now, so ya better watch out!"

"Okay," he said. "You're on for a game, but that bus ride was so long I'm about starving right now."

"What's in your bag?" I asked him, trying to lift the heavy canvas sack. I couldn't even budge it.

"Clothes, fatigues, underwear, and a present for you."

"Underwear? Yucky!" I crossed my eyes and wrinkled my nose. "Can I have my present now?" I asked. "What is it?" I tugged on his hand, hopping like Peter Rabbit in Mr. McGregor's garden.

"Later, kiddo," he said. "You can wait, can't you? Let's go over to Andrew's Café and grab some grub."

My dad stowed Merritt's duffel in the back of the station wagon, and we headed over to Andrew's for cheeseburgers, Cokes, and the best French fries in Michigan, along with a big piece of Apple Pie à la Mode for dessert.

Back then, Merritt was my hero, even though he was just a teenage boy who got into trouble, dropped out of high school and enlisted in the Army once he turned twenty-one. He was hoping for a chance to get his high school diploma and earn some money to attend a trade school when he got out. With an alcoholic father and a mother who suffered from a mental illness, his young life had been tough. During the Christmas of 1963, his dad was in the hospital dying from cirrhosis of the liver.

Merritt and his gang of friends were caught for breaking into a vending machine to steal some candy bars. The court put him on probation, granted his custody to my grandmother, and sent him up North to live with her.

My dad was working in Milwaukee and I could hardly wait for June to arrive, the time we always traveled north to my grandmother's house for summer vacation. When I met my cousin for the first time, I jumped in his lap, wrapped my arms around his neck and kissed him soundly on the lips declaring, "I love you! You're really cute!" His face turned several shades of pink, and I thought it was funny because I'd never seen a boy blush before. From then on, I tagged around behind Merritt like a tick stuck to a dog's fur. He taught me how to play basketball, often giving me a boost up to his shoulders so I could make a long shot. We played endless games of Cribbage, Gin Rummy, Monopoly, and Crazy Eights late into hot summer nights. He endured my constant teasing and sometimes tickled me so hard I almost peed my pants. "You're quite a pest," he often said, grinning at me like the Cheshire cat.

At seventeen, Merritt was slender, almost handsome in his favorite poplin jacket and straight leg jeans, even with the acne he hated spreading across his forehead and the bridge of his nose. Mostly, everyone noticed his eyes, dark brown with long black lashes, incredibly thick and dark; his lashes shadowed his high cheekbones when he looked down.

The first girlfriend he brought home, Veronica McCullough, had brown skin and long black hair she wore in a ponytail. I wanted to hate her when I saw her holding hands with Merritt, but she liked kids. If I asked her, she would cartwheel across the grass, back straight, slim legs circling until she looked like a wheel with spokes rolling—that's how beautiful she could cartwheel. I started wearing my hair in a ponytail just so I could look like Veronica, even though I hated exposing my ears. My grandmother used to tease me sometimes and tell me my ears "stuck out like sugar bowl handles." I thought my ears were almost the size of the Disney cartoon character, Dumbo. Merritt told me "Don't worry, kid, someday you'll grow into your ears." I think he meant that to be reassuring.

We piled into the circle booth at Andrews' Café and I noticed how the waitress rushed over to give Merritt his menu first, beaming a big smile like the headlamps from a line up of cars getting ready for a drag race. Grandma Kate sat next to "her boy" as she liked to call him, every now and then patting his arm as if she couldn't believe he was real.

"So, what's Army life like?" my dad asked.

Merritt regaled us with stories of his arrival at Fort Bragg. "We were screamed at, yelled at, and ushered into a large auditorium where we were yelled at some more," he laughed. When he got to the part about learning how to march, I jumped out of the booth and began marching up and down, lifting one knee up to my chest and then another as I saluted the customers sitting across from us.

"Sit down," my mother scolded. "You're being too rambunctious."

"What's ram-bunk-shis?" I asked my mother, enunciating each syllable slowly.

"It means you're being a pest," Merritt said. I punched him in the arm. He grabbed me and tickled my ribs. "Let go, let me go," I laughed so hard I thought for sure I'd pee my pants.

"Calm down, both of you. I mean it," Grandma said in her most grandmotherly voice. The other customers in Andrews' Café just smiled at our antics.

"Where are they sending you when you get back?" my mother asked, and with this question, our laughter suddenly stopped.

"Do you think they'll send you to 'Nam?" I asked.

I grew up with the Vietnam War, a background for my childhood similar to the war in Iraq now. It was always hovering in the periphery of adult conversations, television news broadcasts, and black-and-white photos slashed across newspaper headlines. Pictures of flag-draped caskets, hand grenades exploding around children running down roads with smoke and dust spiraling up behind them, and soldiers trampling through jungles toting machine guns. The names of the cities were mysterious: Saigon, Cambodia, Hanoi, Danang. I really didn't understand the trauma of war. I almost wanted Merritt to go over there so I could receive mail from abroad, have first-hand stories to tell my friends about his experiences.

"Let's not talk about that now. There's plenty of time for that conversation," my grandmother said, fondly patting Merritt's uniform clad arm. When she looked at Merritt, her wide smile creased her wrinkly face even more. I knew she worried about him, especially when he decided to quit school as soon as he turned eighteen.

I remember the hot summer night when he went joyriding with his friends, crashed a stolen car on the neighbor's lawn, escaped through a broken side window, and slipped into my grandmother's house smelling like sour beer and gasoline. I was so afraid. The police never found out who did it because his friends fled the scene as well. They questioned all the neighbors, but it was too dark to recognize as one neighbor said, "any of those hoodlums." My grandmother was proud now, knowing Merritt was turning his life around. His stint in the Army would give him a chance to get his G.E.D. and study a trade. The specter of Vietnam hovered over these plans, however. If he had to go, there was no telling when, or if, he'd ever return.

The perky blonde waitress gave Merritt his burger combo first, and refilled his coffee before she passed out our orders. "Looks like that gal is makin' eyes at you," my dad said. Merritt laughed and turned a little red. No matter how old he was, he still blushed easily.

I was sitting next to him and noticed he was giving the waitress his shy smile as she filled water glasses around the table. I grabbed his cap from the seat next to me and plopped it on my head. "Hey, look at me!" I chimed, saluting smartly. The cap was so big; it fell over my eyes and slid down onto the bridge of my nose. Everybody laughed. Merritt tugged the cap off me and ruffled a hand through my hair, messing it up some more. "You little goof!" he said fondly. To me, Merritt was a hero and he could do nothing wrong.

Soon, we piled into the station wagon for the ride home. I, of course, claimed the seat next to Merritt, begging him for the present he bought me. "Presents," he corrected and I squealed with delight. The presents ended up being an Etch A Sketch, a Fortune Teller Fish, and a gold bracelet with a heart and key attached to one of the links, along with a small, perfect white pearl. I wore the bracelet until the gold tarnished and the paint chipped off the pearl. I still have it all these years later wrapped in a scrap of velvet cloth, and stored in the bottom of my jewelry box.

As soon as we arrived at my grandmother' house, I raced to retrieve a deck of cards. We played Crazy Eights and Gin Rummy way past my bedtime. My parents didn't know it, but Merritt had a bottle of vodka wrapped in brown paper tucked in the bottom of his duffel bag. It was our secret and I never told anyone, except I did beg him to let me have a sip. He finally let me take a little one. The vodka tasted bitter. It felt fuzzy in my mouth, like trying to swallow a fistful of cotton balls. I giggled when Merritt played the wrong card, almost fell off my chair. When he left the room for a few minutes, I stole a few more sips, even though I hated the taste. My face felt flushed and the room spun like the merry-go-round at Ludington Park. At first, I didn't realize it was the vodka behind the spinning top effect. When Merritt returned, he felt my hot forehead.

"Hey, little one, I better not let you do that again. It went right to your head."

He meant let me take another sip of vodka. He rewrapped the bottle in its paper wrapper, folded it between his fatigues and stashed it back in his duffel. He brought me a glass of ginger ale and soon I felt more like myself.

Merritt never made it to Vietnam. He finished his basic training and after a course in electronics, they sent him to Germany. He was almost finished with his tour of duty and thinking about reenlisting when he ended up being arrested for going AWOL, borrowing a jeep and getting drunk one night while he was on a pass from camp. He wasn't totally responsible for the whole fiasco, so his discharge ended up being honorable; however, he no longer had the opportunity to reenlist. He came home toting his olive green duffel bag, wearing an old pair of jeans and an oxford button down shirt.

This time he arrived on the train, but the only family that came to meet him was my dad and me. I still thought he looked handsome, even without the uniform. I was two years older and he almost didn't recognize me with my French-braided hair and new white dress. I quietly held his hand as we walked to the car. "Why'd you go AWOL?" I asked. He never really answered. He just stood there, awkwardly looking at me from underneath his long black eyelashes, giving me his shy smile.

Merritt went to school to learn how to run a lathe and drill press, and he eventually moved to Manitowoc, Wisconsin, where he got a job in a machine shop. He came home every year for Christmas. I went with my dad to pick him up at the station. He still wore his hair in a crew cut, but he had gained weight around the middle. His cheeks were ruddy, flushed red from the vodka he stashed in his overnight bag, drank on the train while he played cards with his fellow seatmates and bellowed out Christmas carols: God Rest Ye Merry Gentleman, Deck the Halls, and Silent Night. He carried his transistor radio with an earphone dangling from his ear, so he could listen to the news and the slow love ballads he liked. In his jacket, he kept a pocket Bible. I swiped it once, marked up the passages that moved me, the ones about the "lilies of the field" and "seeing through a mirror darkly."

"Why did you do that, little cuz?" he took hold of my hand while I stood there giggling.

"I don't know," which was really the truth. "I guess I just like those verses."

He was twenty-five then and he still talked about Brenda Lee, getting her autograph at the state fair before he joined the Army. He told that story repeatedly, how she touched his hand, stood so close he could smell her perfume, just for that one second while she handed him a 3 x 5 black-and-white photo with her signature scrawled across the front.

He lost his job in Manitowoc and eventually moved to Milwaukee, where he found work at another machine shop. Merritt never let a setback cause a standstill. He never gave up. He even tried his hand at being a shoe salesman as a second part time job. The summer I turned sixteen, I rode a Greyhound bus to Milwaukee to visit my older, married sister. I tried to look my cousin up, without success. I found where he lived, though. It was in a shabby red brick building on the south side, with torn shades and a door that someone had kicked a hole in during a brawl. He wasn't home. I guessed his life wasn't going the way he had planned.

After losing a series of jobs because of his drinking problem, he moved back to Michigan. His mother wasn't doing very well, our grandmother had died long before, and my own mother was suffering from congestive heart failure. Merritt often stopped by to visit my mother and have a cup of coffee with her. He always brought her flowers wrapped in colorful cellophane from the grocery store. "He's such a sweet, boy," she said.

Sometimes he'd drop by my house, bring a six-pack of cold beer and play an occasional hand of Gin Rummy with me, but I was busy with my own life so I didn't see him that much anymore. At thirty-nine, while driving drunk down highway 41, he lost control of his car and crashed into a telephone pole. The driver's side of the vehicle took the brunt of the collision. The bones in Merritt's face were crushed so badly that he had to have a closed-casket funeral. I never had the chance to tell him good-bye.

Merritt never accomplished great dreams or performed tremendous deeds. He did not become a famous leader like Robert Kennedy or Martin Luther King, Jr. He was just an ordinary guy who enjoyed a hamburger at the A&W, a cold beer at the corner bar, and reading Archie in the Sunday comics. He worked hard to educate himself, find a job he liked, tried to quit drinking, but lost the battle. His story is common; it certainly has happened before. Out at Holy Cross

Cemetery, his grave has a white marker; a military tribute like the markers that stand at Arlington Cemetery. Although he didn't make it to Vietnam, people who visit his grave may think he was a hero who served his country back in the sixties when we were seeking answers and justice, and fighting another country's war to preserve peace in ours.

Merritt was a man who had a few friends, a kind heart and a belief that he could change himself, only he didn't know how. I always smile when I think about the day we met his bus, when he came home from basic training and we all piled into the family-size booth at Andrews Café. My cousin's path was obscure and hard to travel, but he took the time to stop along the way and make a little girl laugh while she was growing up. For that, he will always be my hero.

The Psychic Buddy

Randy D. Pearson

"Hello, friend," Phillip droned into the telephone, "you've reached the Psychic Buddies Network. What may I see for you today?"

Laughter exploded from the other end of the line, which made Phil's heart drop. *Oh great, another one,* he thought.

"Gee," the voice said, oozing sarcasm, "if you really were psychic, you'd know what I wanted. Huh, smart guy?"

Phil wanted to hang up, but one realization always made him feel better. *After all, this moron is paying $4.99 a minute to insult me. Who's the smart guy now?* "It only works that way sometimes, sir. There's no guarantee with a gift like this. I can't just turn it on like a faucet. Now, if you want to tell me the purpose of your call, I'll be happy to..."

It felt like a tidal wave had suddenly hit Phillip directly in the brain. The psychic energy that could not be turned on like a faucet, as he put it, could most certainly turn itself on and clobber him with a powerful current. He had felt this torrent before, of course. Many times over the years. But this one felt larger than life. It felt like...death. Death waited around the corner for someone, but not this bozo on the phone.

He wanted, again, to hang up on the caller so he could help the one who really needed him. But his job had to come first. So, he needed to appease this fellow. Over his months as a Psychic Buddy, he learned that when he felt nothing for a caller, he could usually fudge his way through. Normally, he needed to ask a few questions, to allow the caller to unconsciously guide him, but he had no time to play the usual games. "Sir, I'm going to save you some money on this call and make it quick. Tell her you love her. Tell her you are sorry and you realize she truly is the one for you. Trust me, it'll work!"

Phil expected laughter, but after a small pause, the guy said, "Whoa... Um, okay, I will. Thanks, psychic dude."

Phil grinned. "Anytime. Call again, but next time, don't waste so much time and money being skeptical."

He then hung up and quickly started to dial. He did not know how he knew the number, but when it came to his gift, he knew well enough not to question it.

Brannon Billsen stood in the upstairs bedroom of his new house, gazing out the window at his large backyard. His focus was so intense that when his wife came from behind and put her arms around his chest, he jumped.

"Amy!" He exclaimed. "I didn't hear you come up!"

She smiled and laid her chin against his shoulder. "Sorry, Bran. What are you looking at out there?"

"Oh," he replied, "I'm still marveling at this place. We've been here a couple months now, but I'm still so tickled by it all. We actually have a huge, fenced-in yard. Sure beats that apartment, huh Aim?"

"Yes it does, Bran. But now that spring is here, we really need a mower."

He turned inside the circle of her arms to face her, laid his hands on her shoulders and delicately kissed her. "Now Aim, don't be taking the magic out of this yet! It'll grow mundane soon enough, my dear."

They stayed in their embrace for a moment before Brannon turned back to the window. Looking beyond the edge of their property, he noticed someone standing in the middle of the adjacent restaurant parking lot. The man, clad in a beige jacket and blue jeans, appeared to be looking up at them. After a few seconds, the stranger turned as a dog trotted past him in a wide arc. From this distance, the guy appeared to be a few inches tall.

"Y'know, I wonder if he can see us up here," Bran wondered idly.

Amy laughed, "I highly doubt it. This window is what, three by five?"

"But look, honey, he's just standing there, staring up at us."

"Oh Bran, you can't even see his face from here, especially at this time of evening. Even in broad daylight, I doubt he'd see much more than a vague shadow. He's probably looking at the stars. I've seen a few people out there, walking their dogs. And besides, the light from our window is most likely obscuring us."

As the stranger led his dog out of the lot, Brannon turned again to face his wife. "It's the light that makes it so we can be seen, Aim." Brannon stared at her for a moment, then smiled devilishly. "Y'know, I think I can solve this little dilemma. I'm going out there. You stand right here, and put on the sexy black negligee. The one with the..."

"Yeah yeah, I know which one!" Even though she joined in with her own version of a devilish grin, she could not hide the apprehension in her blue eyes. "But what if anybody else sees?"

"You'll know it's me. I'll have on my red jacket."

"Oh but Brannon," she protested, "it's late. Besides, we don't know the neighborhood yet. It seems safe enough, but how do we know for sure?"

He smiled a most confident grin. "I'm a manly man, remember? At least that's what you tell everybody.

I'll be fine. Besides, I really want to see you in that negligee! Any excuse is a good one." After tossing her a wink, he turned and vacated the bedroom, pausing to yell, "And try both ways, with the lights off and on, okay? This way, we'll know for sure what people can see out there."

As she removed her clothes, she let the arousal overcome her trepidation. *After all, I'll be flashing the man I love*, she thought as a sly smile crept upon her pretty face. *I suppose this isn't too sick. At least the guy with the dog seems to be gone.* She found the nightgown, and quickly donned it. Being skintight, it accentuated her curves nicely, making her feel extremely desirable. Small wonder why Brannon liked this outfit so much.

She heard the outside door click shut. Knowing he would be in position within a couple minutes, she began to fantasize. She planned on giving him the show of his life.

Then, the phone rang. "Oh great!" She yelled, "what lovely timing! This had better not be Mom!" She picked up the receiver and gave her greeting.

"Hi, this is Phillip Hammel, and I'm with the Psychic Buddies Network. I'm..."

"Hey look," she interrupted, "now's not the time. I'm not interested! Good-bye!"

She started to pull the receiver away from her ear when he screamed, "Wait! Your husband's life is in danger! Don't hang up!"

This stopped her in her tracks. "What the hell are you talking about? Who is this?!"

"Look, " Phil said, trying to calm himself enough to avoid sounding like a crackpot, "I'm a psychic and I had a vision of your husband, Brandon, I think. He is going to be killed unless you act now! Don't let Brandon go into that parking lot!"

Although Phil's words concerned her, she found herself reacting with anger. "Ya got my husband's name wrong, idiot! Look, I don't know who you are, but this is one sick joke! I'm going to call the cops, you bastard!"

He started to say, "Look, I know this sounds crazy..." but she slammed down the handset before he could say any more.

Phil wished he could jump in his car and drive to the scene, to stop this terrible vision from becoming reality. The problem being, his psychic powers worked in unpredictable ways. Somehow, he knew the phone number, but had no idea where they lived. Unfortunately, he realized he probably had done all he could. Though Phil could call her back, he doubted she would answer. He just hoped his warning would be enough to forestall the situation.

Amy slammed down the phone with enough force to make it bounce slightly. *Great, we moved into a neighborhood with wackos in it.* She went to the window, to see if Brannon made it to his position yet. Though she certainly lost the mood, she did not want to ruin his enjoyment. The best thing, she decided, would be to put on the show and tell him about it afterward. Still, the call ate at the back of her mind. *Don't let Brandon go into that parking lot!* It troubled her that he knew Brannon's name, or close, anyway. But what could she do? If she yelled for him, he would not hear it, and his cell phone rested on the end table next to the bed.

At that moment, she saw Brannon walk around the side of the building and into the parking lot. He waved up at her and she returned the gesture. She tried to force a smile, then realized he could not see her face anyway. His head, from this distance, resembled a tiny peach-colored ball with dark hair. If he had not been wearing the red jacket, she would not have recognized him.

Amy began her striptease, moving seductively in front of the window. After coyly pulling at her right strap, she allowed it to drop off her shoulder.

After a couple minutes of her dance routine, she went over and turned off the bedroom light. Assuming no one would be able to see anything, she mustered enough confidence to drop the other shoulder strap, allowing her negligee to crumple to the floor. She got as close to the window as she could, striving to witness any sign of acknowledgment.

At that moment, she spotted another man out on the blacktop near Brannon, so she quickly pulled up her nightgown. It looked to be the same guy from earlier, or at least he wore a similar beige jacket. However, even from this distance she could see the baseball bat in his hand. It glistened in the ambient lighting of the parking lot. He slowly crept up behind Brannon, bat poised above his head. Amy belted out a scream that Brannon could not hear.

Phillip stood with the phone still in hand, sweat beading on his brow. The image in his brain still haunted him; the man being beaten to death with a baseball bat in a lonely parking lot. When he felt another flash hit him, he dropped the receiver. It loudly clunked upon the floor. The noise alerted several of his co-workers, who stared at him like he had a screw loose. His supervisor, a nasty man with absolutely no psychic abilities or scruples, rapidly approached him with an angry snarl spread across his pudgy face.

At this moment, Phil cared nothing about his job. He bent over and retrieved the receiver. That last brain flash gave him a new number to call and he dialed frantically as his boss dropped a heavy hand on his shoulder. "Hey Phil," he yelled, his mouth wrapped around an unlit cigar, "You know the rules. No personal calls on the job!"

Phillip jerked his arm away from the cigar-chewer as the phone began ringing.

Staring up at his house, Brannon sighed. Amy was right. He could not see a darn thing from this distance. She's probably naked, he mused, and here I am, standing in the cold...

Suddenly, he heard a cell phone ring directly behind him. He spun around to see a man standing too close, an aluminum baseball bat raised over his head, ready to come crashing down. As the stranger paused, clearly startled by his ringing phone, Brannon shot his foot into the man's gut, sprinting away as quickly as his legs would carry him. He heard the bat clatter upon the ground as he continued to flee. He ran all the way to his front door, where his wife stood ready to greet him with a python-like hug.

"You're..." Phillip's boss started to say.

"Yeah yeah, I'm fired," Phil responded with a proud smile. "What, ya think I didn't see that coming? I'm psychic, y'know."

About the Authors

Diane Bonofiglio was born in South Philadelphia. She is a first generation American, transplanted to Grand Ledge, Michigan at age 17. She began writing at age 34. Poetry is her passion, although she enjoys writing creative nonfiction, which allows her to put a great deal of her life experiences into her work. Married to Paul, they have three sons, a daughter and three grandchildren (soon to be four).

Wanda Davison is a retired high school teacher who lives in Lansing, Michigan. She writes poetry now and then for fun. Although she has had four poems published, she considers herself a beginning poet.

Lori Hudson lives in Eagle, Michigan, with her husband and daughter, numerous pets and an ex-racehorse. She writes children's chapter books under the pseudonym Judith Wade. Some of her books include the *Mermaid Island* trilogy, and her recent release, *Faelen, The Horse From the Sea*. She has two short pieces published in recent editions of *Cup of Comfort*®. She likes to do stained glass, walk and dabble in flower gardening…when she isn't writing, of course. Visit her online at http://judithwade.net.

Phil Kline is a freelance writer of sales and motivation for American Marketing Association's *Marketing News*, *Training & Development* magazine, *Selling Power, Sales and Marketing Executives International*, and various Michigan magazines. He is the winner of the Robert J. Pickering Award for Playwriting Excellence for his play, *Hey, Dick*. His sales book was published by HRD

Corporation. He is currently looking for an agent for two novels, a mystery and an offbeat quirky story.

Candy-Ann Little is the co-founder of Writing at the Ledges. She became a writer in the aftermath of a tragedy. Her third child was still born. In her devastation, she began keeping a journal. This led to writing about her life experiences and she has recently completed two inspirational romance novels. "I find there's something therapeutic in putting my thoughts into the words and actions of my characters," she says. She enjoys encouraging other writers by providing a forum that is friendly, gentle and supportive. Married to Lee, she is the mother of two teenagers, Melanie and Michael, who demand most of her energy, yet she always manages to set aside time for writing. Discipline is the biggest goal she has learned in her writing life.

K. L. Marsh grew up on the Straits of Mackinac with charming relatives who knew first-hand of the Great Depression and WWII, whose lives and loves ran the gamut from comedy to poetry and who taught her to love a turn of phrase descriptive of both. Since following her interests hither and yon, she resides in Lansing, Michigan, and returns often to scenes of her youth.

Jan McCaffrey is a graduate of Lansing Community College's creative writing program. She wrote a weekly column *Jan's Scrapbook* for the *Grand Ledge Independent* before moving to Amelia Island, Florida in 1984. In Florida, she wrote a column and other pieces for *The News Leader* as well as for a local magazine, *The Islander*. Co-founder of the Nassau County Writers and Poets, she published several anthologies as a group. In 2000, she moved back to Grand Ledge with her husband, Ted. They have been married for 54 years, have three children, six grandchildren and two great-grandchildren.

Randy D. Pearson was born in Lansing, raised in DeWitt and lived in such cities as Okemos, Mason, Grand Ledge, and Dimondale making him quite familiar with small town life. He has been writing creative fiction for most of his life. His earliest creativity was a cartoon book he wrote at age nine as a birthday gift for his father titled, *The Adventures of Marvin and Randy*. He has won several national writing contests, and received honorable mention in an international contest in 2005. Due to this, he can be considered a "published" author, in newsletters and websites, but this anthology is his first bit of writing he truly considers published.

Rosalie Sanara Petrouske founded Writing at the Ledges in 2005 along with her writing partner-in-crime, Candy Little. Her poetry and essays have appeared in several notable publications including *The Seattle Review*, *Passages North*, *The Southern Poetry Review*, *Red Rock Review*, *American Nature Writing*, and an anthology, *New Poems From the Third Coast: Contemporary Michigan Poetry*, among others. She is also the author of two books of poetry, *The Geisha Box* published in 1996 with March Street Press and *A Postcard from my Mother* published in 2004 with Finishing Line Press. During the summer of 2008, she was awarded an Artist-in-Residence grant and spent two weeks in the Porcupine Mountains writing, hiking and immersing herself in the natural world. She has a beautiful fifteen-year-old daughter and a teacher husband who is a master of trivial knowledge.

Donnalee Pontius is the proud mother of two daughters and one son. She has been married for 22 years and has been a nurse for nearly 15 of those years. She loves to write, spend time with her family and their many animals (four horses, three rabbits, four cats and one fish), and enjoys nature. Throughout the years, she has started, restarted, finished and refinished numerous short stories and poems about horses, nature, girls and horses, and a series of comic strips starring an earthworm. Her advice to young writers—never give up and write, write, write.

Alta C. Reed is 86 years young. She was the valedictorian of Custer High School's 1939 graduating class. Married 63 wonderful years to Ivan Reed, they have six children, Donald, William, Linda, Patrick and Michael, 22 grandchildren, and 20 great grandchildren. A member of Gunnisonville United Methodist Church, D.A.R., and Writing at the Ledges, she enjoys politics, family genealogy and antiques. She recently developed Ivan Reed's Mini Museum at the family farm in Carr Settlement. She also recently published a memoir titled *Carr Settlement: Then and Now*.

Janice Sykes was born and raised on a farm, and continues the country life with her husband, Brad. She has been blessed with two wonderful daughters and their husbands, Shannon and Pat, and Sherry and Dave, and spectacular grandchildren: Nathan, Kevin, Anthony, and Owen, as well as her first granddaughter to be born in September, Sophia. She works part-time as a registered nurse and enjoys writing about personal and observed experiences, fiction, non-fiction, and rhyming verse.

Kerry Tietsort is a life-long Michigan resident, who grew up in, and still lives in a small town. He has a wonderful family with his wife of eleven years, two sons, aged seven and six, a two-year-old daughter, and a fifteen-year-old Dalmatian dog. He began making up stories and writing for fun in late elementary school. Writing for him is truly recreational. It helps him express his feelings and document his life. He used to write more short stories, but now focuses mainly on poems and journaling. He also enjoys attending live music performances and trying to play his guitar! Employed as a Probation Officer for the State of Michigan, his other interests include spending time in Michigan's great outdoors, and following Michigan State University athletics and other team sports. A 'charter member' of Writing at the Ledges, he hopes everyone enjoys reading this anthology as much as he enjoyed being a part of it.

C. J. Tody is a multimedia artist, performance consultant, human resource development professional and 'DreamSculpting Interactive' coach who embraces a variety of experiential excursions into creative discovery. This fuels the reinvention often needed to navigate change, which, and along with an abundant love of creativity, imagination, travel, adventure, dance, relationships, and self-development, often seeps into her artwork and writing. She maintains a lifelong residence in central Michigan near loved ones but likes globetrotting, and studied in Europe, Asia, Scandinavia, and the Fortune 500 before graduating from Michigan State University, traversing careers in both the private and public sectors.

Index

Bonofiglio, Diane
    Can I Go to the Woods? 164
    He Loved Me 266
    Night Pond 75
    The Old Barn 166
    The Philadelphia Six 273
    Red Bird 168
    Thankful Hearts 168
    Winter Forest 171
    A Wondrous Winter Scene 172

Davison, Wanda
    Simple Gifts in the Park 46

Hudson, Lori
    An Act of Kindness 238
    Call Waiting 254
    Snowballs 276

Kline, Marion Phillip
    Phil Kline is Dead 80

Little, Candy-Ann
    Death by Broken Heart 83
    Snowflakes 260
    Sunshine Again 262

Marsh, K. L.
    Birds of a Feather 244
    Duncan Bay 17
    French Sunday 258
    Main Street 227
    My Mother's Garden 245
    One Sided 269
    Tired 278

McCaffrey, Jan
    The Covered Bridge 45
    Island Dreams 16
    The Ledges 18
    Muddle in a Puddle 69
    A Quiet Rainy Morning 82

Pearson, Randy D.
    Don't Mess with Tradition 178
    Lasagna and Sex Therapy 19
    Neighborhood Watch 246
    The Psychic Buddy 289

Petrouske, Rosalie Sanara
    Along the River Tonight 14
    In a Café 78
    Letter from a Small Town 224
    The Perfect Ride 232
    So Much Mess 271
    Somebody's Hero 279
    When Autumn Comes 70

Pontius, Donnalee
    Message From Max 218
    Second Tuesday of Next Week 261

Reed, Alta C.
    Childhood of Yesteryear 176
    Fairy Touch 213
    For Sale: Americana 214
    My Gravel Road 173

Sykes, Jan
    A Hay-Day 169

Tietsort, Kerry
    Ghost Shoes 167
    The Heart and Center 216

Tody, C. J.
    Eye O' the Storm 191
    Treasures Beyond Measure 48
    Where Are You? 235